STOLEN TRUTH

HENYA DRESCHER

Black Rose Writing | Texas

ISBN: 978-1-68433-651-7
PUBLISHED BY BLACK ROSE WRITING
www.blackrosewriting.com

Printed in the United States of America
Suggested Retail Price (SRP) $19.95

Stolen Truth is printed in Book Antiqua

*As a planet-friendly publisher, Black Rose Writing does its best to eliminate
unnecessary waste to reduce paper usage and energy costs, while never
compromising the reading experience. As a result, the final word count vs. page count
may not meet common expectations.

PRAISE FOR
STOLEN TRUTH

"Henya Drescher possesses a gift for creating
the best kind of mystery."
–Walter Cummins, *The Literary Review*

"...a brilliantly carved mystery full of
action and intrigue with powerful characters."
–António Gomes, author of *Visions from Grymes Hill*

"A breathless psychological suspense novel."
–Talia Carner, author of *The Third Daughter*

STOLEN TRUTH

CHAPTER 1

Noah's cries cut into my chest. My eyes well up, and my throat thickens. I run a hand along the back of my six-day-old baby's silky, perfectly shaped head, fighting back the rush of sadness that threatens to engulf me. His cries turn to whimpers and then silence.

I jolt awake.

My body breaks out in a cold sweat before I can identify the source of my unease. The first thing that reaches me is the sharp stench of fresh paint, as I struggle through a haze of consciousness, and with it, the feeling that something's off. I strain my ears in the stillness of the house. No cries from Noah echoing down the hallway, no aroma of French roast brewing, and none of the usual noises from the kitchen.

The weak Berkshires sun filters through the sheer curtains, and the nightstand clock displays 1:00 p.m. in neon green.

What the hell?

Since giving birth, I've developed the habit of waking up at 6:00 a.m. to feed Noah. *Why have I overslept?*

I bolt up and recoil from the flare of pain in my head.

"Todd?" I call out.

My pulse races. My mouth is dry. I raise my head again. Dizziness and nausea hit me. I collapse back on the pillow and wait for the roiling in my stomach to subside.

My mind is working overtime. Why did Todd and Connie let me oversleep, knowing how anxious I am about Noah? Since yesterday, he's had a rash and a high fever. I researched his symptoms online. While rashes don't indicate a dangerous condition, high temperatures are a cause to see a doctor. I'd wanted to rush him to the hospital last night … What happened?

I try again. "Todd! Connie?"

I make another effort to get out from under the blanket, but my head spins, and the floor ripples beneath me. I lose my footing, landing with a bang on my knees. The pain is instant. The floor is cold, as I crawl to the bathroom, my scalp damp from the effort. *Please, please don't let me throw up before I get there.*

I inhale deeply. What the hell is wrong with me?

I struggle to remember last night. Todd and I ate dinner in front of the fireplace. He made a salad and broiled chicken. That's all I recall; the rest is blurred against the fog in my mind. But now, inching forward on my knees, all I want is to get to my baby right away.

Where is Connie? In the kitchen preparing Noah's formula?

At last, I manage to make my way to the bathroom before vomiting. Then, still on all fours, I struggle back to get my robe at the foot of the bed. Holding fast to the edge of the mattress, I steady myself, then stumble to the door and jerk it open before I barge into the hallway, ignoring the nausea and fatigue. Odors of paint and bleach get stronger.

"Todd!" I scream into the empty hall. "Connie!" My voice echoes lifeless off the walls. Maybe this is just a nightmare?

With shaky legs, I slog down the hall, one foot in front of the other.

I shove open the door to Noah's room. A gust of wind blows in through the open window overlooking the backyard.

Stunned, I try to make sense of the scene in front of me. I shut my eyes tight, draw a calming breath, and then open them again.

A full-blown panic forms in my throat, exploding in a scream.

Noah's crib and dresser are gone. No trace of his little clothes — the closet is open and empty. His room is bare, except for a rocking chair. Even the color of the walls has changed, from blue to white. Despite the newly painted room, the bleach, and the missing furniture, Noah's scent still lingers in the air. A small part of my mind tells me I can't smell my baby with the bleach and fresh paint, but I know that I do.

I was bedridden most of my pregnancy, so Todd picked out all Noah's baby things. A comforter adorned with a woodland scene, the stuffed blue bunny with its soft ears, the diaper bag with the teddy bears. Now they're all gone. And so is Noah.

I move my hand to my abdomen, and then to my engorged, leaking breasts. *Where are you, my little man?*

Stumbling out of the empty nursery, I force my legs from room to room, each step growing heavier than the last, each door representing a new hope.

I push open Connie's door, which gives a squeak. The room is spotless, the bed made, complete with tight hospital corners. But her belongings are gone—the room stripped. Even her bathroom is spotless. But her scent lingers, lavender and something sweet, like bubblegum.

My heart tightens. I'm accustomed to Todd disappearing for a day or two without explanation, but where's Connie? She's always here. She delivered Noah. Then she stayed on. Uncommunicative and hovering, Connie is efficient but not comforting. But now her absence unsettles me.

I descend the stairs on rubbery legs. The kitchen and living room appear undisturbed. The heavy silence weighs me down.

Hyperventilating now, I make my way to the garage. My candy red '65 Mustang, complete with silver rally stripes, still sits there, but Todd's Toyota is gone. And in the middle of the driveway, the only thing left from Connie's rusted Jeep is an oil stain.

I try to convince myself that she must have gone out with Noah and will return soon, and that Todd has gone to work. But I know it's wishful thinking. They've never left me alone. Something is wrong. One of them has always been close by, at times making me feel resentful.

Two days earlier, over dinner, I said something to Todd that I'd been repeating since Noah was born. "Still, I don't feel comfortable having Connie live with us."

"Just a few more days. You can use the help."

"I can easily manage taking care of my own baby." I tried to keep the sharpness from my voice.

He remained quiet; eyes glued to his grilled salmon. We spent the rest of the meal in silence.

Now, the late November wind bites into my skin. "Todd."

I wait a moment.

"Connie." My throat burns.

Thunder rumbles, as I make my way along the side of the house to the backyard. My breathing is ragged. I hardly have enough oxygen to call Todd's name again.

Pushing the pain in my lower belly out of my mind, I make my way back to the front of the house, where I stand in the middle of the driveway and slowly make a three-hundred-and-sixty-degree turn. And then again. And then again. Emptiness and silence surround me. Just the rasp of my breathing and the trees swaying in the wind.

For a moment, I think I hear Noah crying in the distance. An unmistakable sound. A noise encoded in a mother to hear through walls — or through miles of wooded terrain. My breasts leak in response. Ignoring my aching body, I dash into the woods toward what I'm certain is the sound of my baby crying. *I'm coming, Noah. I'm coming.*

A happier picture buds in my imagination. Connie has taken Noah for a walk. I gain strength from it.

The cry sounds again. Panting and clawing my way through thick bushes, thorns snagging my robe, I head deeper into the woods, hopping over tree roots and rocks and splashing through patches of mud. Connie and my baby are out here. I trip and fall, scraping my palms and already throbbing knees. Unable to rise, I claw wildly at a vine.

Wheezing, I manage to get to my feet, each gasp of air burning my throat.

Just then, the baby's cries stop.

A twig snaps. Is someone behind me? A sharp tingle of fear crawls up the back of my neck. I whirl. Nothing but the soggy crush of leaves under my feet — nothing but the distant crack of thunder.

The first buds of hope die. No Noah. No Todd. No Connie. Just a chorus of trees rustling in the wind that, to my ears, sounds more like hissing.

•　　•　　•

Against the wind, I make my way back toward the house. Maybe Todd left a note on the fridge door. A little spark of hope ignites in my heart. As I approach the front door, I see something small and white on the ground.

Amidst the wet leaves is one of Noah's white socks, soiled from the earth. I it and hold it to my nose, inhaling my child's sweet scent. A vivid image of Noah lying in his crib flashes before my eyes.

Collapsing, I fold myself into a tight ball, and let out an animal howl, thinking how cold my sweet little boy will be without his sock.

Eventually, the shudders that rack my body subside, and, with Noah's sock still clutched in my fist, I limp through the front door to the kitchen.

There is no note.

The world is spinning around me, again, and I take the stairs up to our bedroom on all fours. Bracing myself against the wall, I rise and make my way to Todd's closet, which only yesterday was filled with neatly hung clothes and precisely lined up shoes on the floor. Now, it is empty. With jerky motions, I yank out bureau drawers, confirming what I already know.

I'm running different scenarios through my head. Nothing makes sense. Back downstairs in the laundry room, I dig through a pile of dirty clothes. There is no trace of anyone's clothes but mine.

I fumble my phone from my purse, which hangs in the kitchen by the back door, and punch in Todd's cell. Pacing five steps to the sink, four to the table, then back to the sink, I listen to a voice message. *The number you have dialed is no longer in service.*

Next, I try Todd's real-estate office in Albany, but I get the same message. And to top it all off, I can't reach Connie. Her cell's disconnected, too.

Where are they? Noah needs to see a doctor. What if his condition has worsened? I can't bear the thought. Then I realize something: stripped of Todd's and Connie's and Noah's things, the house looks as if no one else lives here but me. And it finally dawns on me that Todd is not going to call, explaining he took Noah for a ride, and that he's sorry he caused me grief.

And with that understanding, I dial the Becket Police Department.

"My baby has disappeared." I fight to keep my voice calm. Tears burn. The words rush from my mouth as I tell the officer what's happened.

"Can you repeat that? I'm having a difficult time understanding you." The police officer sounds bored, as if disappearing babies are something of a daily occurrence.

Between sobs, I do my best to explain. I give him mine and Todd's name.

"An officer will be there shortly," he informs me.

"How fast? This is an emergency."

"About twenty minutes."

My shoulders sag with the tiniest bit of relief. Help is coming.

I begin counting the minutes.

CHAPTER 2

The house is quiet, a hollow echo of how I feel. But other sounds magnify — the creak of the old building settling, the wind slapping the clapboard. After several minutes of pacing, I go outside to wait. Lightning crackles across the sky. I glance at my watch. Seven minutes. Ten minutes. Fifteen minutes. With each passing moment, my panic rises higher and higher.

My arms ache to hold Noah, my little bundle of joy and happiness.

He started coughing and sounded congested. I wanted to rush him to the hospital last night … Todd said we would. Then everything dissolved into a fog. What happened last night?

From the first moment I saw Noah, I was completely smitten. He was perfectly formed, a cherub straight from heaven. You always hear that babies are ugly at birth, wrinkled and red and resembling little apes. Not my baby. Noah is beautiful. His resemblance to Todd is striking. Noah has his father's large eyes and beautifully shaped head.

I had a difficult pregnancy. I was bedridden for eight months. Level three. That's how the doctor described it to me. This meant I couldn't stand for more than five minutes. My activities limited to taking showers, puttering around, and resting. Not until I held my squirming newborn son in my arms did I finally relax. I knew then that if anything happened to him, I wouldn't survive.

It's funny. As soon as I met Todd, I began to see myself as the mother of a brood of children, picturing my offspring lined up by age, Todd and I standing proudly in their midst. And Noah, our first, gave me so much pleasure, I didn't even mind rushing to him in the middle of the night whenever he cried. I welcomed the warmth of his soft little body, loved nursing him and then rocking him gently back to sleep.

A year ago, my best friend, Luanne, suggested I try Dating.com. I was burned out from a recently ended relationship and not at all sure I was ready for another battle with love. But I opened an account and scanned the profiles of men I might be interested in meeting, telling myself I would just check it out. But Todd's ad caused me to take notice.

In his photo, he was looking straight into the camera with a wide smile and a twinkle in his eyes. But it was what he'd written that really caught my attention. He said that he was marriage minded and wanted to have a baby right away. I remember thinking, *This guy's going to save my life.*

I don't like to think of myself as a wimp, but I met Todd at the most vulnerable time of my life. I was hounded by uncertainty after breaking up with George—uncertainty and, as much as I hated to admit it, burgeoning anxiety that took the form of debilitating anxiety attacks and a reluctance to leave the house wherever possible. And, tragically, for someone who loved cars as much as I do, a fear of driving, too.

Our first telephone conversation lasted half an hour. Todd brought up babies right away. He was charming and interested in me. That was eleven months ago. I got pregnant two months later. I was grateful for the stability and security Todd was offering. I thought I loved him. And I was sure that having a baby would fix everything that was wrong in my life.

Now, as I plod up and down the driveway waiting for the officer, I play back the months Todd and I spent together. He never told me much about himself, turning stiff when I wanted to know more about his past, his family. His memories, he had said, were vague. His parents drowned when he was young. His grandmother raised him. I hadn't pushed the point. I knew what loss felt like.

Still awaiting the officer, I recall the day Todd and I decided to stop at a diner after I'd had a checkup to confirm my pregnancy—although I knew already. I experienced all the signs: sore breasts, fatigue, a late period. We'd gone to the office of a doctor a friend of Todd's recommended, a Dr. Bryson in Albany, who gave us the good news. But my happiness was somewhat marred by Dr. Bryson's diagnosis of gestational hypertension, a condition characterized by high blood pressure during pregnancy. He stressed that the earlier in pregnancy hypertension appears, the greater the risk of problems developing, restricting me to bed rest for the duration of the pregnancy.

"Salad with grilled chicken on top and a glass of milk for the lady," Todd told the waitress when she came to take our order.

When I started to disagree, because I resented him ordering for me, Todd reached over and grabbed my hand, silencing me.

"And a hamburger for me. Well done, please."

"Why did you do that?" I said after the waitress was gone, massaging the place where his nails had dug into my palm.

"Bree, you're eating for two people now. What did you have for breakfast?"

"Eggs and toast."

He shook his head, disappointed. "Not enough. You need to eat more. What fruit did you have today?"

"Uh. An apple."

"Not enough." He pushed the glass of water I hadn't touched yet toward me. "You need to hydrate yourself and our baby."

Though I appreciated Todd's concern, I was also wary of having him take such command. Not wanting to argue, though, I let my gaze drift through the window to the parking lot. My heart hammered when I saw George, illuminated by a streetlamp, leaning on the hood of a 1970 burgundy Corvette across the street. It was twilight, but he still wore his aviator sunglasses. This was the first time I'd spotted him lurking in my vicinity in a week. My neck tensed as I glared at the car. It was the same Corvette I'd overhauled for him when I still worked as a mechanic at Gene's restoration shop.

"Bree, are you okay?" Todd asked.

I swallow hard. Our relationship ended three months before I met Todd. George took our breakup badly and had taken to stalking me. His possessiveness and short temper were something he'd hidden well at first—early on, his abuses were subtle, so small, they spread over me like microscopic parasites. But they grew. And by the time I woke up to his meanness, I'd lost my job and lived in fear, constantly looking over my shoulder.

I'm not sure why, but I never told Todd about George. Maybe I was ashamed for making such a bad choice.

Todd's eyes shifted from me to George. "Bree, what's going on here? Who is this guy?"

At first, I shrugged it off, telling him I didn't know the man watching us. But he pressed harder. Finally, I broke down and told Todd about the endless phone calls, the threatening notes. The restraining order that hadn't worked. The phone calls to the police that hadn't helped.

When I was done, three creases I'd never seen before appeared across Todd's forehead. He stared out at George. I grabbed his arm. "Please don't."

Todd took a deep breath and released George from his stare. He gave me a small smile, and patted my hand. I turned my attention to my meal. The next time I looked, George and his showy car were gone.

And that's when Todd reached into his coat pocket and pulled out a small black box. Inside, nestled in velvet, was a diamond ring, with tiny sapphires surrounding the diamond. He held it out to me like a sacred offering. "What do you say?"

I found myself speechless, but nodding, nonetheless. Todd slipped the ring on my finger. All at once, the tension inside me melted away. The world seemed brighter. Even so, a small voice inside my head cautioned that this was moving too fast. But that didn't stop me.

When Todd insisted I move in with him immediately, I agreed without hesitation. It made sense, after all. Todd said he would take care of everything. He filed for a marriage license in Berkshire County. I moved into his rambling 1790s farmhouse in Becket, Massachusetts, in the middle of the woods. Twenty miles from town, the house stands high on top of the mountain. Its wraparound porch overlooks treetops and mountain peaks — but there are no other houses in sight.

A week later, we were married by the same Dr. Bryson that had declared my pregnancy dangerous, Todd assuring me the man was ordained. Everything seemed to be falling into place. *Todd and I will have a good life. We'll be happy together*, I thought.

A few days later, before Todd changed my phone number, Luanne called to tell me that George had been found outside of his apartment beaten and bloodied and had ended up in the hospital.

And now, here I am. My lips tremble as I continue to pace the driveway. Every minute is unbearable. Swiping at the seemingly constant flow of tears, I glance at my cell. Twenty-five minutes have passed since I called the police. So, I call again.

"Someone will be there shortly," the bored-sounding dispatch officer assures me.

I take a deep breath, let it out slowly, and make another call. Aunt Rachelle took over the parenting role after our parents died. I was fourteen. My sister was eighteen. Rachelle's been there for us whenever we've needed her, a clear and calming influence. But under Todd's sway, I haven't talked with her since I discovered I was pregnant.

I try to contain my tears, but the sobbing starts before I can say anything.

"Bree, is that you? Honey, what's wrong?"

"Noah …" I say, before breaking down again.

"Noah?"

"Yes. My son."

"Your son? You have a son?"

"Yes, yes, Auntie, I have a son!" Events are spinning around me. Too much to explain all at once.

"Honey, calm down," my aunt says after a long silence filled with my choking sobs. "It's just that I haven't seen or spoken with you for almost a year. You changed your phone number and seemed to disappear. And you certainly never let me know you were pregnant. And now … What's going on? Are you okay?"

"Noah is gone, and so is Todd. They're both gone."

The silence lasts longer than it should. I imagine Aunt Rachelle's lips pressed together. I know what she's thinking.

Finally, she says, "Bree —"

"You have to believe me." For months, I stroked my growing belly in amazement as little Noah poked and stirred, pushing an elbow, or his little feet—a concealed force that rearranged the landscape of my flesh.

She sighs. "Honey? Um, are you still seeing Dr. Palmer?"

"No."

"I'm sorry," my aunt says. And nothing more. No questions about Noah. Or Todd. Or how I feel. Instead, her silence expands, filling the space between us with the unspoken: *Are you sure this is happening to you?*

Maybe it was a mistake calling her, knowing she wouldn't believe me.

"I'll get back to you after I've spoken to the police," I tell her.

"I love you, honey," she says before hanging up.

I go back into the house, restless, moving from room to room, opening drawers and closets, the fridge. Only yesterday—was it just yesterday? —our refrigerator was stocked with leftovers, fruit, and vegetables. Now the shelves are nearly bare.

It's been forty minutes since I first called the police.

Eventually, I find myself in the garage. Five wooden shelves cluttered with tools and garden implements run along one wall. I scan the space, but I don't know what I'm looking for.

Again, I speed-dial Todd's cell, and again I get the same impersonal disconnection message. I glance at the time. Forty-five minutes.

Something niggles at the back of my brain. I press my palms against my eyes until dark pinwheels spear my vision. Memories rush in, unbidden, small fragments that make me cringe. Most of the time Todd was impatient and irritable. He complained about Noah's nighttime waking, his crying at two-hour intervals and not falling back to sleep until I nursed him, rocked him, sang to him.

Noah disturbed him whenever he wanted quiet, Todd said. And on Noah's fifth day, I caught him shaking our baby. But when he spotted me, Todd immediately plastered a smile on his face and kissed Noah, making me question if I'd even seen it after all.

As much as I've tried to push these facts about Todd out of my head, now I'm forced to admit that his behavior to me was never quite right—and that Noah's arrival made it worse.

Leaving the garage, I head through the kitchen and up the stairs to Noah's room. From the threshold, I gaze into the now unfamiliar space, Noah's sock pressed to my nose. I breathe in the smell of my son's skin, and the pain of his absence contracts my heart more powerfully than the contractions that heralded his birth just seven days ago.

CHAPTER 3

The cruiser rolls to a stop, and an officer slides out at a leisurely pace. I rush to the front door.

"Thank goodness you're here." Hysteria starts to rise again.

Big and hulking, the officer peers down at me through dark, wrap-around glasses. I see him taking in my messy hair, the scratches on my skin, my muddy, bare feet. I follow his eyes to where my robe has a tear at the bottom, a piece of twig still stuck there. I tighten my dirty robe and fold my arms across my swollen breasts.

"I'm Officer Gordon," he says. "May I come in?"

I stand aside, and he steps into the foyer. He removes his glasses, stops in the middle of the living room—his black eyes, set close together, dart from side to side. He takes a small, spiral notebook from the breast pocket of his uniform jacket.

"What is your full name?" he asks.

"Bree Jane Michaelson."

"You say your baby and husband are missing?" He pushes his hat back on his head, assumes an authoritative stance, and regards me with raised eyebrows.

As I tell him about Todd and Noah, it sounds unbelievable, even to me. Suddenly, I'm choking with grief that wants to escape. And escape it does, erupting into a howling I can't seem to stop.

Officer Gordon moves swiftly to the kitchen and returns with a glass of water. I try to sip it, but my hands are shaking so badly I spill most of it down the front of my robe. Still, I get hold of myself.

"Are you okay to talk, now?" the officer asks.

I nod.

His pen hovers over the small notebook. "Had the two of you quarreled?"

"No. Everything seemed just fine last night."

He scrapes a hand across his square jaw. "May I look around?"

I nod and lead him up the stairs. We are accompanied by the squeaking of his gun as it rubs against the holster.

At the entry to Noah's room, I point. "See? The furniture is gone. The crib stood under the window there, and the chest of drawers, there." I gesture to the opposite wall. "And you can still smell the fresh paint. The room was blue, yesterday. Someone painted it last night while I was asleep."

"Hmm," Officer Gordon says. He jots something in his notebook. "And you say you don't live here alone?"

"Our midwife, Connie, she lives with us. But she's gone, too."

His right eyebrow raises a fraction. "Too bad, ma'am, that you had to wake up to such a horrible discovery. The fact that you managed to sleep through the commotion of moving furniture, and the painting of the baby's room …"

Heat spreads over my body. The officer clearly thinks I'm crazy. I suck in air and let it out slowly. But the tightness in my chest remains.

"I woke up disoriented, and then I vomited. I was drugged."

"What makes you think that?" he raises a suspicious brow.

"I know from experience," I tell him about the date rape in college. The disorientation, the weakness, the dry mouth. A friend found me naked and unconscious in the back of my dorm. The school psychiatrist explained I'd suffered a state of dissociation from ingesting Rohypnol.

A look of sympathy flashes across Officer Gordon's face, then recedes.

After checking all the upstairs rooms, he follows me down to the kitchen.

"What time did you say you woke up?" His pen is poised over the spiral notebook.

"One o'clock this afternoon."

He doesn't answer. His silence seems like a rebuke.

"Just because you can't find evidence doesn't mean I'm lying."

"I'm not suggesting anything, ma'am. What is your husband's full name?"

"Todd Robert Armstrong." A thought strikes me that "tod" is Middle English for "fox." That seems so appropriate given the man's sneaky behavior.

"What make of car does he drive?"

"A silver 2015 Toyota Corolla."

"When was the last time you saw him?"

I take a deep breath to relieve the pressure I feel building. "Last night."

"What was he wearing?"

"Black jeans and a hooded sweatshirt," I say. "He has blond hair, streaked with gray, and gold eyes."

Officer Gordon rubs his jaw. "May I see pictures of your baby and your husband?"

"I have pictures of Noah but not of Todd. He didn't like to pose."

The officer follows me to the living room, but I'd forgotten. The shrine-like arrangement of baby photos disappeared with everything else. In its place is a single picture of my sister, Margaret, and me. We are standing in front of our childhood home. Margaret's blond hair was uncharacteristically curly that day from the humidity, and she stood straight-backed, chin lifted, as though facing off with the future. Next to her, in my tennis whites, I stand a head shorter, and wear a forced smile. That's because Margaret pushed me away when I tried to hug her, just before my father snapped the picture.

In the picture, Margaret's blue eyes mock me.

I have the sudden urge to swipe the picture off the shelf and send it crashing to the floor. But what would Officer Gordon think of me?

"I'm sorry," I say. "The photos were here, there were a half-dozen, but he took them, too, I guess."

The officer's gaze, full of doubt, zeroes in on mine for a long moment, trying to read the truth behind them. I glance down at my tattered robe, at the network of scratches, purple with bruising and caked with dried blood and mud that crisscross my legs.

I consider how I look to him: swollen feet, my long black hair a massive mess. A demented woman, that's what I look like. Someone he'd have a hard time believing. And why would he believe me without a single photo of either Todd or Noah? I have nothing to prove that I've ever had a baby or a husband.

"Wait!" Remembering the sock, I pull it from my pocket and hold it out to him. "Look, my baby's sock. I found it on the ground, outside."

The officer examines the sock, then hands it back to me.

"Ma'am, it's not enough evidence to go by."

I clasp my trembling hands together to keep them from shaking. "I gave birth a week ago."

"Where did you give birth?"

"At home."

His gaze sweeps the room. "Here?"

"Yes, look at me. I still look pregnant."

And I do, but Officer Gordon doesn't seem to notice. Instead, he asks, "Do you take any medications? For instance, sleeping pills? Did you have a drink before you went to sleep?"

Is he blaming me? "No. I'm nursing." Then I remember Noah's little leg. "You also need to know that Noah has a birthmark on his thigh, the size of a quarter. It's brown and shaped like a heart."

He scribbles in his notebook.

"And he has a fever and a rash." My lips tremble. "I need to find him and take him to the hospital right away."

"I'm doing the best that I can, ma'am."

I desperately want to sit down, to stop shaking.

"About your husband. Can you tell me a bit more about his background?"

"He was raised in Ottawa, Canada. He lived there until two years ago, then moved here." At least that's what Todd told me. The way things stand now, I'm not sure I whether I know anything at all.

"And the woman who lived here with you? What's her name and phone number?"

I give him Connie's cell number. "I think her last name is Bridgestone." I realize how lame this must sound. What mother turns her baby's care over to a woman whose last name she's not even sure about? Right now, I don't know how to explain that, even to myself.

"Have you seen any suspicious looking characters in the area?"

"No."

"Any hunters? People like to hunt in these woods."

He's right. Landowners in rural areas of the Berkshires sometimes spot hunters and fishermen on their property. Many times, I've awakened to the sound of early-morning gunfire.

"No. I've never seen them here, though I've heard shots in the distance. It's been a while, though."

"Okay, then. I'll go inspect outside, around the house," Officer Gordon says. "But my advice to you is to stay by the cell phone and wait for your husband to call."

I follow him to the doorway, feeling defeated. I know he's thinking the whole abduction is an invention of a disturbed mind. He might even think I'm experiencing the aftereffects of pseudocyesis—false pregnancy.

Even so, part of me wants to beg him to stay and search the house again.

But it's pointless.

Before leaving, Officer Gordon reaches into his pocket and pulls out a dog-eared business card. "Once the report is filed, we'll do an investigation," he says.

My shoulders slump as soon as the door closes behind him. His lack of urgency and what I suspect is a lack of belief in my story have gutted me.

From the window, I watch him walk towards the back of the house, then return and head toward his cruiser. Before getting in, he takes a long look at the house. When his eyes meet mine, he holds my gaze for a moment, then touches his hat and, tugging open the car door, slides into the driver's seat.

CHAPTER 4

Every act becomes an effort. An effort to make the bed. An effort to cook. An effort to shower. How long has it been since Todd and the baby disappeared? It takes me a minute to work it out. Just a day? Scenario after worst-case scenario spirals through my brain.

I'm dazed and groggy and barely upright, cell phone clutched in my hand, waiting for Officer Gordon to call with new information.

Last night, I expected to fall into an exhausted sleep the moment my head hit the pillow. Instead, I tossed and turned for hours, the sound of my baby's cries ringing in my ears. My breasts leak. Who is feeding Noah? If it's Todd, is he smart enough to test the temperature of the formula before giving him the bottle? His lack of interest in our son gives me little confidence he would do the right thing.

I find myself combing over everything I can remember from the moment I met Todd. What did I miss? How did I miss it? And when exactly is the last time I saw Noah?

Right. Just two nights ago. Again, I think about his fever, wondering if Todd took him to the pediatrician.

I keep going over everything that happened that night. Did I do or say anything to provoke Todd? Nothing I come up with makes sense. And how could he, even with Connie's help, make such a clean sweep of any evidence of their or Noah's existence?

Two days ago, I lived quiet and content. Two days ago, I changed Noah's diaper, kissed the tender skin of his thighs, and watched him sleep. Then, just like that, my world was turned upside down. The little things I worried over — Todd's lack of interest in me, in Noah, the annoyance of Connie's constant lurking presence — seem insignificant now. I'd accept all these, just to have my son back in my arms where he belongs.

I push off the bed like a woman twice my age, limbs aching under my weight, and find myself, once again, standing in Noah's room, his sock pressed to my face, breathing in his fading scent.

In the kitchen, I stare at the phone, feeling the burden of wasted time, an urgency that drives me to call Officer Gordon.

"Do you have an update on the investigation?" I ask.

"It takes time." Officer Gordon's voice, a gruff tenor, gives the impression of paternal disapproval. "I only filed the report late yesterday afternoon."

"But we're losing valuable time. Shouldn't you be putting out an AMBER Alert?"

"Under normal circumstances, I would. But in your case, we have no leads. We need to have a photo ID, and a birth certificate would help."

Again, I have the feeling that Officer Gordon thinks I'm delusional. At this thought, my breathing becomes labored, and I can sense the onset of a panic attack.

"But, please, you have to do something!" I cry.

"I assure you I'm on top of it. I've scouted the area and spoken with a few of your neighbors. But they live pretty far away from you, and those inquiries haven't revealed anything suspicious."

After hanging up with Officer Gordon, I move like a zombie from room to room. The walls close in on me. The big house feels so empty; it makes me so feel small.

The only thing I can think of doing right now is driving to the police station and confronting Officer Gordon in person. That might make a difference. At least it's better than staying put and just pacing around the house with wild imaginings circling my mind.

While I shower and dress, I realize I want to call Luanne — she's the closest friend I have. I know she's wondering what happened to me. The last time we spoke was when she told me of George's attack. Then Todd changed my phone number, and we haven't talked since. Of all my friends, Luanne is the only one who knew my parents. We grew up in Albany, went to Logan High, and ran track together. Freckled, round-faced, Luanne is vivacious and daring enough to take on anything she sets her heart on. After college, Luanne moved to Manhattan to pursue acting. I miss her.

But, I think, it will take too much time to explain everything to her. I'll call Luanne after I return from the police station, I decide. Maybe by then, I'll have more answers.

I open the garage door to see the sun peeking through the trees. I zip my leather jacket up to my throat and shiver.

I haven't driven my Mustang for eight months, not since Dr. Bryson ordered me to bed.

I yank hard on the door several times. It finally opens with a metallic squeal. I make a mental note to buy grease to lubricate the hinges. But that will have to wait.

Settled in the driver's seat, I take a deep breath, relishing the scent of gasoline and motor oil. It reminds me of all the hours my father, a physicist turned mechanic, and I spent bent over this very engine. The Mustang was his, purchased when he was in college and maintained with his own hands until the day he died.

Growing up, I spent any time I could following him around the shop. I liked fixing cars just to be around him and cherished the moments I saw praise in his eyes. Eventually, I grew to love tinkering with engines, whether he was there or not. It's not that I wasn't a good student. I was. But like my dad, ultimately, I preferred concrete solutions to theoretical ones.

I place my hands on the wheel and try to swallow, but my throat is dry. I'd fooled myself into believing the anxiety would magically vanish once I moved in with Todd. On the contrary. It became worse than ever. Despite making me feel protected, his quick impatience and irritation often made me feel like I was teetering on the edge of a high cliff.

He told me a few times that he loved me, but that was obviously a big, fat lie. A husband who loves his wife doesn't disappear in the middle of the night. With their baby.

Shaking a bit, I turn the key in the ignition. I almost feel relieved when the engine refuses to roll over. My driving anxiety makes me worry I'll lose control of the wheel and cause an accident. And traffic jams make me feel trapped. The fact that Becket is a small town of only about two thousand people, and is nearly devoid of traffic, doesn't help at all.

I take another big breath to calm myself. That's when I notice it: the smell of Connie's sweet, candy-like perfume. I remember, now. She used my car a month or so ago, when the battery in her Jeep died.

I feel myself tensing again, but another deep breath gets me out of the Mustang. I walk to the front of the car and smooth my hands over my stomach, feeling the softness there. Connie said it would take weeks before my belly snaps back to the general shape it was before I got pregnant. A flush of longing for Noah rushes through me, but I push it down. There's business to attend to.

The hood creaks when I pop it open. Immediately, I see it. The battery is corroded. It's a wonder Connie was able to get the Mustang started when she borrowed it. At the end of twenty minutes, I've removed the cables and cleaned terminals and the cable ends with baking soda and water and a good scrub with a wire brush. I try the ignition again. This time it kicks over.

My Mustang groans as it bounces up the twisting dirt road, then down the hill and away from the house. I speed along Route 8, which cuts through a terrain of dense trees and small houses. Monstrous gray rocks jut up from the earth, entwined with briar vines.

I'm entirely involved in keeping myself calm as the road flies by under my wheels. Then my cell phone rings. I screech to a halt at the side of the road, flinging bits of mud in my wake. When I see who's calling, I shake my head—but I answer anyway.

"Bree," my aunt says, "are you okay?"

"Don't worry, Auntie." I keep my tone steady. "I'm holding up."

"That's good, honey. I'm glad to hear that." She sighs. "I worry about you."

Tears prick my eyes. Not now.

"Bree?"

I know what's coming. I crank down the window. In the crisp, cold air, I smell winter.

"You're not having another episode, are you?"

"I can't talk," I say, tightly. "I'm in the car, on the way to the police station."

"In the car? You're driving? That's so good, honey. I wanted to tell you, though, a police officer called yesterday, asking questions."

"Officer Gordon?"

"Bree, I have to ask this: You did have a baby this time?"

"Yes!" I say, trying to erase the doubt in her voice. But knowing my history, why would she believe me? Or anyone for that matter.

"It's just that, you know, last time . . ."

"I had a baby! I was pregnant, I went into labor, and I gave birth!"

"Don't get upset with me. It's going to be okay, honey."

A false assurance and we both know it.

"I miss you," she says.

"I'm sorry. Soon as I can, I'll come and visit," I promise before hanging up. I should have called my aunt months ago to tell her what was going on. I know that. But Todd discouraged my keeping up with my family, my old friends. And, with all I'd been through, honestly, it ended up seeming easier that way. But now, no one from my old life knows anything about my new life. Or what had been my new life. Until two days ago.

A thunderstorm looms. A few deep breaths calm the panic welling up, and I steer the Mustang back onto the road.

A few detours and wrong turns later, I arrive in downtown Becket. Just as I'm about to turn into the police station parking lot, I spot a red, barn-like structure. A sign above the door says, Becket Country Store.

Wait a minute!

I slam on the brakes.

CHAPTER 5

A few months ago, Todd, or maybe Connie, had pizza delivered from the Becket Country Store. I remember looking out the bedroom window and seeing the delivery boy walking up to the door. Would he remember seeing whichever one of them answered the door? Maybe. If he does, that will prove to the police that Connie and Todd lived with me.

The bell over the front door of the country store tinkles as I enter. A man sitting at the counter looks up from his plate and eyes me too long. Pulling my gaze from his, I feel my stomach grumble. The aroma of carrot soup and fresh baked bread reminds me I haven't eaten much in two days.

The girl behind the counter, early twenties and thin as a matchstick, with short spiky hair, glances at me as I edge forward. She pauses in her conversation with a woman wearing a ponytail and holding a baby on her hip. I smile at the child. He turns his head and nestles facing away from me.

"How can I help?" the girl asks.

The baby begins to fuss, causing my breasts to ooze.

"Ma'am, can I help you?"

I pull my gaze away from the baby. "I … I had pizza delivered a few months ago by a young man. Is he here?"

"That depends. We have two delivery boys," the girl says. "What did he look like?"

"Tall and skinny." I press my arms against my swollen breasts. "His hair was dark, shoulder length."

"That would be James. But he's not working today. Can I give him a message?"

"No, no. Thanks. I'll be back." Finally. A witness. I hope.

Nodding at the woman with the baby, I leave the store and walk across the parking lot to the police station.

An overweight officer sits behind a scarred desk, choking down a thick sandwich that reeks of salami. He tells me I can wait—Officer Gordon will be back soon. I sit on a green plastic chair and flip through a *Guns and Ammo* magazine, not seeing what I am looking at.

Ten minutes later, the door swings inward, and Officer Gordon enters, his badge on a lanyard around his neck, his gun holstered on his belt. He frowns when he spots me, then motions for me to follow with a hand holding a Styrofoam cup. "Hold my calls, Bernie," he says over his shoulder.

I trail him into a small office overlooking the narrow parking lot and dense woods and lower myself into one of two chairs across from his desk. On it, in a small, framed photo, Officer Gordon stands with his arm around a pretty woman who holds a small boy on her lap. His son. I figure he would have sympathy for me.

Officer Gordon leans back in his desk chair, which groans beneath him. "How can I help, Miss Michaelson?"

Might as well get right to the point. "You were pretty vague on the phone," I say. "Could you tell me what exactly is being done about finding my baby and husband? What leads you're following?"

He reaches for his notes, turning a few pages. I get the feeling he's trying to stall. Finally, he leans forward. "Unfortunately, Miss Michaelson, we've gone over all the details you've given us and, so far, have come up with nothing."

He turns more a few more pages. "Have you found any photos of Todd or the baby?"

"No," I say. "As I told you already, Todd was camera shy. And any pictures I had of the baby are gone. Even from my phone." I was stunned—again—when I scrolled through my phone for the dozens of pictures of Noah I'd taken only to find them missing.

But when I explain that to Officer Gordon, he looks almost bemused, as if he's listening to a woman with a great imagination, rather than a frantically worried mother.

Still, he makes a note in his file. Then he says, "Look, I'm trying hard here. But you have to understand that it's difficult to investigate without evidence."

I understand my predicament. As far as I know, the only people who have ever seen Todd and Connie were Dr. Bryson and me. And no one besides Todd and Connie has ever seen Noah. I find myself thinking how happy Todd looked when I told him I was pregnant. He immediately sprang into action. "Greg, Dr. Greg Bryson delivered a friend's baby," Todd said. "We'll use him." Todd also suggested it was best to wait until after the first trimester before telling anyone about the pregnancy.

In answer to my objections, he pointed out that it was bad luck. I didn't know about that, but I did know that miscarriage was most likely in the first three months, so I was willing to wait. And by the end of the first trimester, Todd had convinced me that I was better off without contacting my family and friends. "Make a clean break so you can start fresh," is how he put it. I was so relieved not to have anyone bringing up my past, that I agreed, thinking I would contact Aunt Rachelle and Margaret when I had established my own little family. When I was "normal."

"What about the midwife?" I ask Officer Gordon. I'm a drowning woman on a mission. "Have you found anything about her?"

He looks again at his notes. "Connie Bridgestone?"

I nod. "I think that's what it is."

His eyebrows rise, folding his forehead like an accordion. I understand. How is it possible to have someone live in your house for months and not be sure of her name?

He shakes his head. "I'm sorry, but she doesn't show up in any of our databases, either. We've even searched the FBI database." He folds his hands on the desk. "How did you get in touch with her?"

"I didn't. Todd did." More and more, I'm seeing how I've failed in all of this. Letting someone else take charge of my life seemed like a good plan at the time. But now?

"And what did you know about her?"

My heart is sinking. My far-too-late realization that I have let Todd take care of everything numbs me. He insisted on putting Connie, another referral from a "friend," in charge of my delivery and of Noah. Although Connie seemed competent, I was uneasy with her from the beginning, her disapproval seemed to be constantly looming.

I hang my head. "Nothing. Just what Todd told me. She had worked for friends of his."

There's a pause. I don't look up. I'm embarrassed to meet the officer's eyes. Finally, he says, "Your gynecologist was Dr. Greg Bryson, right? That's what you said?"

I nod.

"Well, we can't find any record of a Dr. Greg Bryson. He's not affiliated with any of the hospitals or medical centers in Albany. We've even contacted the American Medical Association. But no go. And the address you gave for his office must be wrong. No one by that name has ever had an office there."

I can hardly breathe. How is that possible?

We only went to the office once, when Dr. Bryson diagnosed my condition. After that, he visited me at the house. It seemed odd to me at the time. But I accepted it. After all, having a doctor make house calls had its advantages. And I didn't want to look peevish objecting to such a convenient arrangement.

Officer Gordon reaches for his Styrofoam cup of, takes a small sip, and wipes his lips with the back of his hand. "You said your husband's name is Todd Armstrong. I'm sorry to tell you this, but your husband doesn't show up anywhere either, at least not by that name."

"Impossible." I nearly jump out of the chair.

"As for your son, you must understand, six-day-old infants don't mysteriously disappear without some cause."

"Eight. My baby is eight days old today," I say through clenched jaws.

He shakes his head, as if Noah's age is immaterial. "Unless there are previous reports of your husband abusing you or domestic violence calls to your address, there would be no reason we would suspect foul play."

As the hopelessness of my situation sinks in, I want to throw myself to the floor, sobbing. But I don't want Officer Gordon to think I'm crazier than he does already.

Looking at me steadily, he says, "The question is: Why would your husband take off in the middle of the night with the baby and the furniture? And the midwife? In my conversations with your friends and family members, they all indicated they've never seen your baby, neither have they seen you pregnant. And they've never met Todd. To help you, I need proof that this child actually exists. Do you have any such proof?"

There's a tone in his voice, almost accusatory. I find myself shrinking. He has made up his mind about me. I don't know what to say. Besides my leaking breasts and soft belly, do I have any proof?

I turn my eyes to the window. The sky is thick with dark clouds. Rain hasn't come yet, and neither have the answers I'm desperate for.

"When it comes to children," Officer Gordon continues, "we jump into action. But without leads, evidence ..." His voice trails off. Then, "The baby's name, you said, is Noah? Well, have you found his birth certificate, yet?"

Noah was born at home. I didn't like the idea at first. But Todd had convinced me that today's midwives were well-trained professionals. "Midwives deliver more U.S. babies than ever," he said. "If something goes wrong, which it won't, we're only an hour away from Berkshire Medical Center in Pittsfield."

I accepted his input as evidence of his caring, and I acquiesced. No one but Aunt Rachelle had ever taken care of me so completely.

That was how I saw it then. Now, the realization that I relinquished all the decisions about Noah causes my heart to sink like a boulder. And, no, I never saw the birth certificate. *Stupid! Stupid!*

At a loss for words, I shake my head. "Please," I say. "You must help me. There has to be a way."

He glances at his notes and drums his fingers on the desktop. At last his eyes refocus on me.

"It's impossible for me to help you. I don't have your husband's cell number to monitor. No pictures. No license plates."

Then his forehead suddenly creases as though he's remembered something.

"See, I collect pieces of information until a few of them fit together. Your parents died in a car accident when you were fourteen."

What? I eject myself out of my chair. It crashes to the floor behind me. "What does that have to do with my missing baby?"

"You came here to find out what I've learned in the course of the investigation. Well, I have gained insight into the circumstances surrounding your, um, missing baby." Flipping through his file again, he extracts an official looking document, but holds up his hand, as I start to open my mouth in protest.

"You see, this is a serious matter you're presenting, and I'm making it my business to learn everything I can about you." He points at the document. "It says here that you once tried to commit suicide."

"That doesn't mean I'm making this up, and it doesn't mean you should doubt my story. My baby *was* stolen from me. Who do I talk with to get your department to help?" My voice shakes with rage and worry and fear.

Ignoring my outburst, he calmly slips the document back into his file and shoves it to the side. "So, you see? We can find out anything we need to know, and there's nothing about a husband and a baby."

Defeated, I pick the chair up off the floor and sit back down. Then I remember the pizza delivery boy. "I do have proof," I say. "We had pizza delivered from next door a few months ago. Either Todd or Connie paid for it. The delivery boy, James, he can vouch for me."

He sits up straight. "Oh, I know James. James O'Leary." He makes a note. "Okay, I'll check with him."

I can see there's something else on his mind. He's drumming his fingers on the desk, again. "You say your husband owns the house?"

I nod.

"What makes you think that?"

"He told me. I had no reason to doubt him."

He gives me a wary glance. "Do you know an Agnes Payne?"

I've never heard of her. But even as I shake my head, I see his cop's eyes calculating my reaction.

"Who is she?"

"She's the owner of your house."

As I let his words sink in, I stare at his thick fingers — now laced around the cup, they're too short for his large hand.

"And Mrs. Payne says that you're in fact the one who rented the house, and that you paid in cash for one year."

"Not possible. I never met the woman. She's lying!"

He raises his eyebrows and waits, but I don't know how to respond.

"Sorry, I've done all I can, for now," he finally says. "But I'll check with James and get back to you."

The police are supposed to serve and protect. I had hoped so, but after this interview with Officer Gordon, I'm fairly certain I'm on my own with this. But I have one more question.

"What about the sock I found in front of the house. Isn't that proof enough?"

"Not really. Agnes's last tenants had a baby. They could have left the sock behind. Go home now," he says, and leads me to the door.

In the parking lot, I wrap my arms around myself. But the chill comes from within. I came to the police station to find answers. Instead, I'm leaving with more questions than ever.

CHAPTER 6

I head back to the country store, get a cup of coffee, and do a quick search on my cell. Google supplies me with Agnes Payne's address in Great Barrington. But no phone number.

Fueled by caffeine and adrenaline, and oddly untroubled by my driving anxiety, I punch the gas and speed along the winding roads toward Great Barrington, still reeling from everything Officer Gordon told me.

I consider what Officer Gordon said about having gone door to door, only to find that no one close to us had ever seen Todd. How could they, though? Each house is a quarter mile away from the next.

Another thought strikes me. Todd did all the shopping. Unless he traveled to another town, someone in Becket or Great Barrington had to have seen him. And once in a while, Connie, when Todd was around, would go out for hours at a time. Where did she go? Wouldn't someone have seen her as well? I start to get excited, but then remember that I don't have any pictures of them to show anyone.

A rabbit scurries across the road. "Damn!" My arms stiffen at the wheel, and I hit the brakes hard, skidding a bit, which causes something to slide out from under the seat and lodge against my boot. Heart still pumping, I bend down and close my fingers around a hard, thumb-sized item. Too nervous to take my eyes off the road, I shove the thing into my coat pocket and concentrate on driving.

Set amidst rolling hills, with its historic buildings, Great Barrington has a picture-postcard look—a church built in the Gothic Revival style and a small library to match. No chains have replaced the gourmet restaurants, the trendy boutiques, or the ice-cream parlor on Main Street.

It's lovely, for sure, but I'm not in the frame of mind to appreciate the town's charms. Instead, I'm frustrated at the wrong turns I make on the way to Agnes's house. But I find it, shortly after eleven, on a tree-lined street, one among a neighborhood of meticulously maintained turn-of-the-century homes.

Agnes's quaint Colonial is surrounded by maples and spruce trees. A rectangle of neatly mowed grass edges the front. A late morning breeze pushes at me and carries the perfume of hydrangea across the yard.

Dead leaves crunch under my boots as I stride toward the front door and give it a firm knock. No answer. I knock again, as a dog barks in the background.

Still no one. Deep breath in. Deep breath out. The barking continues. What now? I chew my bottom lip. I decide to wait.

Once I settle behind the steering wheel, I pull out my cell phone and dial a number I know by heart. Luanne answers on the first ring, sounding out of breath.

"Hi," I say.

"Well, what do you know? Out of the blue. It's like you fell off the earth. No phone calls from you for, let's see, for how long? Many moons, anyway. And then I get a phone call from an Officer Gordon, asking me questions that don't make sense. What happened to you?"

I reach toward the passenger seat, grasp Noah's sock, and begin to wail.

"Bree," Luanne says, "you're scaring me. Calm down and tell me what's going on."

I let out a long, shaky breath. "Todd ... and ... Noah have disappeared."

"Wait? Todd? Is he the guy you were dating before you cut me off?"

Suddenly, a chill overtakes me. I turn on the ignition and dial up the heat.

"Bree?"

"Yes."

"Who is this guy, anyway? How come I never met him?"

"You're not helping."

"Don't I have the right to be upset with you?"

"We're getting off the subject."

"Oh, and who is Noah?"

"I had a baby with Todd. We're married."

"What?" Luanne's voice rises a couple of notches. "This is a joke, right?"

"It's not. It's real." With a shudder, I tell her everything, right up to this morning's conversation with Officer Gordon. "So, the police couldn't find anything on Todd. He doesn't show up anywhere. Since no one saw him or the baby, Officer Gordon thinks I've lost my mind. And ... and I don't blame him."

She doesn't respond for a long time. Then she clears her throat. "For someone with a high IQ, you are kind of clueless when it comes to men."

"I'm not in the mood." My sudden anger is not directed at my friend, but at myself. After my experience with George, I should have paid more attention to the signs.

"Okay," she says. "Well. No evidence, no motive, no suspects, no witnesses. You know how that sounds, right?"

"Crazy, huh?" I say. "Officer Gordon couldn't even accept a missing person's report without evidence. There's no proof that Todd and Noah ever existed. But they did. And the big question is, why would Todd get up in the middle of the night, make it seem like he never existed, and then take off with Noah?"

I fish out a tissue from the glove compartment. "I don't understand. Why would he go to such lengths to make it seem as if he'd never lived there? And Connie, too."

"Wait. Connie?"

"Todd fished her out of somewhere to deliver Noah and take care of us."

There's silence on the other end. I imagine Luanne wrinkling her freckled nose, as she always does when something doesn't make sense. I miss her.

"I know," I say. "I wasn't paying attention, was I?" I swipe at the dust on the dashboard with my tissue. "In my defense, I was busy with a high-risk pregnancy."

"Don't be hard on yourself." I hear Luanne gulp something. "But how did you know it was high risk?"

Yes. How *did* I know? "A doctor Todd chose," I admit. "Someone he supposedly knew recommended the guy."

Looking back, I remember feeling uncertain about Dr. Bryson's diagnosis because I felt fine. But who was I to question a medical professional?

"So? What now?"

"I don't know. Officer Gordon is useless — and he obviously thinks the same of me."

"Um … maybe you should speak to someone."

I roll my eyes. I know what Luanne is alluding to. "I don't need to have a headshrinker digging inside my brain. I've had enough of that to last me a lifetime."

My friend sounds hesitant as she poses her next question. "Given what happened before, this is difficult, but — are you leveling with me about Todd and having a baby?"

"How could you ask me that?" I retort. But at the same time, I'm thinking, *How could she not ask?* Luanne, of all people, knows my history. Still, her question is like salt on a raw wound.

"Don't be upset with me," Luanne says. "It's possible you've had a relapse."

"My aunt. The police. Now you. You all doubt me?"

"Put yourself in my place. I never met Todd, never even heard his voice. Never saw you pregnant. Never saw the baby. And for nearly a year you practically dropped off the earth." Luanne's voice, though quiet, carries an edge. "Even Rachelle has never seen the baby or Todd."

I rub a greasy spot on the radio with the pad of my index finger. How can I convince Luanne that I'm not hallucinating a husband and a baby, when, as she's pointing out, I did have a mental breakdown a few years ago — and my aunt and my psychiatrist convinced me to check into a facility.

"Bree, listen, we're just talking, okay?" Luanne's soothing voice calms me a bit. "But what are you going to do?"

"Start digging."

"Sounds almost impossible."

"Pretty much, the way things look now. But I can't sit around and wait for the police to do nothing."

"Do you want me to come out? I can jump on the next train."

"Not, now," I say. "But thank you. For now, I need to sort things out by myself."

After we say goodbye, I sit outside Agnes's house, staring at the trees swaying in the wind, thinking about what Luanne said. She doesn't believe me. Officer Gordon doesn't believe me. Neither does my aunt. I'm more alone now than ever.

CHAPTER 7

I wait another thirty minutes for Agnes to arrive, then the need to use a restroom forces me to the nearest convenience store. When I return, I park at the curb again, and, hoping the woman has returned in my absence, crunch back up the walkway.

I knock, and, sure enough, at the window to the right of the door a curtain slides aside and a woman's face peers through. I force a smile. The woman disappears from the window and opens the door, blinking her myopic eyes against the daylight. A small parrot perches on her shoulder, all scarlet and jade. Long earrings dangle from her overstretched earlobes.

"Are you Agnes Payne?" I ask.

"Is something wrong at the house?"

"I'm Bree Michaelson."

She takes my offered hand with a liver-spotted one. "Yes, of course you are. I'm not senile."

Odd. What does that mean?

My eyes follow the parrot, who hops from side to side on her shoulder.

"This is Romeo," she says, gesturing at the bird. "So, is something wrong at the house?"

"Nothing. The house is fine. But I need to ask you a few questions. Do you mind if I come in?"

Agnes steps back and gestures for me to follow her into a crowded living room, where an overstuffed floral sofa faces a small television on a stand, and a large bird cage fills a corner of the room, which is warmed by a fire crackling in the fireplace.

Memories of my parents rise up, unbidden. Anything burning reminds me. The stench of rubber and human flesh. I was thrown from the car during the impact, sustaining a head injury and several broken bones. But my parents were trapped—trapped in a burning car. I'm good at compartmentalizing, but fires are still a trigger.

As I swallow the thick lump in my throat, the black Great Dane that was lying on a second sofa comes over to give me a friendly sniff. I stroke his smooth head, and Agnes says, "This is Charlie. He belongs to my grandson, Damon. He lives half a mile from you on Elm Court. Have you met?"

I shake my head.

"He's a good kid, works hard. He's a private investigator, does something with insurance fraud."

Charlie rolls over on his back, and I bend to stroke his belly.

"Charlie, go sit on the sofa," Agnes commands.

The parrot gives an approving squawk. Charlie trots over to the sofa, leaps up, and flops down with a sigh.

She gestures to a wingback chair upholstered in a faded Indian print. "Have a seat," she says, as she sits on the floral couch across from me.

"Do you mind if I ask you a couple of questions?"

I watch as the parrot hammers its beak on her shoulder. "Don't mind at all."

Just then, my cell buzzes in my pocket. Hoping against hope that it might be Officer Gordon, I dig it out, holding up a finger in a "one moment" sign to Agnes.

But when I see who it is, a familiar weariness settles over me. My sister Margaret has done her best to cut all ties that might bind her to the past. But that hasn't stop her from calling me or Aunt Rachelle on occasion to voice her strong opinions. And when she does, even though she's only four years older than me, she makes me feel like I'm a child again. For a moment, I picture her at eighteen, sitting on Aunt Rachelle's front steps, her thin body folded into itself like a weighted-down twig, shedding tears over our parents' death. For which she has never forgiven me.

I let the call go to voicemail, realizing that Aunt Rachelle must have given her my new number. Figures.

Agnes looks at me curiously.

"I'm sorry," I say. "I've turned it off, now. So, I wonder, could you tell me who rented the house last year?"

Agnes squints at me, stroking Romeo's head as if seeking reassurance. "It was you," she says, in a slightly belligerent tone. "Unless you have a double."

"Are you sure it wasn't a man who rented the house?"

"I'm old, dear. Not forgetful."

"I didn't rent the house. I've never met you before."

"Are you on medication, dear?" Agnes gives me a skeptical look with her rheumy eyes. But there's no judgment in her voice, now. No belligerence. Just concern. "I used to be a rehab nurse. I helped patients who'd suffered anything from a stroke to massive trauma. I wonder if you've had any sort of shock. Or head trauma?"

I shake my head. There's a heavy silence.

Then I ask, "How did you get paid? And when exactly was the house rented?"

She frowns. "What's this all about?"

I'm on the edge of breaking down again. This woman was actually a pawn in Todd's deception. How can I get the information she may not even realize she has? "Please, I need your help. My husband and baby disappeared the other night."

"What? What husband? What baby? You told me you'd be the only resident."

"Well, how did they, I mean I, how did I find about your house?"

"Oh, about a year ago, my grandson placed an ad for the house on Craigslist. You called. I'm sure you were the one I met. Same height. You are very tall. Easy to remember. You handed me cash for twelve months' rent. And that was the end of that. You even told me there was no reason to worry, that if anything got broken, you'd have it fixed."

My face blazes at the thought of the deliberation and preplanning this suggests. "Mrs. Payne, what was I wearing?" It's easy to see Agnes is half-blind, but I'm grasping at straws, now.

Seemingly weary of explaining things, she just sighs, and Romeo flutters away. "You know, Bree, if it wasn't you who came to rent the house, then the one who did bears a remarkable resemblance to you. Are you okay, dear?" Agnes is studying me carefully. "You don't look well."

I blink away tears. Right this minute, I don't want sympathy. I want revenge. Actually, I'm damn angry. But all I say is, "I'm fine; just allergies."

The Great Dane unfolds himself from his couch and comes over and nudges my hand. As I scratch behind his ear, his tail whips in wide arcs.

The dog has given me another thought. "Was your grandson with you when this woman … ah … when I rented the house?"

She folds her bony hands together and places them firmly in her lap. "No. I was alone."

I sense my time with Agnes Payne is running short. "Have you or your grandson ever stopped over at the house for anything?"

"Never had a reason to, dear. We trust people, and you looked nice enough."

"What about a lease. Did she … I mean, did I sign a lease? Did you request ID?"

"Didn't see the need. You had letters from former landlords that showed you were an excellent tenant. You offered to pay in full up front. It was a pretty straightforward transaction. Now, if you don't have any other questions …"

Agnes pushes up out of the soft cushions of the couch. Clearly, my welcome is expired.

I stand and extend my hand. "Thanks for taking the time to talk to me."

Agnes shakes my hand gently, then releases it. I give Charlie another pat on his handsome head and follow her to the door.

"One more thing, Mrs. Michaelson, are you planning to stay on? If so, your rent will be due soon."

I make a quick calculation in my head. If the house was rented almost a full year ago, Todd, or the woman pretending to be me, moved in almost as soon as he met me. I'm beginning to understand a little more. The reason renters pay in cash is that they don't want a paper trail.

"No problem," I say. "I'm interested in staying longer. Can I pay you month to month?"

"Certainly, dear."

At my car, I feel like I've overlooked something … yet I can't put my finger on just what. I turn back, but Agnes has already shut the door.

CHAPTER 8

A black depression follows me all the way back to the empty house. I try to push the hopelessness out of my head. No room for pity. No room for guilt. Two days have passed. The pressure of finding Todd and Noah presses on my temples. Did Todd take him to the doctor to check his rash and fever?

I'm sure both the police and Agnes think I'm stark raving crazy. And yet, for a fleeting moment, I consider calling Officer Gordon again. But I have no new information to give him.

In the kitchen, I swallow two Advil, then fire up my computer. I may not have any information, but I won't rest until I've found some. Everybody leaves a digital trail, and Todd isn't any different. A search of his full name yields thousands, though. I enter a free database that sorts those thousands by age, state of residence, prior addresses, and relatives, but don't get a good match, don't turn up any criminal record or driving history.

I never even thought of memorizing Todd's license plate number, or Connie's. In my defense, why would I? But I know now that I allowed myself to be blinded. And as a result, I have been robbed of my child.

As far as Todd's search, I'm at a dead end. It's as if the guy never existed.

On the National Center for Missing and Exploited Children website, I look at articles about abducted babies. A two-year-old boy hasn't been seen since January 2014. Another two-year-old was abducted by his mother in August of the same year. The list of missing children of all ages goes on and on.

My finger poises over a link. It headlines, "If your child goes missing." There, I find that in addition to calling local law enforcement, parents can call the NCMEC hotline. But I soon realize that, with no picture and no hospital or birth record, they won't be able to help.

After an hour, my shoulder muscles clench into ropy knots from leaning over the computer. My eyes are tired and achy. I might as well be chasing shadows.

Maybe if I write down what I remember about Todd, I'll be able to get a better picture of him. It doesn't take all that long, which is testament to how little I learned about my husband in the scant time we were married. In the meantime, the kitchen has gotten as chilly as my mood, and I'm hungry. I turn on the oven for warmth and make myself a cheese sandwich. It tastes like cardboard, but I swallow it down with a glass of milk and feel slightly better.

Thus fortified, I spread my notes on the table and study them. It's odd, I reflect, how impatient Todd was with Noah, when he'd seemed so happy about my pregnancy. Those pieces don't fit together. And another odd thing for someone so insistent on being a father: immediately after Noah's birth, when I wanted to take Noah to the pediatrician, Todd kept putting me off. "Connie is perfectly capable of taking care of Noah," he'd said, stiff beneath his even tone.

"Todd, I'm serious. Babies need to be checked by a pediatrician within three to five days."

"You worry too much. Connie says he's fine."

"But she's not a pediatrician."

Then Noah developed the rash, followed by that high temperature, and I pressed Todd again, saying we should take the baby directly to the emergency room. This time, he placed a hand on my shoulder, gave me a direct gaze, which I read as sincere concern, and said, "Connie says he'll be okay for tonight, but tomorrow we'll take him to a pediatrician."

The next day they were all gone.

I shove my chair back and start pacing. And what about Connie? A clip of the last few months runs in reverse in my head. The gazes Todd and Connie gave each other when they thought I wasn't looking.

The time I caught her massaging Todd's shoulders. I thought it was odd, but I ignored it because Connie is in her sixties, and I saw no real threat there.

Thinking of Connie gives me an idea. There is one way to prove I delivered a baby—a doctor's examination. Why didn't I think of this before? A quick internet search gives me a list of gynecologists. I make an appointment with a Dr. Reardon in Pittsfield for next Friday, his earliest opening.

Then, my thoughts turn to the Mustang. Over the years, I've done everything from replacing the car's timing belt to rebuilding a toasted alternator. Tinkering with car engines, running my fingers along tight hoses and lines, relaxes me, even comforts me. It makes me feel close to my father.

My dad was a master of seeing mechanical possibilities. The most important lesson I learned from him was that all sound puzzle-solving starts with a hypothesis, which is the basis for exploring a situation from all angles. I couldn't have asked for a better teacher. I can hear him saying, *Bree, working with your hands requires complex thinking. Understanding how machines work is a virtue.* Maybe tinkering with my car will kick my problem-solving process into gear.

I go down to the basement to get my mechanic's overall to cover up my clothes. Like the rest of the house, the basement is empty of everything that would suggest anyone but me lived in the house. The absence of Todd's weight bench, dumbbells, and punching bag— which he resorted to when things didn't go well at the office ... but there is no office! *Where did he go every day?*—make the basement feel shadowy and unfriendly. I grab my overall from its hook and head back upstairs, the clatter of my boots on the wooden stairs echoing in the empty house.

In the garage, I run my hand across the Mustang's candy red hood and consider my hypothesis, which is simply that Todd had a reason to leave the way he did, and he had his departure in mind before I was even fully committed to playing my part in his game.

Having articulated that clearly for myself, I give myself over to the Mustang. My hands hum with electric energy as I loosen, clean, and inspect parts. At one point, a strand of hair falls in front of my eyes.

As I sweep it out of my face with the back of my hand, a light bulb flickers in my brain. What is it about hair? Then, a memory rushes in. The wigs!

A few days ago, while Noah and Connie were napping and Todd was grocery shopping, I decided to clean the closets. That's when I spotted the supermarket bag wedged in the corner of Todd's closet. Tugging it down, I found a stash of wigs and glue-on mustaches and beards.

When he got home, I met him at the door and asked, "Why do you have those wigs in your closet?"

"What were you doing in my closet?" he asked, a wariness flickering in his eyes.

"Just keeping myself busy while Noah napped," I said. "Why? Is that a problem?"

"Oh, no. No. Not at all." Todd answered too quickly and widened his smile. "This is so silly. A leftover from Halloween parties. Didn't even know I still had them."

I wanted to believe him. And at that moment, I convinced myself that I did.

The next day, the bag had gone.

CHAPTER 9

I look up from the Mustang to see a blue Jeep turning into my driveway. The vehicle crunches over the loose gravel and comes to a stop near the open garage door. I put my wrench down and wipe my hands with a cloth. A large man with a buzz cut, wearing jeans, cowboy boots, and a weathered jean jacket jumps out, followed by a black Great Dane.

"Charlie!" I call. The Dane lopes over and plants his paws on my shoulders, tail whacking the air behind him, a tsunami in the making.

"Down, Charlie!" the man calls, his intense brown eyes holding mine.

Charlie drops to all fours next to me, panting and looking cheerful, while the man, Agnes's grandson, I assume, studies my disheveled appearance, all the way down to my grease-splattered overall.

"Hi," I say. "Are you …?"

"I'm Damon. Damon Morgan, Gladys's grandson. You're Bree?"

I nod. "I am."

He walks forward, filling my field of vision. At six feet tall, I've always considered myself a substantial woman, but I feel positively tiny next to him.

I wipe my hands again and shake his offered hand. His clasp is firm and warm.

He eyes my Mustang, its hood still open. "Problem with your car?"

"I'm just making sure everything is humming along."

He raises his eyebrows and, noting the tools lined up on next to the car, smiles. But it seems he's not in a rush to say anything further.

We stand there for a moment, listening to the quiet. The sun is sinking low in the sky. A chipmunk scurries across the driveway. Trees sway in the wind, but the soft whoosh of leaves does nothing to comfort me. Obviously, his grandmother sent him. Is he checking up on the house? Going to evict me?

He clears his throat. "We're practically neighbors. I live on the other side of the hill."

"That's what your grandmother said. I'm surprised she hasn't asked you to come and check the house before today."

He sighs. "We have a deal, Grandma and me. She's independent, likes to take care of her own affairs. So, I try to stay out of her way."

"And now?" I press.

"Yeah. Well, she asked me to check in on you." His smile is apologetic.

I cross my arms over my chest. "She wants to know if you think I'm crazy. Is that it?"

He shifts his weight from one leg to the other. "I admit, she's concerned. But *crazy* is not one of the words she used. Besides, she and I agree that Charlie is a good judge of character."

The dog whacks his tail on the ground at the mention of his name. I reach to stroke his satiny black head.

"Fair enough." I throw him a conciliatory smile.

"Actually, she told me you might need help. I don't know what she meant by that. But here I am."

"I could use some help," I find myself admitting, "and I'm just about due for a cup of tea. Would you like to come in?"

The Great Dane stares up at me, wagging his tail.

He smiles. "Sure."

Charlie trots behind us through the garage into the kitchen, where I invite Damon to have a seat at the pine table. After I put the kettle on and place a bowl of water on the floor for Charlie, I excuse myself to clean up. Upstairs, I strip off my overall, scrub my hands, splash water on my face, and run my fingers through my hair, making myself as presentable as I can before the kettle whistles.

Back in the kitchen, I pour out our tea. The Great Dane parks his haunches on the floor next to me when I settle myself at the table opposite Damon.

He takes a sip of the tea, soft brown eyes gazing at me from above the rim of the cup, and nods to me, waiting for me to begin, so I do.

"Your grandmother thought I was the one renting the house. But it wasn't me."

"My grandmother is in her early eighties, and vision is a bit of an issue," he says, placing his cup down. "But her mind is sharp." Then, he leans toward me. "Bree, the truth is, Grandma thinks it's really odd that you claim you weren't the woman she met. Who else could it have been, she wants to know. And she said you looked troubled."

"Of course, I looked troubled." My voice sounds loud to my ears. "Wouldn't you be if your entire life disappeared overnight?" It all comes flooding back: Todd's strange behavior the night before he left, the stripped rooms, Officer Gordon's disbelief, and, to top it all off, learning Todd doesn't own the house, and I don't even know his real name.

"Sorry, I didn't mean to offend you."

I wave away Damon's apology. "Your grandmother's wrong. It wasn't me."

"But if it wasn't you …?"

"I have no idea." My throat tightens around the words. "All I know is that this was my husband's house. At least, that's what he told me."

His face is hard to read. "And where's your husband now?"

I sigh, frustrated. "I don't know." My fingers tighten around my cup; its warmth seeps into me. I consider telling him everything. Would he believe my story? So far, nobody has. Heck, it's hard for me to even believe it myself. But I definitely need to talk to someone who doesn't think I'm delusional. Who knows, maybe Damon's fresh eyes will spot something I've missed.

"Your grandmother told me you're a private investigator."

"Something like that."

"Are you? Or not?"

"I am. Do you want to tell me what happened to you?"

I take a deep breath, then the words tumble out. "My husband disappeared with my baby, and I have no idea where they are, because he never said anything about leaving, but I woke up yesterday, no, two days ago, and found myself alone in the house, which had been emptied—cleaned out—of all their possessions, and Connie's gone, too."

"Tell me everything from the beginning," he says.

Nervous energy propels me out of my chair, and I start to pace. Charlie scrambles up and follows me, his claws clicking on the wooden floor. While pacing, I begin to the assemble words that will explain what I don't understand myself. Damon taps notes into his phone as I talk. I try to keep the story short, but he's having none of it. So, still pacing, I unspool the long version, beginning with meeting Todd, my pregnancy, the move to the Berkshires, the marriage, the birth, and finally, Connie, Todd, and Noah's disappearance.

When I finish, I sit back down, Charlie settling beside me, and pick up my now-lukewarm tea. I place it down again. I drop my hand to my lap, and Charlie reaches up and licks it, gently. The warmth of his concern wraps around me like a hug, and, without warning, I lose control of the stream of tears I've held back since I started talking.

When I get hold of myself, I look up to see Damon scratching his chin. Does he think I'm nuts, too? Tears spring again. I feel so vulnerable in front of this complete stranger. But I have no one else to talk to.

He places his phone on the table, picks up his cup, and studies it. For a moment, I think he's going to flat out tell me he doesn't believe me. Then, peering at me intently, he asks, "Why do you think your husband disappeared?"

"God knows," I say, throwing my hands up. "I can only assume I served a purpose. Did he use me to sire a child? If so, why me? The whole thing sounds insane. But it's happened. I need help, and I have no idea where to go from here."

"I understand you called Gus."

"Gus?"

"Officer Gordon."

"Yes. How do you know?"

"This is a small town. Gus and I practically grew up together. He's a good guy."

"Not good enough to help me find my missing baby."

"You've got to understand the limits of what the police can do, especially if the missing person is an adult. It's not illegal for a person to go missing. And ..." He pauses, as if taking care about how to say this. "As far as I can see there is no evidence that there was a child, which complicates matters for Gus."

I smooth my hand over Charlie's silky head, remembering how it felt to hold Noah in my arms, this tiny, squiggly little thing. His lips pursed, his face red. I never wanted to put him down. I resented Connie holding him. I wanted him all to myself.

Damon is watching me. "What about your cell? No pictures there, either?"

"No. They were wiped, too." I shake my head. How could this have happened?

"Look," I say, "I know my story sounds unbelievable. It ... it just doesn't make any sense. But I'm trying my best to figure it out. I've researched this afternoon, plugging Todd's name into people finders like ZabaSearch.com and Pipl.com. The problem is that I don't know enough about him to use their filters effectively."

Damon nods. "Did you ever overhear any of his phone conversations?" His brown eyes hold me with an intensity that makes me want to look away. "Or maybe Todd or Connie had visitors?"

"He never really talked about his business. He was close-mouthed about everything. He said he was in real estate. But that doesn't seem to have been true."

"What about Connie?"

I'm embarrassed, again, to admit how little I knew about the woman in charge of my delivery and baby. "She was efficient and pleasant enough. I'd describe her as nondescript. Someone who blends into the background. But she also was really possessive of Noah."

I pause, then state the obvious. "I was sucked in, and I've lost my baby because of it."

"If that's what happened, then it's not your fault, Bree."

I feel a bit lighter after I confide in him, a weight off my shoulders. It's a risk, but I ask, anyway. "Damon? Would you consider helping me? Professionally, I mean, of course."

He strokes his chin, again, as if assessing my question.

My shoulders sag. "Please?"

Finally, he responds. "I have a heavy caseload."

"You don't believe me." I knew it. Why did I think this would be different than any other conversation I've had in the past two days?

"I didn't say that. I'll do my best to free up time for you."

"So, you do believe me?"

"Let me poke around," he says, ignoring my question. "But the way things look, it's going to be difficult to move ahead with any sort of investigation."

Charlie nudges my leg with his snout, and I lower my hand back to his head.

"I understand," I say. "No names, no pictures, a house that, according to the landlady, I rented on my own. It's just a fairytale you're listening to."

He gives me a sympathetic smile. "Not quite. Let me ask you a few more questions. You said that Noah was born at home. Do you have a birth certificate or fingerprints?"

I shake my head and, for the umpteenth time, feel stupid and gullible.

He makes a note, then asks, "What's the last thing you remember?"

I have to clear my throat to get the words out. "I put Noah to bed on Tuesday night, checked on him around seven-thirty, and then Todd and I had dinner."

I fall silent for a moment, remembering. "Todd offered me another glass of wine," I whisper. "Then I started to feel woozy." Then, suddenly I remember being carried up the stairs and the swimming sensation I'd had.

I tell this to Damon.

"What do you think happened?"

"I ... I ... think Todd drugged the wine. I know what it feels like to be drugged because it happened once when I was in college."

If he's shocked, he doesn't show it. He takes another sip of his tea and waits for me to continue.

"Todd had to have had an accomplice," I say. "And not just Connie. Someone had to move the furniture out. Someone had to paint Noah's room, clean the house. I bet there are no fingerprints anywhere to be found. And about Connie? I know it's weird, but I've sensed there was a measure of affection between her and Todd, something almost romantic. But I dismissed it because she's so much older than he is." I sigh, pick up my teacup. Put it down.

Damon straightens in his chair. "There are several scenarios why people up and disappear," he says. "Three main types of missing people — people who are not really missing, just don't want to be found, people who get abducted, and runaways. Those folks who don't want to be found have a reason. If there really is a Todd, he could have owed money, committed a crime, or he might have had other secret he wants to hide."

This added information makes all sorts of gears engage in my head.

Charlie rests his chin on my knee. He stares at me with raptured delight as I scratch his ears.

"There's one more thing," I tell Damon. "I just remembered a little while before you arrived. I found these wigs, and also glue-on mustaches and beards, in Todd's closet the other day. He wasn't too happy about me finding them. That's the feeling I got. But he did come up with an excuse. He said he used them for Halloween."

"You still have them?"

"No. When I went to look the next day, they were gone. But also, what about the fresh paint? You can still smell it in Noah's room."

"That only proves someone painted the room. It could have been you."

"It wasn't me."

When he doesn't respond, I play my final card: "Look at me," I say, and lift my shirt to show him my belly. "My stomach still looks like jelly, and, I'm not going to show you, but my breasts are heavy with milk. I leak when I see a baby. What other proof do you need?"

When he doesn't answer, I say, "I called a gynecologist in Pittsfield. A Dr. Reardon. I made an appointment for next Friday. He'll examine me, and I'll have proof that I gave birth."

Out the window, I see twilight giving way to evening, and I sense Damon getting ready to wrap up our discussion. I need him on my side. He's a private investigator. He knows what he's doing. And he could help. I feel it in my gut. He seems honest, thoughtful, and strong. "Will you help me? Tell me your fee. I can pay you."

A long pause. He's either trying to let me down easy or considering whether he should help.

"My baby. Noah. He's only eight days old." Tears prick the corners of my eyes. "And he's out there somewhere. He needs me. I need to find him. And I need your help." I let my words hang in the air between us. Then I add, "I'll pay you double your fee. Please."

"If I take the job, there's no fee unless I find your baby."

I'm confused. "That's unusual, isn't it?"

"I don't do my job for the money," he replies tersely.

"Then why do you do it?"

"Personal reasons." Damon looks at his watch, then pushes himself up out of his chair. "One more thing. Even if what you say happened really did happen and that gynecologist's exam proves you had a child, you're faced with another dilemma. The disappearance of your child might then look suspicious. *You* might look suspicious. And this investigation might take a turn you won't like. Do you understand what I'm saying?"

His words sink in slowly. It's something I hadn't considered. I'll have to think about it later. For now, I have one more request.

"Would you do me a favor before you leave?"

Damon has started for the door but stops and turns. Charlie looks back and forth between us. "What's that?"

"Could you look around the house and tell me if you see anything that strikes you as odd? As a trained investigator?"

He hesitates.

"Please? Just a couple of minutes."

"Okay. Sure. From my experience, they always leave something behind. Let's look."

I lead the way, flipping lights on as I go. Damon's right behind me, and Charlie trails him. We move from room to room, opening drawers and closets. As we approach Noah's room, the now-familiar pressure of grief rises, making my heart pump a little harder.

"There's nothing left here, except for the rocking chair," I choke out.

In the bathroom, he points at a prescription bottle with a snap cap. "Is this yours?"

"No. I've never seen it before. What is it?"

He picks up the bottle and pours out a couple of oval-shaped, yellow pills. "Zoloft. One hundred milligrams. Pretty high dose."

"I don't take pills of any kind."

"It has your name on it." He extends his hand. "Zoloft is used to treat several symptoms such as depression, panic attacks, post-traumatic stress disorder."

I grab the bottle. "I don't understand." He's right. The bottle has my name on it and the dosage, and that's all. "This has to be a mistake. Besides, it doesn't look right. The doctor's name and pharmacy should be posted."

I don't remember seeing Connie or Todd taking any pills. This bottle has my name on it. Seemingly another mystery I have to solve. But when I say so, Damon just shrugs.

After we've looked downstairs, we step into the garage, which smells comfortingly of old motor oil and paint. Cabinets and narrow wooden shelves stretch from floor to ceiling, crammed with cans and other tools, my mechanic's tools among them.

"My granddaddy built those shelves," Damon says. Then, pointing at the tools, he adds, "All his. We decided to leave it here. No use to me or Grandma."

Damon opens a few cabinets, scanning each one. Then he runs his palm over a shelf.

It's when he bends down to inspect a lower shelf and pushes an old watering can out of the way that he finds it.

"What is this?"

I blink at the gray, steel box. How has it escaped me? Todd's safe. When I'd asked him about what was in it, he'd shrugged it off, as if having something locked away was insignificant. And when I'd pressed him on it, he told me it was where he kept papers and photos from his dead parents. But when I showed interest in looking at those photos, he'd abruptly said it was too painful for him to revisit the past.

I tell him what little I know about it. "And isn't it strange? The value Todd put on it … it's not something he would likely leave behind."

Damon bends down and examines the safe. "Not easy to open. This is an Australian-made home safe with a La Gard 3750 digital electronic lock. Do you know the combination?"

"No. Can you unlock it without that?"

"Hmm. Safes can sometimes be compromised by guessing the combination. If it's an easy-to-guess combination, like a birthdate, or a street address, or driver's license number. What about Todd's birthdate, or yours, or Noah's?"

I supply him with Noah's birthdate, and Todd's — which I doubt is even his real birthdate. Damon tries those and a few other combinations without any success.

"Sorry," he says, "I can't help you out with this."

His phone buzzes. He pulls it out and glances at the screen. "I have to run, but you need to get that safe looked at. There might be something in there to help your case."

"Please. Could you do it?"

I'm not sure what convinced him, but Damon throws me a look, gives a sigh, and says, "Okay, I can take care of opening the safe, but I don't know how long it will take."

He fishes in his jeans pocket and produces a business card, which he hands to me. The card lists his full name, Damon Payne, with his photo centered above that and below, the words *Private Investigator.*

"Thank you." I hold out my hand.

His phone buzzes again.

"I need to get going." He takes my offered hand and squeezes it lightly.

He walks to his Jeep carrying the safe, Charlie padding behind him. I watch the lights of his vehicle turn the corner, and then start for the door, when a chill comes over me. What about those pills? Who prescribed them? Where were they purchased?

Movement from the corner of my eye catches my attention, but when I turn, I see nothing out of the ordinary. I spin on my heels, shut the door behind me, and double lock it.

CHAPTER 10

Darkness presses against the window. Heavy raindrops punctuate the stillness in the bedroom. It's 3:00 a.m., and all I want is to get a decent night's rest. No use—I'm as wide awake as if I'd downed ten cups of coffee. All I can think about is that Wednesday has turned into Thursday, into Friday, into Saturday, into Sunday. As I pace the bedroom, I count each day in my head. I want to scream in frustration. I can't stop thinking about Noah, wondering where he is, not knowing where to look.

I end up at the computer again, willing Todd's name to appear, when a thought strikes me. Did Todd try to kill me? Maybe he didn't expect me to wake up. Would he come back to finish the job? At this thought, my heart leaps and sweat blooms on my skin. On the other hand, killing me would cause him serious problems. If I turn up dead, there would be questions and an investigation that might lead to him.

A dark, cold sickness hovers over me as I gaze out the window. The sun is starting to come up now, making the flat, gray sheet of clouds look gauzy. My brain buzzes.

Clearly, whatever feelings I had for Todd were simply a reflection of what I wanted him to be. So, who is he? As if watching a movie projected onto the screen of my brain, I recall a few details that make me wonder how I could have ignored my doubts about him. By leaving the way he did, Todd forced me to see a flaw in myself I never wanted to acknowledge—gullibility, a hard lesson learned too late that things aren't always what they seem. And that is far worse than being fooled.

The depth of my helplessness and inadequacy weigh heavily, making it difficult to breathe. *What kind of a mother would let her baby be taken away from her?* I ask myself for the thousandth time. In the distance, a cock crows and cows low as they chew their way through the shrinking green fields. Familiar sounds that no longer bring comfort. Home should bring security, comfort to both me and my child.

My emotions spin around for a few more seconds, then I drag my attention back to my laptop. This time, I key in Damon's name. His credentials are a mile long, including working with major governmental agencies. Most importantly, I learn he's a retired federal special agent—a criminal investigator. He's the perfect candidate to help in my search.

A long, hot shower restores my vigor. Then I dress and go downstairs. The sun paints a single oblong of light across the living room floor. I consider the upholstered sofas facing each other, the coffee table between them, the painting over the mantelpiece, and the bookcases flanking the fireplace—all of which I'd assumed were Todd's, but which I now know to be Agnes Payne's things. Surveying the living room, I realize it doesn't feel as cozy as it once did. Still, I drag my fingers along the tabletop and eye the streaks I created on its dusty surface. Today, I'll clean, I think.

After a soft-boiled egg, which I chew and swallow without tasting, I wash the dishes, wipe the countertop. Then, dust rag in hand, I start my assault on the rest of the house, paying careful attention to the insides of cupboards and hidden corners, remembering what Damon said about criminals always leaving something behind.

Eventually, I find myself standing in front of Todd's empty closet. I get down on my hands and knees, poking my fingers back as far as I can reach. And that's when I feel something hard wedged between the closet wall and the edge of the carpet. Tugging it free, I crawl out to find, in the palm of my hand, a small, three-ounce brown glass bottle. I hold it up to the light. It's empty. I unscrew the top and sniff a familiar odor: peppermint. The smell causes my eyes to water slightly and I'm trying to remember where I've smelled it recently.

Downstairs, I place the bottle in a kitchen drawer, making a mental note to try to bring to remember the last time I've encountered this scent. Right now, I'm on a mission to finish combing the house from corner to corner.

Back in the living room, I pull books from the bookcase one at a time, leaf through the pages, dust, and return them. I continue this mindless job, until I spot a slender book of love poetry. Todd gave it to me when I found out I was pregnant. I reach up to the top shelf to retrieve it and end up knocking a pile of books over onto the floor. A piece of paper drifts down with them. I scoop it up.

It's a worn cash receipt for $42.35 from Café Madison in Handrock, New York. I stare at the date. November 4th. Two weeks before Todd disappeared. The bill includes two lasagnas, one piece of strawberry-rhubarb pie, one maple cake, and two coffees.

My heart thumps. Though seemingly insignificant, this could be my first lead.

How did this little piece of paper end up between the pages of a book? Todd rarely reads. Connie, on the other hand, was always reading. In fact, I now remember walking in and startling her with a book in her hand. She hurriedly shoved something between the pages of that book, but I didn't think anything of it at that time, just figured she was marking her place.

Settling at my laptop, I copy the address from the receipt into MapQuest. Handrock, it turns out, is a tiny town on the Canadian border.

I consider what I've learned—or, rather, conjectured—so far. It seems Todd planned to leave me, had the help of a woman who looks like me to set up his disappearance, used me to bear his child, and, maybe ate at a restaurant in New York near the Canadian border. Plus, there's the mysterious bottle of Zoloft, the wigs, the peppermint oil, and Todd's safe. None of which I'm able to add together in any meaningful way. I need help from a professional.

It's only eight-thirty, but I dial Damon's number anyway, and leave a voicemail.

CHAPTER 11

The receipt from the café reminds me about the young man who delivered pizza to our house. Officer Gordon has never gotten back to me about that. So, Monday morning, after a phone call confirming that James O'Leary is at work, I make my way to the country store. At the door, a man, who seems to recognize me, makes a stiff and unsmiling *after-you* gesture. Avoiding further eye contact, I hurry inside. Every head turns, every eye tracks me as I move through the store. Becket is a small town. Maybe they've gotten word that I'm the crazy woman who lost her baby. Or, maybe, just the crazy woman.

My boots clack on the wood planks as I make my way to the counter. The spiky haired girl is behind the counter, again.

"Hi." I offer up a smile. "Is James O'Leary here?"

She looks at me, but before she can answer, I hear someone call my name.

I spin around and come face to face with Officer Gordon. His arms are folded across his chest. He says, in a tone that sounds like a command, "I need to have a word with you."

"Now?"

Officer Gordon holds up his hand, signaling me to wait. "Latika," he says, to the counter girl, "let me have a tall one."

Her smile is radiant as she hands him a steaming Styrofoam cup of coffee and a muffin. "On the house," she says.

"And could you please call James to come to the front?"

Two minutes later, the tall, skinny young man I saw bringing pizza that night makes his way up from the back of the store. Officer Gordon walks over to him and says a few words. The young man eyes me for a second, says something to the officer, then turns and heads back to whatever he was doing. I take a step to follow the young man, but cup in one hand and muffin in the other, Officer Gordon forestalls me.

"Won't be necessary," he says, nodding to James's retreating back. "And would much appreciate it if you could spare a few moments of your time."

Anxiety twists my gut. Something terrible has happened to Noah. For a moment, the idea that the officer has learned that my baby is dead causes bile to rise in my throat.

Outside, the sky is low and gray, and the air smells of rain. I follow Officer Gordon across the parking lot to the station. I sit while he perches on the edge of his desk. "As you know," he begins, "our first priority is to find out what's going on with your … situation." He takes a loud slurp from his coffee.

I'm not sure what he means. "I thought you couldn't help, since I don't have proof."

"We don't take a missing baby lightly. It's most troubling."

I'm not sure what to make of his tone. But I have another question. "What did you just say to James O'Leary?"

He picks up a pen from the desk and rotates it in his fingers. "I asked if he'd seen you before. He says you're the one who answered the door and paid for the pizza."

"What? I've never met him. I just saw him from the bedroom window. Like I told you."

"Miss Michaelson. He says you were the one at the door."

I take a deep breath. This is like my interview with Agnes Payne all over again.

He changes direction quickly. "You still maintain that your baby is missing?" When I nod, he says, "I understand you've made an appointment with Dr. Reardon?"

How does he know? Damon said they were good friends. Did he tell him?

"Miss Michaelson?"

"Yes, I did. It's for this Friday."

"Good. Once we know that you, in fact, have delivered a baby, we can properly start our investigation."

The way he looks at me makes me break out into a cold sweat. Is this what Damon was warning me about? Will I be their first suspect?

"Okay." He rises. "Thank you for your time, Miss Michaelson. I'll be in touch."

I push up from the chair.

"Oh, and Miss Michaelson?" I turn to face him. "I trust you'll make yourself available if I need more information from you?"

It sounds like a veiled version of "and don't leave town." Dread builds in my gut. He's already made up his mind. My only hope now is to find out what's in the safe Todd has left behind. Maybe something in there will incriminate him and absolve me of any wrongdoing.

I step through the double doors and outside into the gray day. I've missed several calls from my sister. I'll call her back later. I dial Damon's number twice, getting his voicemail each time, leaving a message the second time.

Now, I regret having Damon take the safe. I could have gone to a locksmith to have him figure out the combination. And since it must have been him who told Officer Gordon about my gynecologist's appointment, I'm not sure I can trust him.

CHAPTER 12

When I get home, the late morning is hazy. The rising sun has painted the trees a dull shade of yellow. Inside, the house seems to hold its breath.

A thought occurs to me: if my life with Todd has been a sham, then our marriage could have been fake, also. Typically, the person who performs the wedding ceremony submits the license to the county office within a few days of the ceremony. The marriage certificate is then issued and sent, usually within a month. I don't remember ever seeing a marriage certificate.

I call the vital records office for Berkshire County and get an address to send my request for a copy of the record, with instructions to include a check for thirty dollars.

Then, I move robotically through all the rooms. The minutes blend into each other, and I'm growing sick with pain and uncertainty. I weep, so frightened for Noah that I can't catch my breath. The conversation with Officer Gordon has left me unnerved.

It's six days since Todd's disappearance, and I often find myself in Noah's room. In my mind, I pray for my baby's safety. I pray I'll survive what the future has for me because I'll need all the strength I can muster to help me find my way out of this.

Into my seventy-second hour with almost no sleep, I'm dazed and groggy and barely upright. But even in the snatches of sleep I manage, my brain doesn't shut down entirely. I go to the living room and lie on the sofa. As soon as I close my eyes, though, a vivid image of Noah's sleeping face appears, and my heart squeezes with love, as I see my fingers stroking the silky skin of his rounded forehead.

With the shades drawn, no light filters into the room, so I have no idea what time it is when my cell rings, startling me awake. I grab my phone, only to see a blocked number. Should I answer? For a fleeting moment, a hope arises that it's Todd, with a good explanation.

"Hello?" My voice sounds eager to my ears. But there's no response other than the sound of ragged breathing. Then the call is disconnected, and I'm left with the unease that the call hints at something ominous, that I should be afraid. On the other hand, I try to convince myself, it could have been a wrong number. But if it was, what was the heavy breathing all about?

Damon. I have to get a hold of him. I look up his address, then drag my aching body to the shower, hoping the warm water will deliver relief. The payoff is marginal. Still, half an hour later, I grab the envelope with the check for the marriage certificate, start the Mustang, and cautiously make my way toward the main road to town.

After depositing the envelope at the post office, I head toward Damon's house. The fact that he disclosed information I shared with him makes me wary about putting any more of my trust in him. But he's a professional—and he has Todd's safe. Plus, the receipt from Café Madison might mean something, or it might not, but I want to show it to Damon.

The car bounces along a potholed drive, until I find myself in front of Damon's house, which has a stone façade and an old-fashioned lantern over the door. When I get out of the car, the cold air the carries the scent of pine. Gold, red, and brown leaves blanket the lawn and the driveway. I walk up to the door and ring the bell. After a few minutes, it's clear he's not home.

I scribble him a note, which I wedge note between the door and doorframe. It seems almost futile to ask him yet again to call me, but maybe my showing up at his door will prompt him to get in touch faster.

Back home, the isolation weighs on me, and I suddenly crave a talk with Luanne. When I call, I only get her voicemail, and I remember that she's recently started a new production on Broadway that's likely keeping her busy.

I haven't run in months, but I need to get out of the house and clear my head. I put on my sneakers, stretch my legs, shrug into my sweatshirt, and stomp out the door.

The crisp Berkshires air pricks at my face. But ignoring that, and my painful breasts, I charge forward. My legs carry me onto a trail that leads into the woods. I'm on automatic, anger, fear, and frustration pushing me forward. Sticks and other woodland debris are scattered across the slick, leaf-covered path. Gray roots crisscross the trail, threatening to send me crashing if I don't pay close attention. The occasional creak of trees sounds lonely.

After about a mile, I get the feeling that I am being watched. It's a distinct physical sensation that starts at the base of my spine and slinks up to the back of my skull. I stop and look around. Nothing but the pale sun peeking through the trees, creating patterns of light across the sodden earth.

I hold my breath for several moments, hyperaware of everything around me: the flutter of birds, the swoosh of leaves. A twig snaps, sending a spasm of fear thumping in my chest. I search for something to grab, a stick or a rock. Then I tell myself it's only my imagination and continue my run, my breath rasping like an old steam engine on its last legs.

Suddenly, something crunches behind me. I whirl around to confront my follower. Instead a deer gallops back down the trail in the direction from which I'd come.

CHAPTER 13

After double locking the front door, which is starting to become a habit, I lumber up the stairs on heavy legs, pausing a moment at Noah's door. The house is a memory trap: just passing Noah's room makes my heart constrict. I push his door open. My gaze stops at the rocking chair, which stands all alone in the otherwise empty room. I spent hours in that chair watching Noah sleep. When he wasn't sleeping, I cradled his plump little form, which felt like rays of sun warming my chest and kissed the silky wisps of hair that hugged his perfect head.

Now, I pull his sock from my pocket and press it to my face. There's really no scent left, but I imagine it, anyway. *Where are you, my little angel?*

I step out of Noah's room, pull the door closed, and enter my own. The bed is cold when I slip under the comforter, and I curl into a shivering ball. The loneliness hits me, as I think of my son spending another day without me.

I let my hand rest on the side of the bed where Todd had normally slept. I'd grown so used to feeling the heat of another's body beside me, of having legs tangled with my own. I loved Todd for giving me Noah. Will I ever get back that feeling of contentment, of being so complete?

At some point, I wake with a jolt. In the dark, I listen with my whole body. The silence of the house seems to have changed, become alien and hostile. At first, it's just a feeling, a creeping sense of dread, a prickling down my spine. Then, somewhere downstairs, a floorboard creak. I lie for a moment, frozen.

Old houses make noises, I tell myself.

Still. My body is on full alert. I'm alone in this particular old house, a quarter of a mile away from the nearest neighbor.

There it is again, a scraping noise followed by a thump. Then, I hear a door close.

Heart racing, I toss the covers aside and tiptoe toward the window. The woods are a curtain of darkness in the distance.

Fighting to move without making a sound, I reach for the baseball bat under the bed and start toward the hallway — which is dark. Why? Since Todd disappeared, I always leave the hall light on at night. Did I forget to turn it on?

I can barely see, but the open bathroom door halfway down the hall lets a sliver of pale moonlight through, allowing me to see that Noah's bedroom door is open, and so is the door to Connie's room. I am certain I closed both doors.

When I hear a rattle, followed by another faint thump, coming from downstairs, I take a deep breath, grip the bat with both hands, and silently descend the stairs, my back hugging the wall. The going is slow. The muscles in my legs burn. All the while, I stay alert for more sounds. When I reach the first floor, I find all the windows closed and locked, as are the sliding doors leading to the backyard from the basement.

I brace myself, push through the garage door, and take in the damp smell of rain and gas. The automatic garage door is closed, but my unease persists. I inhale and then exhale. Nobody has been here, I tell myself. It's just my overactive imagination.

Then I feel it. A cold draft. Bat still gripped, I sidle to the garage window. By the dim light of the moon, I see it's open a crack. As I move to shut it, I hear the crunch of tires on gravel and look out to see red taillights, just before they disappear down the end of the drive.

CHAPTER 14

After a few hours of fitful sleep, I ease myself down the steps to the kitchen, brew coffee and force myself to swallow a few spoonsful of cereal with milk. The feeling that I am in danger is gut-deep and getting deeper.

Needing a friendly voice, I dial Luanne's number. She sounds groggy.

"Did I wake you?"

"No," Luanne murmurs.

She's lying, but it's a kind lie.

"Just a minute." I hear her talking to someone, then she's back. "Are you okay?"

"Am I interrupting something?"

"Not at all. How are you? Should I be worried? Are you still looking for Noah?"

I pace to the sink and back. It's her tone. She doesn't believe me.

I hold back a sigh and instead tell her about finding a receipt from the café in Handrock.

Her disbelief is even louder in her silence, but I ignore it and carry on anyway.

"Also, there's Todd's safe, which I found, although it doesn't make sense that he'd leave it. Right now, my best chance of finding out what's in that safe is Damon. But he's not returning my calls."

"And who, exactly, is Damon?"

"My landlady's grandson. He's a private investigator."

"Well, I think I can help you with something," Luanne says.

"Really? How?"

"But I need to ask you again—"

"Don't!" I pick up a neatly folded dishtowel, unfold it, and refold it in perfect squares.

"Okay, don't be mad at me."

"I'm not mad at you."

"Give me a second." I hear her talking to someone again. "Okay. Can you describe Todd enough for someone to draw him?"

"Sure. Why?"

"I told Andy, the guy I'm dating, about what you're going through. Turns out, his best friend, Howard, is a forensic artist. Andy suggested getting the two of you together, so Howard can sketch Todd's face. And from that, you can do a face recognition on the internet. In fact, here's a thought—you can post his picture on Facebook and see where it takes you."

Even though I know Luanne doesn't believe me, I love that she's reaching out to help in such a practical way.

"Great idea," I tell her. "But you didn't say you were dating someone. Is it serious?"

She lets out a giggle. "Too early to tell. So far, he seems like a nice guy."

"Tell me about the illustrator."

"According to Andy, he's a whiz. You think you can drag yourself to Manhattan today?"

"Absolutely!" Immediately after hanging up, I jump in my car and am on my way.

CHAPTER 15

It's early afternoon, and I'm walking Lexington Avenue under a bright sun. The narrow street is crowded. Car horns signal frustrated drivers. A light wind ruffles my hair and pigeons fight over crumbs on the pavement.

I enter the coffee shop and sit facing the window. Half an hour later, I drum my fingers on the table and glance at my watch. Luanne is late.

A sigh of relief escapes my mouth as she finally breezes in, a big smile on her crimson lips. Her golden hair hangs loose around her face, and she's wearing the New York City uniform of tight black jeans, army boots, and a short, black leather jacket.

"Bree." Luanne's voice rings out with joy, reminding me how much I've missed her.

She grabs me in a tight hug, and I know with absolute certainty that I'm not alone. My eyes suddenly sting with tears. I sniffle into her jacket, before she holds me at arm's length and studies me. "When was the last time you ate?"

I shrug my shoulders, not trusting myself to speak.

"I'm ordering coffee," she says. "You?"

I hand her my empty mug, and she saunters to the counter and gives her order to a woman wearing a sweater stretched on her muscular frame.

She returns with two muffins and two steaming lattés. I devour the muffin like a woman eating her last meal.

"So?" Luanne says as she wipes crumbs off her lips.

"I feel like such an idiot."

She wrinkles her freckled nose. "Don't be hard on yourself."

"Well," I say. "Maybe I'll be hard on him, instead. I'm going to find the bastard, Luanne. With or without the police. And your idea to have sketches of Todd and Connie drawn is brilliant. I'll show them around town. See if anyone has seen him."

She's silent for a moment. Then she says, "I never met the man. Okay. So, you find Todd. What then?"

"I confront him and make him tell me why he did what he did and get Noah back where he belongs. With me."

"You think he's going to make nice? Reminisce about the good old days? Beg your forgiveness and tell you where Noah is? Even if ... I'm sorry, Bree, but I have to say it. Even if there is a Noah."

"There is, Luanne. I understand why you doubt me. But I appreciate you helping, anyway. For my part, he's my baby, and I *will* find him."

More silence, long and drawn out.

"Okay. Any thoughts as to why Todd did this?"

She's humoring me.

"I don't know. I wish to God I did."

I glanced at my watch. My appointment with the illustrator is at three. "I've got to run."

"How about spending the night at my place?" Luanne asks. "It's been a long time since we hung out."

I'd love to spend time with my friend, but once I have Todd's image in my possession, I'll be anxious to put it to use immediately. "Let me take a rain-check?"

"Sure," she says. Then, "By the way, your sister called me. Listen, it's not my business, but she says you aren't answering her calls."

My stomach clenches up. "What did she want?"

"She says your aunt's not feeling well. You should call her."

•   •   •

I point at an *FBI Facial Identification Catalogue* I spot on Howard McFarland's desk. "Do I need to look at this?" I'm sitting across from the illustrator, ankle on my knee, bouncing my foot at breakneck speed.

"Not yet," he says, smiling. "I prefer to begin to work without it. I like to keep the catalog around just in case witnesses have a difficult time. It comes in handy, for instance, when young children or non-English speakers struggle to describe something they've seen. A three-year-old girl might not know how to say, 'close-set eyes,' but she could point to a picture."

Noticing my nervousness, he says gently, "I'm not going to ask you to relive anything. We'll just have a free flow of information. Let's begin with what Todd looks like."

I'm not sure where to start. Todd was my knight in shining armor — in the body of a Grecian god, topped with a smile that made me shiver. His face, lined in the right places, made him look vulnerable. Always freshly shaven, his thick, honeyed hair always brushed neatly.

When I don't speak, Howard prompts me. "Give me general stuff, like age, weight, hair and eye color, and skin tone."

It's hard, though, bringing Todd to mind. It hurts. But I bite the bullet and, picturing him, I begin. "He's in his late thirties, with brown eyes … No, more towards gold, and bronze skin. His longish hair is dirty blond with gray at his temples. And if I had to guess, I'd say he weighs about two hundred pounds."

"Okay, you're doing good." Howard is sketching as he speaks. "Describe his face," he says. "Any scars? Every small detail counts."

I continue to describe the father of my child to the best of my recollection. "Square jaw, eyes close set. His lower lip is fuller than his upper lip. He has long, black eyelashes, and a long, straight nose."

"Great description," he says, showing me his preliminary sketch and inviting me to tell him what to add, take away, change. I give the growing image my entire attention: Did I say thin eyebrows? No, thick. Thicker. And his chin, sharper. Cheekbones? A little wider, maybe?

And so it goes, until, after an hour, Howard hands me the sketch. "What do you think?"

My fingers tighten on the sheet of paper. To my surprise, looking back at me is Todd.

I spend a full minute studying the drawing. In Howard's version, Todd looks peaceful, as if life has treated him rather kindly over the years. But on closer examination, his eyes are cold, calculating. How is it that I hadn't noticed this all the months we were together?

Staring into the eyes of a man I thought I knew, I entertain a dream more violent than any film I would be willing to watch. In it, I picture myself tracking him down, knocking on his door, a gun tucked into the waistband of my jeans. When he answers, I fill him with hot lead. But not before he tells me where to find my baby.

Looking back at the picture in my hands, I know I'm missing something. I can feel it, my failure to register a crucial bit of information that will help lift the fog surrounding my brain and bring it into focus.

Then it hits me, the perpetual sore on Todd's chin and the patchy rash over his upper lip. Although Todd dismissed my questions about his skin as sensitivity to his shaving cream, my mind hauls up the three-ounce brown glass bottle I found on his closet floor. The peppermint smell was just like the spirit gum we used in high-school theater productions when we had to affix wigs or false facial hair.

"Bree?" Howard prompts.

His voice jerks my attention to the present.

"Do we have to make any changes?"

I tell him about the sore and the rash.

Once he adds them, I nod. "You drew a great likeness of this bastard, thank you. Do you have time to draw one more face? It's a woman."

When Howard agrees, we repeat the routine, but bringing Connie to mind proves difficult. I'm sure about her height, her short curly hair, and the large, tinted glasses she always wore. But those made it difficult to discern the shape and the color of her eyes. I do my best, though. Finally, I have to resort to choosing the shape of her face from the book. When I do so, Howard looks up at me and says, "She has the same face shape as yours!"

She does. I never noticed. If she were taller, I would think it was Connie who impersonated me when renting the house from Agnes Payne, and again when paying for the pizza from James O'Leary. I shake my head. She wasn't that tall. And she was so much older than me. No one could mistake us for one another.

Howard hands me his finished sketch. I thank him, but it's not as accurate as Todd's, although I can't pinpoint what's off about the features. I fault myself for not paying closer attention to her when she lived with us. But Connie seemed so secretive and slippery, her face always averted when she addressed me, always speaking in short, clipped phrases.

Oh, well. Her sketch is better than nothing. Leaving Howard, I go to Staples to make copies, then head back to Becket.

CHAPTER 16

It's Wednesday morning. Thirteen days have passed since Todd and Noah disappeared. After that vaguely threatening conversation at the police station, I don't intend to keep my appointment with the gynecologist. That means it's only a matter of days before Officer Gordon will want to know the results.

In the meantime, Damon hasn't returned my repeated calls, so I still don't know what's in the safe.

What I do know is that I'm not the helpless, dependent woman I've been for most of my life, and I'm not going to wait for a man to rescue me, this time. I'm going to rely, instead, on the confident self I am when I'm working on car engines. And that confident self is going to find Noah. Right now, that means taking the sketches of Todd and Connie, along with the restaurant receipt, and driving to Handrock.

I pack lightly, taking just what fits in my knapsack, which I toss in the trunk of my car, before giving the house a final glance and driving off. I plan to stop at Aunt Rachelle's house in Albany on the way to see first-hand why Margaret is worried about her.

During the drive, I think about how that's going to go. Will my aunt try to persuade me to move back? How do I explain Todd and Noah? How do I explain why I haven't visited her in so long? I have no idea how I'll explain all that to her. But as uncomfortable—not to mention, desperate—as I am with my situation, I have to make the effort. I owe that to my aunt for all the care and love she's given me over the years.

I have to make two stops first, though.

• • •

I hurry down the path toward the entrance, walking beside well-tended lawns, the scent of mold and damp and something vaguely fetid following me. I think of my parents and the stench of burnt flesh, and then I'm standing in front of two slabs of granite, a vase of flowers on each. I can see my aunt's hand in keeping fresh flowers at my parents' graves.

I read the familiar words: their names, their birthdates, their death date. November 29th. The seventeen-year anniversary of my parents' death is next week. I was fourteen years old when it happened. The accident created a shattering change in my life.

Seventeen years. I didn't expect to still be alive. For many years, I wanted to die and be buried here, beside my parents. But I lived.

There's something powerful about visiting their graves. It's a reminder of how everything can change in a split second. Of how fragile life is. What lingers emotionally after such an event speaks louder than any skid marks or jagged, twisted metal ever could.

I'm pierced by a sudden pang of regret for not stopping to buy them bouquet. My mother loved red geraniums.

When I awoke in the hospital, it was my aunt, sitting by my bedside, who told me my parents had died. My last memory—not what my aunt or sister told me after the fact—was not of my parents, but of the impact. The screech of tires and the ugly crunch of metal smashing into metal.

After that? It's all a fog, present but impossible to grasp. Traumatized, I recuperated in the hospital for a week. But the trauma lives on. My sorrow, my lack of wholeness is evident in my pattern—first George, then Todd—of trying to fill the void with men who take control.

Obviously, Aunt Rachelle's pragmatism about people hasn't had any influence on me. It is my mother, who thought people were born pure and good and that evil was a product of learning, who has shaped me most. I thought Todd was pure, his motivations for a family the same as mine. But he is evil for what he did to me and to our son.

•   •   •

After saying my goodbyes to my parents, I head toward my second stop. Taking the third exit toward downtown Albany, I find the seedy part of downtown bustling. Splashing through puddles, I pass several antique stores, a hardware store, and a real-estate office. Cars fill almost every parking space.

The street is slick with the cold rain that has been falling since early morning, and I'm lucky to find a parking spot close to my destination. I get out of my car in front of a two-story storefront of old red brick and sandstone flanked by a Chinese restaurant and a body-piercing shop, where a crowd of glassy-eyed teenagers hangs out, looking aimless.

Despite my uncertain memory, I recognize the building. How is it possible that I allowed Todd to bring me to this squalid-looking place? I tug open the street door, climb up two sets of stairs, and head for the glass facade of the office. Instead of Dr. Bryson's name, the bronze plaque on the door declares that this is Pitki & Dorie, C.P.A.

I walk in, anger and confusion simmering inside of me. The small lobby has a vinyl floor and three plastic armchairs around a table cluttered with stacks of outdated magazines. I can hear a television from behind the office door. A middle-aged woman, with olive skin and big round eyes, seated at the reception desk gives me an inquiring look.

I give her my best smile. "Do you mind if I ask you a question?"
She stares at me without blinking.
"How long have you been in this office?"
"Why do you want to know?" she asks, immediately suspicious.
"I'm looking for the gynecologist who used to rent this office."
"There's no gynecologist here."
"I can see that. But he attended my pregnancy."
"Don't know about that. But there's no doctor here."
"Do you mind telling me how long you've been here?"

"What's this all about?"

"Please. I need to know."

She reaches under her blouse and adjusts the strap of her bra. "Um … two years."

"Two years? But I was here a year ago. To see Dr. Bryson."

"Not here, you weren't."

The phone on her desk buzzes. She picks it up, says, "Yes. Yes. Okay," and hangs up.

I pull out the sketches. "Please, one more minute of your time. Have you seen these people?"

She points a crooked finger at the door. "I have to ask you to leave. Now."

Since it seems there's nothing else I can do here, I slowly make my way toward the door, gritting my teeth to keep myself from screaming in frustration.

Someone must have seen something. It's a long shot, but as long as I'm here, I'm going to test my luck. The teenagers watch as I stride by them. I force the air out of my lungs and set my gaze straight ahead and begin my task, of going from store to store asking proprietors and clerks if they know anything about the accounting firm, or if there was ever a gynecologist in this block, or if they've seen anyone in the building moving in about a year ago.

All I'm met with are suspicious looks and shoulder shrugs. No one wants to get involved in this part of town. A shiver slinks down my spine as I drive away.

CHAPTER 17

After a twenty-minute drive, I turn into my aunt's neighborhood, passing older, well-kept homes, with full front porches and beautiful lawns. When I arrive at Aunt Rachelle's and exit the car, a wave of frigid air slaps my face. I look up to see the chimney spewing white smoke, while pinewood scents the air. For a moment, I stand beneath the massive chestnut tree and note the clumps of brown-eyed Susans and domes of jewel-toned mums decorating the front of the house I've called home since I was fourteen.

"Oh, my darling," my aunt says the moment she opens the door. She pulls me into a tight hug.

The frustration and sorrow inside me erupt in great, gulping sobs.

"I'm sorry, sweetheart," she whispers softly. Five minutes later, she places a large bowl of soup and a steaming half loaf of bread in front of me. She eases her body into the chair across from me as though it requires lots of effort, then leans forward, looking me over — trying to establish how much has changed.

I'm doing the same with her, but before I can ask how she's feeling, she says, "It's odd I never met that young man of yours. What's his name? Todd? And you say you gave birth to a baby?" It sounds like an accusation.

I swallow a mouthful of soup and steel myself for confrontation. "His name is Noah," I tell her. "Although nobody seems to believe he exists."

Frustration crosses her face, which looks thinner than I remember. "But the police have no evidence to support your claim?"

Sighing, I nod my acknowledgement of that fact. "Officer Gordon thinks I've hallucinated Todd and the pregnancy, that I'm crazy."

"Bree, why are you doing this to yourself?"

"I had a baby," I say firmly.

My aunt watches me for a minute, silent. In that moment, the late afternoon light coming through the window makes her seem paler.

When she speaks again, she's changed the topic. "Did you stay away from me because of the fight? It's been almost a year. I didn't know where you were. And you had your number changed, and I couldn't reach you, at all."

Last time I saw Aunt Rachelle, we had a fight about me dating Todd, how fast it was all going, and how he wasn't willing to meet her. My aunt's words ring in my ears, even now: "I'm just trying to remind you that Todd is the first guy you've gone out with since you broke up with George, which means you haven't had enough time to recover, never mind to figure out who you are on your own. And this young man seems awfully secretive, too. Doesn't that worry you?"

"I feel safe with him." That was my answer. And now I understand how stupid that sounds.

Now, my aunt says, "I know nothing about your life in the last nine months, then one day you call out of the blue, crying that your baby is gone, the police won't help, that no one saw your boyfriend — or is he your husband? — or the baby. And you want me to believe ... what, exactly?"

Pushing up from her chair, she turns and starts cleaning the stovetop. "I worry about you," she says, her back still turned to me. "You need to learn to choose carefully. We both remember what you had to go through with George. Is he still stalking you?"

"No." I try to sound convincing because I don't know if he's stopped. Was it George in the house the other night? Is he the reason I feel I'm being watched?

The air in the room is heavy. My breathing gets thicker. I shouldn't have to try to convince my aunt, who's been like a mother to me, that I had a baby. Yet, I can't be angry with her for doubting me. Not after the last time.

"If I were you," she says, as if reading my thoughts, "I'd go see Dr. Palmer. Stay here for a few days and set up an appointment. I'm sure he'll make room in his schedule for you."

"No." Frustration and anger creep into my voice. The hell with everyone who doesn't believe me, including my aunt.

Aunt Rachelle lets the spoon clatter into the soup pot. She turns and stares at me. "That's not an answer I want to hear."

"I'm sorry."

She returns to her chair and adopts a gentler tone. "Maybe you really believe you had a baby. Maybe there are too many unpleasant memories for you to deal with. We went through this a few years ago. What is so different this time?"

I pull up my shirt, all the way. I have nothing to hide from my aunt. "You don't believe me? Look at my stretch marks. Look at my breasts."

She looks, considering my flaccid belly and still swollen breasts. "That doesn't prove ..."

"I don't know how else I can make you or the police believe me."

"You can have yourself checked by an obstetrician."

The panic attack comes upon me suddenly, without warning white dots to appear in front of my eyes. Breathe in through my mouth, one, two, three, four. Exhale through my nose. All I can think of is Officer Gordon waiting to arrest me for killing my baby. The only way I can prove I had a baby will make me the prime suspect in his disappearance.

My aunt pushes her chair back, rushes to my side. Her hand is rubbing my back. "Honey, you're having a panic attack." My aunt's voice is gentle. "Why don't you stay the night?" She moves to the sink, dampens a dishcloth in cold water, and presses it to my forehead.

I take the dishcloth from her and wipe the sweat off my face and neck. "Thank you, but I can't. I have to ... be somewhere." I'm not about to tell her about the restaurant receipt, that I'm on my way to Handrock. The whole thing sounds flimsy, even to me. But what choice do I have?

"Bree." Her voice is stern, now. "Snap out of your emotional upheaval and start thinking clearly. I don't know what you've been doing these past months. What I do know is that you lost your job when George harassed you at work, then you showed up here with a story about a man I never met, and now there's a baby that no one has ever seen."

"You're right. I'll pull myself together."

Aunt Rachelle reaches across the table and lifts my chin, gently. "You look tired. When was the last time you had a good night's sleep?"

"I'm fine, but what about you? How are you feeling?" She looks tired. I see why Margaret is concerned. But I need her to say she's fine.

She waves her hand. "I'm fine. It's you I'm worried about, so don't try to distract me. I insist you get help. It will make me feel better. If you don't ..."

I pull away from her hand. Is she threatening me? Would she go so far as to have Dr. Palmer commit me to a mental facility? I should never have told her about Noah. My mind is spinning, trying to work out how to remedy my mistake.

"Okay," I say, smiling in a way I hope is reassuring. "That's not a bad idea. I'll get in touch with Dr. Palmer. But I have a few things to take care of first."

A flicker of doubt crosses her face. "Do you promise?"

I go over to her, bend down, and wrap my arms around her. "I love you," I say.

Aunt Rachelle raises her hand to my cheek and strokes it. "Go upstairs and make yourself comfortable."

If my staying the night will placate her fears and buy me time to do what I have to do, it's a small price that I have to pay. Besides, the Café Madison will still be there tomorrow.

Upstairs, I find nothing has changed in my old bedroom. The eyelet ruffles on the sheets and curtains and the fading posters on the pale gold walls are just the same as they were fifteen years ago. Even the photos are the same. My eyes stray to one of Margaret and me as children. In it, I am riding on the shoulders of my smiling father.

The bookcase above my old writing desk still holds the books of my youth. There is a set of Jane Austen novels, the *Great Gatsby, Romeo and Juliet,* and several books of poetry.

I open the desk drawers, even though I know they'll be empty. I took all my possessions with me when I left the last time. But in the bottom drawer, a plain silver ring and delicate silver chain that holds a heart shine up at me. How did I miss these? Then I remember the guilt that made me think leaving these pieces would be best—did I even deserve them? Two months before her death, my mother bought the pieces to reward me for getting good grades.

That bittersweet memory brings back the argument I had with my parents, moments before the crash. The subject of our argument has been erased from my mind, along with other details of the accident—but the emotional fact of it remains.

Unwilling to think more about the last months of their lives, never mind those last precious moments, I tuck the jewelry back in the drawer and return my gaze to the photograph, recalling how my sister has always blamed me for their death. I never told her about the fight, but I found out that, while I was in the hospital, she heard me talking in my sleep. And that's when the accusations started, my sister insisting that our parents would be alive if I hadn't distracted my father while he was driving.

I have accepted Margaret's blame. And the guilt that comes with it. Until, finally, it seems I don't know how to live without either of them.

My cell phone vibrates in my pocket, interrupting this dark train of thought.

Damon. Finally. He's cracked the safe. But he refuses to tell me what's in it over the phone, insisting on speaking with me face-to-face. And he won't be home until tomorrow, late afternoon. I guess Handrock will have to wait.

CHAPTER 18

Aunt Rachelle walks me to the front door. She tugs the edges of her sweater close to her neck even though it's warm in the house. I am in my car five minutes later; the feel of her warm kiss still on my cheek.

An hour and a half later I'm back in Becket, a town I thought I've left behind until I find Noah. Damon's car is in the driveway. Lights are on inside, giving the house a soft and welcoming glow. It's 6:30 p.m. and it's already dark. I knock on his door.

"Hi, Damon," I say when he opens the door. "What's in the safe?"

Despite the chill outside, he's wearing a white T-shirt above his worn-out jeans. His hair is wet, and he smells like pine soap. The shadows under his eyes suggest he hasn't slept in days. He gives a weary smile.

A chill feathers its way up my spine. "So?" I ask. "What's going on?"

"Come in." He leads me into a spacious living room with a large window looking out to a backyard rimmed by woods. I can't see any other houses.

The living room is sparsely decorated with a brown leather sofa and two matching chairs. The walls are beige, and a large painting of a barn hangs over the fireplace. Cherry floors gleam in the soft light cast by a floor lamp.

"I like your house," I say, looking around.

He points to the sofa. "Please, sit."

I rest on the edge of the sofa. "You don't look good."

"It's been hectic the last few days."

I glance around and don't see the safe. "What did you find?"

An awkward silence follows. He blinks a few times. No question, he wants to say something but just can't figure out how to put it into words.

I wait.

Just then, Charlie comes barreling out of the kitchen and crashes into my knees, pushing me back into the sofa.

"Charlie! Down!" Damon yells.

Charlie moves away, but his tail continues to whip wildly.

"Wait here," Damon tells me.

He leaves the room. Charlie follows.

I rise and begin to glance around. Next to the fireplace, floor to ceiling shelves house a collection of books. I trail my fingers over their spines. There are books about home building and woodworking, books about renovations and photography. There are also pictures — photos of Damon in his police uniform, looking much younger, and one of a boys who appears to be three years old, holding a red truck. His gray eyes gaze straight at me. He looks familiar. But from where? Ah. he has the same round eyes and small ears as Damon.

But before I have the chance to examine the rest of the photos, Damon returns, carrying the safe.

"Let's go to the kitchen," he says.

"Is everything okay?" A bitter taste washes through my mouth.

"Coffee?"

I shake my head. "Just water, please."

He places the safe on the table, then opens the fridge and pulls out two bottles of water. He hands me one. I take a swig.

We sit, and Charlie rests on his haunches, his large head resting on Damon's thigh.

"We need to talk." Damon throws a quick glance at the safe, then squints his chocolate brown eyes at me. The same color as the little boy's in the picture.

Opening the safe, he withdraws a sheave of paper and hands it to me wordlessly. I scan the documents. My stomach cramps. I can't believe my eyes.

Everything that has happened so far has led to this. A surge of bitterness hits me. Todd's deceptions keep piling up. My hands start to shake, and the papers slip to the floor.

I sweep them up and wave the documents at him. "You think I'm lying. No, you think I'm crazy! And now you have proof." I didn't mean to shout, but I'm furious. If he were to ask me why I was institutionalized the first time, I would have told him I was out of my mind with grief over my parent's death. The second time ... well ... that was another story.

I raise my eyes to Damon's, whose gaze is shadowed with a new look—worry fused with doubt. In the dead silence, he takes a gulp of water and waits for me to continue. A horrible picture crystalizes in my head, and I press my fingers to my eyes. Willing myself not to cry in front of him.

"I don't know how these documents got into the safe." It's all I can think to say. "According to these papers," Damon replies, "the second time you were institutionalized was after you'd had a false pregnancy. Do you understand what's happening here?"

"I do. Todd orchestrated the whole thing, making sure that no one would believe me. So, you—or whoever opened that safe would say I never had a baby. But I have nothing to prove to you that I was framed." I start shivering.

For some reason, I tell Damon I changed my mind about going to the gynecologist.

"Why?"

"Were you the one who told Officer Gordon I was going to see the gynecologist?"

"No, I wasn't."

He seems sincere.

"You were right. If I have a letter of proof of delivery from the doctor, Officer Gordon will investigate me. He already seems like he's leaning in that direction. So, I'd become the number one suspect. And I won't be any closer to finding Noah."

Damon shrugs. "Officer Gordon is new on the job. Maybe he's eager to prove himself, and even you know your story is difficult to prove. If I do decide to help you any further, I'll do so only because I believe you. But I need more than just your word."

My mouth opens, then closes, as I remember that I do have proof. Of a sort. "Look at these," I say, pulling folded copies of the sketches Howard had done for me out of my pocket. "I had a forensic illustrator draw these for me."

He stares down at the pictures drawn in charcoal on a thick gray art paper, his eyes darting between the pictures. "Todd and Connie?"

"Yes."

His jaw tightens. Something in his face has changed.

"I'm sorry," he says. "It still doesn't prove anything."

"I didn't dream up these faces."

I watch him for a moment, and when he doesn't answer, I change the subject. "How do you suppose Todd was able to obtain my medical records from the Albany Psychiatric Center?"

Of course, it's an inane question. With written consent and an indication of the reason for the request, the Medical Records Office routinely provides reports to their patients. On top of the stack of papers I see the consent form and the letter. My signature is at the bottom of both. I know I didn't sign these papers. Yet the likeness to my handwriting is eerie.

The pit in my stomach has turned into a bottomless chasm. I remind myself that if Todd was capable of planning a disappearing act with my son, and went through the trouble of cleaning the house of all traces of himself and Connie, he was capable of forging my signature.

"I didn't consent to have these documents released."

Damon meets my gaze. What does he see when he looks at me? A crazy woman. I pull the restaurant receipt out of my pocket and hand it to him. "While I was cleaning the house, I found this between the pages of a book."

He scrutinizes the piece of paper and scrunches his eyebrows. "What does this prove?"

"For starters, it's not mine. I've never been there."

His cell phone goes off.

"Damon," he answers. He nods his head a few times. "Repeat." He retrieves a notepad from the kitchen counter and starts writing. An expression crosses his face that I can't read. "Okay … got it."

"I'm sorry," he says as soon as he hangs up. "A client." He picks up his water.

I pick up where I left off, trying to convince him with admittedly skimpy evidence. Or occurrences. Or coincidences. "Someone is following me," I say. "I went for a jog in the woods the other day. I heard someone, but I couldn't see who it was."

"Could have been a deer or other animal. Do you have a reason to fear for your life?"

"No, not really. But there was someone in the house a couple of nights ago, too."

Damon's cell begins to chime, again. He glances at the screen and dismisses it.

"Will you help me find Noah?"

He shakes his head. "You've got no proof, and the bottle of pills I saw in your bathroom. You told me you woke up dizzy and disoriented. Those are side effects from taking Zoloft. Nausea, dizziness, drowsiness."

"Give me the benefit of a doubt." My voice cracks. "My baby is gone, and I don't know what to do."

When he doesn't answer, I chug down the rest of the water, scrape back my chair, and stand. The anger I've felt since coming out of that heavy fog of confusion and grief begins to bubble up. I put my hands on my hips and face him squarely. "I get the impression you'd made up your mind before I got here."

He frowns as if considering his response.

"No, don't bother," I say quickly. I can feel the heat in my face. "This was a mistake. I should never have asked you for help."

He clears his throat. "Look at it from my point of view. Your whole story sounds unbelievable."

I glare at the papers on the table and, with one quick sweep of my arm, they scatter to the floor.

Charlie stands up and whines. Damon pats him, and, reassured, the dog sits back down — albeit, still looking nervously at me.

"Where is the bathroom?" I demand.

Damon points to a door on the other side of the kitchen.

I lock myself in and lean toward my sad image in the mirror. Those hospital documents have set a parade of memories marching in my head. After watching my parents burn to death, I became fearful of everything. I refused to leave the house, as if death awaited me beyond the front door. That meant no school, no friends. And no amount of persuasion from my aunt helped. Finally, she took matters into her own hands. That's when I was hospitalized the first time.

Staying in my room made me feel safe. The nurses had to coax me out during mealtimes and therapy sessions. I was so sick with myself that I vomited, often. I wanted to get better, I did. But I didn't know how and exposing my inner thoughts to the doctors did little to help.

Even now, I'm not exactly cured. But I've learned to force myself out when I need to. Funny, isn't it? When Dr. Bryson prescribed full bed rest, I was actually relieved. I had a good excuse to keep my unborn baby and myself out of harm's way, to nurture the agoraphobia I'd once worked so hard to push away.

The second time, I admitted myself. I was twenty-three, and my depression and agoraphobia, compounded by the need to give new life, was just too much to deal with. I received meds to alleviate my dark moods, which left me lethargic. At first, I welcomed the numbness, but then I wanted to start feeling again, so I stopped taking the pills.

No wonder my story is so hard to believe.

I take in a big, shuddering breath, turn on the faucet and splash cold water on my face.

When I emerge from the bathroom, Damon is standing by the kitchen sink.

He turns around and runs a hand over his buzz cut. "Bree, listen—"

I lift my hand to silence him, then gather the documents and shove them back in the safe.

"I have to go." Safe hugged to my chest, I head toward the door, anxious to get out of this house and away from his doubting eyes.

Damon grabs me by the hand. "Bree, wait a minute."

I yank away and run for the door. By the time I reach my car, I'm panicking. Was it a mistake to entrust Damon with the safe? What if he goes to Officer Gordon and discloses that I was hospitalized? What would happen then?

Just then, my cell phone rings. It's an unfamiliar number. "Who is this?" I ask.

"Lee, Lee Thompson, honey. Your aunt's neighbor."

This call cannot be good news. "Is my aunt okay?"

"No, I'm afraid she's in the hospital. St. Peter's."

My panic morphs into frantic worry for Aunt Rachelle. I yank open the driver's door and slide in, my pulse pounding against my eardrums. Shaking, I turn the key in the ignition. Nothing. I try again. Still nothing. I scream and punch the steering wheel. Pain sears my knuckles. Other than the sound of my breathing, loud and winded, the silence is piercing.

I head back to the house and knock on Damon's door.

"My car won't start, and I need to get to the hospital," I cry as soon as he opens the door ignoring his frown. "My aunt is in the hospital. I have to get there. Please. Can you drive me?"

He rubs his jaw as his frown deepened. Long pause. Then he nods slowly, although clearly unhappy at my request. "Which hospital?"

"St. Peter's, in Albany."

CHAPTER 19

We don't utter a single word on our way to the hospital. We finally arrive at nine-thirty, I tear off my seatbelt and jump out as soon as Damon stops at the front door.

"I'll have your car towed to your house," he says before peeling off on screeching tires.

I dash toward the emergency room at a run. Since the accident, I've hated hospitals, although, voluntarily and involuntarily, I've spent my fair share of time in them. I sprint through the automatic doors to find Lee Thompson waiting for me, looking nervous inside his crumpled clothing.

"It was so lucky Rachelle gave me your new phone number," he says.

"I'm so glad she did," I say, giving him a gentle hug. "Can you tell me what happened?"

"Rachelle called, said she was feeling funny, pain in her arm. I ran right over and found her on the floor."

"Have you spoken to the doctor?"

"No. They rushed her back. No one has come out to talk to me, yet."

"Did you call Margaret?"

"Yes. She said she'll fly out on the next plane."

I do a quick calculation in my head. It's about six-thirty in California. She should be here sometime after midnight.

Just then, a tall doctor, who carries his narrow frame in a stoop, emerges through the swinging doors. He introduces himself as Dr. Bakash, and I identify myself as my aunt's niece.

"How is she doing?" I try to keep the hysteria from my voice.

Stroking one eyebrow with a long, brown finger, he says, "What your aunt has is quite common. We did an angiogram to determine if her arteries are blocked and, if so, where. The test showed she has an embolism, a blood clot that formed in her left atrium and migrated to a coronary artery, which caused her to sustain a myocardial infarction."

"Can you translate it to English?"

"It's a heart attack. But she's going to be all right."

I manage to quickly choke them back. "What happens now?"

"Blood thinners should prevent existing blood clots from growing and new ones from developing."

I turn away, staring at the other wretches in the waiting room, an impromptu assembly of people brought together by misfortune.

"May I see her now?"

"Yes, you may. But make it short. She needs to rest."

I leave Mr. Thompson sitting in the waiting room and head toward the ICU. The lights are intense—headache-inducing bright. Aunt Rachelle lies in her curtained ICU bed, a sheet pulled up to her chest. She looks so small. A tube snakes out of her nose, another from her arm. The wire attached to her chest displays a complicated video with an uneven green line that travels across the screen like a vessel across unsuitable terrain.

She looks pale. I'm afraid for her, afraid of the proximity of death. I take a step back, thinking that if I went out into the hall, I could pretend that it's not my aunt in this room. Instead, I suck in a breath and move closer.

Sitting next to her, clutching her hand as I wait for her to awaken, I let myself cry. I should have been there for her.

Earlier today, at her house, I saw several bottles of pills on the kitchen table, but I didn't bother to ask what they were for. I swallow against the guilt and squeeze her hand.

She squeezes mine weakly and opens her eyes.

I try to smile. "Auntie?"

She looks into my eyes and whispers, "Bree, honey. Don't cry. I'm okay. It was just a little scare." She closes her eyes. "It's okay," she says, as if to reassure herself, as well as me.

I continue holding her hand until her even breathing tells me she's asleep again.

An hour later she's moved upstairs. I insist on a private room. Once I make sure Aunt Rachelle is comfortable, I give Lee Thompson a report. He shakes my hand and says, "I'll be on my way, now, but call me if you need anything." I thank him and watch him go.

With nothing to do but worry, I pace the floor, thinking about my sister. I already know the greeting I'll get when Margaret shows up at the hospital: a quick sweep from head to toe, then an awkward hug that spells obligation, rather than warmth, followed by a barrage of questions aimed at making me feel bad.

Sure enough, several hours later, hearing a commotion behind me, I turn to see my sister rushing in. Diamonds flash on her tanned fingers.

Margaret scowls when she spots me. "I want to see Auntie, now," she says after a quick hug and a couple of air kisses.

I point to Aunt Rachelle's door. "Right there."

Before she enters the room, my sister says, "We need to talk after I've seen Auntie."

I unclench my clenched fists. "It's two in the morning, and I'm tired. I'm going to Auntie's house. Will you be staying there too?"

"Yes."

"Then, we'll talk tomorrow."

CHAPTER 20

When I wake up, it's afternoon. I peek into Margaret's room, which is across the hall from mine. She isn't there, but it's clear she hasn't been gone long: Bundles of clothing lay scattered on every available surface, and there's a wet towel on the bed.

I make a pit stop in the bathroom, where there are now countless creams, combs, oils, perfumes, soaps, and shampoos. All high quality, much different from than I'm used to.

I call and leave a message on Margaret's cell, then make my way to the kitchen, where papers are strewn all over the table, which is littered with soda cans. Unwashed plates and bowls and mugs are left on the kitchen counter. It took my sister less than a day to make the place look like a bomb has gone off.

Aunt Rachelle would hate it, I think, with a guilty pang, and I get to work putting the cans in the recycling and washing the crusty dishes. Then I check the fridge. Finding wilted lettuce and rotten vegetables, I toss them. Next, I sweep the floor. When I'm finished, I turn back to the table, stacking the magazines neatly and recycling the newspaper.

Beneath the newspaper, an official-looking document sits in plain sight. At first, I'm not sure what I'm looking at. I skim, but it's the fourth page that makes my heart bang against my rib cage. I sit down slowly in the chair beside the table. Damn. Of course, it's plain as day.

I glance at my watch. Nearly four o'clock, and Margaret hasn't called back yet. I dial her number again. This time she answers. "Listen," she says, before I can get a word out. "I have a few things to take care of. I've visited Auntie. Let's meet at eight. I should be done by then. The Corner Pub, okay?" She doesn't wait for me to agree, just clicks off.

•   •   •

At eight-fifteen, an Uber drops me off in front of the Corner Pub, oddly named, since the place is in the middle of the block. Inside, the bar is stuffy but quiet. I step in, scan the room, and spot my sister seated on a bar stool, sipping a glass of white wine.

"You're late." She stares at me as I wonder over. If it's anything the way I feel, the instant shock on her face underscores how awful I must look. It has been a long day, beginning with driving from my aunt's house back to Becket for an emotional reencounter with my past, then back to Albany to visit my aunt at the hospital. All that in one day. Yesterday morning I set out to Handrock, placing my hope in one little piece of paper to get me closer to my son. And I'm still not there yet.

"Sorry," I say, hoisting myself onto a stool. "My visit with Aunt Rachelle was interrupted by a nurse taking her vitals and blood work. Then I was waiting for the doctor to explain things to me. But he never showed up." I catch the bartender's attention and hold up a finger. He's next to me in an instant. I order a glass of white wine.

"You could have called to let me know you'd be late."

I glance at my sister. Even in the dim light, I can see she doesn't look well.

"Did you get the chance to speak with the doctor?" I ask, nodding my thanks to the bartended for the glass he's setting on the counter.

"I managed to track him down. Dr. Kabash."

I take a swallow of the wine. "What did he say?"

Her answer is brusque. "Nothing really new. Apparently, the blood thinners she'd been taking didn't stop the heart block. She had a mild heart attack. She needs new medication. Then she can go home."

Then she raises her eyebrows at me, and I can tell she's going in for the kill. "So, what's going on with you? When I finally get your phone number, you don't return my phone calls. And Auntie tells me that you are looking for a baby?"

"Noah. My baby's name is Noah. Todd took him away from me."

"Todd? This is ridiculous," my sister continues. "No one has seen this man."

I nod. "I had a forensic illustrator draw a picture of him and Connie."

"Connie? And who is Connie?" My sister rolls her eyes. "See? That's what happens when you disengage yourself from your family."

"The midwife. She delivered Noah. Six days after Noah was born, Todd and Connie disappeared, along with my baby."

Margaret rolls her eyes again and sighs loudly, fingering the shiny rock on her finger.

I take a sip of my wine, and flash on an image of my sister in her bed with a boy, after school one day. I don't remember where my aunt was at the time.

"So, where did you meet this phantom man?"

"Dating.com."

"I told you at the time not to do that, not to go searching for men on that … that site. You've consistently had bad judgment about men, always wanting to be rescued. A damsel in distress. These are the kinds of signals you project."

Sitting in the uncomfortable silence, a part of me wants to defend myself. But what's the point? Conversations with Margaret are always awkward. Although, in this case, I hate to admit she's right.

I continue to nurse my wine.

Margaret takes this as an invitation to continue her diatribe. "And as far as the baby goes, you and I both know that you've committed yourself to work out your issues with false pregnancy. But here it is again. An entire imaginary baby, this time, though, not just an imaginary pregnancy."

"But this time it's real!" I exclaim. "And I have the drawings to prove that Todd and Connie do exist."

"Drawings? Drawings mean nothing," she points out. I start to talk, but she raises her hand to silence me. "Okay. I'll humor you. Where are the drawings?"

"I left them in the car. I'll show you later."

She exhales in exasperation and pushes her hair away from her face, which reminds me of our mother, her blond curls like a splash of sunshine. But the memory quickly fades, as I see the worry lines etched around my sister's eyes and mouth. She looks worn out, even with all the makeup she has on. Is that a bruise on her cheek? And the remnants of a black eye? All the foundation she's used hasn't concealed either one.

When she notices I'm staring at the bruises, she attempts to cover them with her hand.

I confront her. "Margaret? What happened?"

She averts her eyes, turning her attention to the bar. "Oh, nothing. Clumsy me, I tripped on the basement stairs and fell."

The documents I found on the table at my aunt's house tell a different story. My sister filed for divorce and an order of protection, claiming she's an abused wife.

"If there's anything you need to talk to me …"

She immediately derails me. "Auntie and I are worried sick about you. It's you we need to talk about."

The bartender is busy polishing glasses at the other end of the bar. Even so, I suppress the urge to explain the last nine months to Margaret. After our parents' death, when I needed her most, my big sister pulled away from me. Much as I wish it was different, I don't feel safe being emotionally vulnerable with her now, any more than I did then.

But she's not finished with me. "You've made bad choices picking men in the past, but doing a disappearing act? How do you think Auntie and I felt about that?"

She starts in on her second drink. I bow my head. I wish I could argue. But she's right. I do let men control my life.

"Bree?" she presses when I ignore her.

I really can't take it anymore. Turning the conversation back to her, I ask, "How long will you be staying?" By the look of the clothes she brought with her, it seems like she's planned an extended visit.

"Margaret, I saw the documents you left on the table. Are you okay? Are you in danger?"

She leans toward me, hands twisting nervously. "I'll be camping at Auntie's for a while. I've moved back to my old bedroom." There's the tiniest break in her voice. "Besides, Auntie needs me right now."

"What about your veterinary hospital?"

"I sold it," she says. "I can always open up another clinic in Albany."

I try again, reaching out to put my hand on hers. "If you ever need to …"

She yanks her hand back. "We should be leaving," she snaps. "I'm going back to the hospital for a while."

"I'll be leaving tomorrow morning." I place a few bills under my glass.

My sister squints at me, suspiciously. "Where are you headed?"

"I have to take care of a few things." With that, I slide off the stool and scoop up my purse.

Twenty-five minutes later, I reach up to the top shelf in the closet of my former bedroom, bring down a small lockbox, take out my pistol — which is fully loaded — and slip it into my bag.

CHAPTER 21

With the blinds drawn, Aunt Rachelle's hospital is dim, lit only by the nightlight above her bed.

I take her cold hand in mine. "Auntie?"

She stirs and her eyes flicker open, then blinks a few times as if registering who I am. When she does, she smiles and closes her eyes again. I sit with her a few more minutes, watching her chest rise and fall under the thin blanket.

Just as I think it's time to leave, my aunt opens her eyes again, and tightens her hand around mine. "How are you doing, Bree?" she asks in a low, raspy voice.

"I'm fine, Auntie. Don't worry about me."

"I know you're going through a hard time. I hope you sort it out soon with Dr. Palmer."

Before I can answer, a nurse pops her head in and smiles. "Time for a check-up," she says, bustling in to poke my aunt with various instruments.

I stand and step aside. "I have to go now."

"Bree? You do intend to keep your appointment, right?" My aunt watches my face carefully.

I nod.

As her eyes search mine, a sticky tension stretches between us. "Okay," she says, "But we have a deal. If you don't keep your end of it, I'll keep mine."

With a promise I don't intend to keep and a heavy heart, I turn and walk quickly out of the room.

By the time I reach my rented Dodge Charger, I've managed to blink away most of my tears. After programming my destination into the GPS, I punch the gas and head toward the highway north of town. It will take about three hours to get from Albany to Handrock. This undertaking could lead to another dead end. But I keep my mind on Noah, on the prospect of seeing him again, the thing that keeps me from falling to pieces. Maybe the answer is closer than I thought — that much I allow, because hope is all I have now. That, and my wish that Noah is well taken care of, that he is warm, fed, and safe, wherever he is.

The wide-open highway cuts through mountains and forests. On both sides, the ground rolls and swells, red oaks and white Spruce clinging to steep slopes. Rows of jagged peaks are visible on the horizon. Intermingled with the evergreens, fall foliage ruptures in burnt sienna, wine, and scarlet. I keep in the flow of the light traffic, trying to control my anxiety.

About an hour later, I exit onto a small country road in a hammering downpour that makes it difficult to navigate. Finally, the village of Handrock announces itself with an old clapboard sign and the rain abates. I roll down the window, and the scent of wood smoke fills the car. Several turns later, and I am in downtown, where I find a stretch of stone buildings more than a century old, home to antique stores and corner bars. It's past five, and most of the storefronts that line the Main Street are dark and shuttered. The few people still out on the street shelter under dingy awnings or within doorways.

At one end of Main Street, a squat motel appears. A neon light blinks its vacancy. Two beat-up pickups are the only vehicles in the parking lot. I swing into a space beside one of them.

Inside, the motel office reeks of cigarettes. A long-haired man stands behind the counter reading a newspaper, which he holds at arm's length.

"Hi," I say with forced cheerfulness.

He clears his throat and looks up, blinking, his eyes magnified behind thick lenses. "Welcome to Lakeview Motel."

I wonder if there's actually a lake in the vicinity. "I would like to get a room."

"How long will you be staying?"

I shrug. "Don't know yet."

His fingers punch at the keyboard, while he mumbles under his breath. "I have one room on the lower level," he says. "And I have one room on the second floor. The room on the lower level is a suite. What do you prefer?"

"First floor, please."

"Eighty bucks a night." He smiles, revealing a set of yellow teeth. "Cash."

"By the way," I say, after I hand him the bills. "Do you mind looking at these sketches and telling me if you've seen these people?"

When he nods, I pull the pictures out of my coat pocket, unfold them, and present them to him. He glances at them. Then, suddenly his smile evaporates. "Sorry. Can't say that I do." He shoves the sketches back at me.

I try to put him at ease with a smile. "What's your name?"

"Billie." He pulls out a package of tobacco from his breast pocket and stuffs a wad up into his upper gums.

"Billie, I'm Bree. Would you mind looking again?"

"Nope. Once is enough." He glances out the window at my rental. "Need help with your bags?"

I shake my head and flash him another smile. Might as well stay on his good side. "Can you recommend a decent place to get dinner?"

"Only two places in town to get good food. Café Madison is on Steel Road, off of Main Street, and Sylvie's Diner is down the road a ways to the left."

"Which one of them do you suggest?"

He eyes the clock hanging on the opposite wall. "Being that it's Friday and past five, Café Madison is closed. They're open only … oh … till five-ish, depending on the owner's mood." Then he chuckles. "In that case, all's that's left is Sylvie's. Meatloaf and mashed potatoes are the special tonight. It sure fills a hungry stomach and mighty tasty at that." He gives another chortle.

He hands me the key to my room, I thank him, and spin on my heels—right into a large bearded man, with black eyes like charred potatoes, who stands directly behind me. He smirks. "Hello, little lady. What's a pretty thing like you doing in this shit of a town?"

"Knock it off, Wayne," Billie snaps. "I reckon you don't want me to go telling your wife about your foul mouth."

"Cool it, buddy. Just joking, is all." The bearded man looks down at the sketches in my hand and raises his eyebrows. "What's this?"

"She's looking for these people," Billie says. I think I see him wink. "Told her there's no one in these parts resembling the people she's looking for."

Wayne squints at the sketches again. "Really? She's looking for them?"

I hold them out so he can have a better look. "Have you seen them?"

"Looks to me like you're looking for trouble, little lady."

Is that a threat?

"Wayne," Billie says in a warning tone that makes Wayne throw his hands up in the air and leave, banging the door behind him.

I fold the sketches and stuff them back in my pocket, then head back to unpack my car.

I drop my stuff at the motel suite. It has a small living area, a kitchenette, and a separate bedroom. The furniture looks as if it has been dragged from the curb, but I don't care. At this point, I feel hopeful, and nothing is going to spoil my mood.

•　　•　　•

Sylvie's is an old roadside diner, with a large, dirty parking lot, which is inhabited by a collection of dilapidated pickups. A group of scraggly men sit on the bench out front, looking bored. Their chuckles drill a hole in my back until I the diner's door closes behind me.

Friday-evening faces—sagging, gaunt, resigned—pivot in my direction. I find a seat opposite a red-eyed, middle-aged blonde, whose head is buried in her laptop. A waitress approaches her table, carrying a tray stacked with food. The server is a big woman; her long, auburn hair is pulled back and fastened with a clip. She and her customer exchange a few words before she approaches me.

"Good evening. I've never seen you here, before."

I glance at her name tag. "Good evening, Viola."

"I guess you're just passing through, ha? No one in their right mind would want to stay here."

When I don't answer, her face turns serious. "Sorry. Didn't mean to meddle. What would you like?"

"According to Billie, the meatloaf and mashed potatoes are the special tonight."

"A woman who knows her appetite."

"Don't remember the last time I had a good meal."

"Then let me get right to it," she says, her grin deepening the wrinkles around her eyes.

As she turns away, a vaguely familiar-looking man enters the diner. He walks with a smooth gait, and has a slight stoop, as if worn down by decades of hard living. His denim jeans and shirt are clean, but well worn, as are his boots. I try not to stare as he pulls up a chair at a neighboring table. He reminds me so much of Dr. Bryson.

Who was Dr. Bryson? I wonder, not for the first time. Obviously, he was in on the scheme to keep me bedridden, which meant I was entirely under Todd's control. After a few minutes of fruitless thoughts about the mysterious "doctor," I look up to see Viola approaching with my meal.

"Thank you," I say to the waitress.

"My pleasure. Is there anything else I can get you?"

"No," I say. "But could I trouble you to look at a couple of sketches?"

"Sure."

I pull out the drawings, quickly, and hear the tiny clatter of an object falling from my pocket to the linoleum floor. I unfold the drawings and hand them to Viola, then reach below the table feeling for what I dropped. My fingers close on a small object. I sit back up and look at it.

It's a flash drive.

Where did it come from, though? And then I remember the small item that slid out from under the driver's seat when I'd slammed the brakes to avoid hitting that rabbit the day Noah went missing.

"Are you okay?"

I raise my eyes to Viola and deliberately keep my face relaxed. "I'm fine," I say. The little flash drive weighs only an ounce or two, but it feels heavy as a stone in my hand. I slip it back into my pocket.

I nod to the sketches. "Have you seen them? They could have come here to eat."

She squints at the drawings, then averts her eyes, face clouded, unreadable. When her gaze returned to me, she gives me a long appraising look.

"Who are they?" she finally asks.

"My husband and the woman who delivered my baby. They're missing."

"Missing?" Her eyebrows reposition upwards, then press towards the center of her nose, and she hands the sketches back to me.

"Viola!" someone calls from the back.

The waitress turns. "Be right there, Tommy."

"Before you go, can I have the check please?" I'm anxious to get back to the room and see what's on the flash drive.

Viola writes my check and slaps it on the table. She starts to say something, then shakes her head and presses her lips tightly together.

She waves at a couple with a baby and hustles back to the kitchen.

I pick at my food, wondering why the drive was in my car. Connie did use my car at least once, that I know about. Could it be hers? Does this flash-drive hold the key to finding Noah?

As walk to the register, I fight an irrational urge to go over to the man's table and ask him if he's Dr. Bryson.

That's ridiculous. Of course, he's not. I pay for my meal and leave.

CHAPTER 22

Displayed on my laptop, the video that was saved on the flash drive is dark and grainy, a mishmash of shadows. And at first, it's hard to tell what it is I'm actually seeing. Even though it's difficult to make out the faces, it's apparent from the marching boys and the commanding voice shouting orders at them that this is a military exercise. The video turns blurry and pixelated, and my attempt to adjust the contrast for maximum definition fails.

Next, a group of boys stand in front of a gate, barbed-wire fence stretching left and right, a field bordered with a line of dense trees behind them. I pause the video and lean in, my attention captured by the children. There are about twenty of them, arranged by size, smaller boys in the front, the taller ones in the back. Positioned in the center of the back row stands a tall, unsmiling woman. I can't make out her face, but, like the man in the diner, there's something familiar about her. Unlike the Dr. Bryson lookalike, though, I have no idea who she reminds me of.

I press Play again. For a second, the screen goes black, then I see two youngsters, a girl and a boy, playing with guns. A man's voice says, "What do you do with the weapons?"

I can't hear the children's answer. It's muffled by a noise that sounds like thunder.

Then there's a pulsing light shimmering in the sky. A couple of seconds after the light flashes, a figure materializes. It's a man. He's tall, but that's all I can make of him. He's shouting something. A chorus of young voices responds.

For several seconds, the video goes black again. Every nerve in my body stretches taut.

The next moment, I see young boys marching in formation through a large field. Their lower faces are covered with black bandannas. Rifles are slung over their slender shoulders. A great cry goes up, and they break off into several units, shouting. The light fades. Moonless night engulfs them.

I continue to stare at the screen long after the disturbing images have halted. A strange twisting starts in my gut. Children marching. Children holding guns. And that tall woman. Who is she? Who is the man?

I pick up my pen, twirling it in my fingers, while I ponder what to do next. Should I call the police? I'm not so naïve as to think I can make Officer Gordon believe this tape has anything to do with Todd's disappearance.

What if …? I could email Damon a copy of the flash drive. But the way we left things suggests he may not look at it anything I send him. But I have no choice. I compose a brief note, explaining how I came upon the flash drive, attach the video to the email, and ask him to please contact me once he's viewed it.

After that, I get ready for bed, but, for the longest time, I can't fall asleep. From the darkness, problems pop out at me like so many sinister Jacks-in-the-Box.

Finally, though, just before nodding off, I imagine holding my little boy in my arms once again.

CHAPTER 23

I park the Dodge across the street from Café Madison, at the other end of town. Unlike Sylvie's Diner, this place looks cheerful and inviting with its gleaming glass and frilly curtains. The exterior of the building is painted a rustic red and has matching awnings. A flag hangs by the door and waves gently in the cold, late morning breeze.

Several highly-polished motorcycles are parked out front. The rest of the vehicles are mostly pickups, crusted with mud.

I climb out of the car and tighten my scarf. The change in the weather has flattened the light to a dull gray. Clouds press low. I cross the street and stride up to the restaurant. Up close, I see the café is in a state of mild despair. Paint has peeled on the wood trim, and the concrete wall is cracked in several places.

Before entering, I hesitate. What am I doing? It seems almost impossible that I would get information from a cash receipt. Instead, trying to convince myself that maybe I'll find answers here, I suck in chilled air, then exhale and push through the glass door.

Two men sit at a table close to the front. They scrutinize me, and I wonder if I look as horrible as I feel. A bunch of customers in jackets and scarves are lined up waiting to order food from a grandmotherly-looking woman behind the counter.

Negotiating my way through the maze of people waiting to be served, I make my way past occupied tables, floorboards creaking with each step. A man in a brown fleece jacket has just vacated a table in the back of the room. I maneuver into the small space and sink onto the chair.

Immediately, a waif-like waitress puts a glass of water in front of me. She stares at me and raises an eyebrow. Her large blue eyes are glassy, and her pupils are dilated, and she has a little smile on her lips, as if she's seen me before. But she hasn't. I haven't been here before. Still, there's something familiar about her. I place my order. Within minutes, a steaming cup of coffee and a banana muffin on a small round plate sit on the table before me.

On my second bite of the muffin, I sense someone ogling me. I glance up, and one of the men seated by the door quickly averts his eyes, cupping his mug of coffee in his leather-gloved hands. His inky, curly hair shoots out from the sides of his head, a strange asymmetry that stops him from being handsome. The bearded man seated next to him, who sports a mustache, appraises me, narrows his eyes, and scratches the scruff on his chin, then gives me a slow, knowing smile. I realize it's Wayne, the man I met at the Lakeview motel. Every instinct in my body signals he is dangerous. His stare, like two black holes, is unflinching. I want to turn away from him, but, with all the unhappiness and frustration of the last few days stirring inside me, I glare at him, instead, daggers shooting out of my eyes. Finally, he turns away.

I unclench my teeth and return to my coffee, then pinch off a bite of muffin and stick it in my mouth, chewing without tasting.

The waif-like waitress comes back. "How about a refill?"

I nod and rub my hands together to rid myself of the icy feel in my bones. Suddenly, I get it: what looks familiar about her is her eyes. Viola had the same constricted pupils, the same rapid blinking.

"Cold out, isn't it?" Her voice sounds like it's covered in gravel.

"Yes, it is," I say. I'm still warming my hands when she returns with the coffee pot. "Can I ask you a question?"

She smiles. "I'll do my best to answer."

I fish in my purse, bring out the receipt, and slide it across the table. "Could you tell me if there's a way for you to know who ordered this meal?"

The waitress gives it a perfunctory glance, then refocuses on me with a suspicious stare. "I'm sorry. I can't do that since they paid in cash. Even if I could, it's against our policy to disclose such information."

Odd. This is a public restaurant. What difference does it make if she divulges this information?

"Can I trouble you for another minute? To look at a couple of sketches?"

She plants one hand on her skinny hip. "What kind of sketches?"

I pull out the photocopies and smooth them. "Have you ever seen these people?"

She reaches up to her hair and twirls a lifeless strand. "What's this all about?"

Subzero fingers crawl down my back. There's something strange about this restaurant; something I should remember and can't.

"I'm looking for my husband," I say, tapping Todd's picture. "And the woman is his sister."

She turns her glassy stare to the men seated by the door. "I've never seen them," she says without meeting my eyes again. "Is there anything else I can get you?"

I shake my head. She slaps a meal check down on the table and leaves.

The men by the door throw bills down onto their table and exit the café together. Both light up cigarettes as soon as the door swings closed behind them. Through the window, I observe them exchanging a few words and glancing back in my direction. I immediately avert my eyes. Moments later, they mount their bikes and head down the street in a raucous roar. A simple encounter, yet I feel strangely agitated.

At that moment, a young woman with long brown hair, carrying a baby on her hip, walks into the restaurant. She waves at the grandmotherly woman behind the counter. They exchange a few words, then she settles at the table next to me. I turn away.

A few minutes later, the baby starts shrieking. The sound penetrates my skull. I have a sudden image of my son crying in hunger. My breasts fill up with milk. I ball my hands into fists, holding back my emotions.

I remember how, for those very few days—six days—I was connected to my baby beyond any bond I'd ever shared with anybody. I want that feeling back.

The crowd at the cash register, keeps me from leaving as quickly as I'd like. I feel trapped. I take in a deep breath and force myself to relax until the bill for my order is settled. Then I grab my leather jacket and purse and dash for the door, battling a rush of hysteria.

On the way out, I bump into a display of boxed cookies and watch in dismay as they crash to the floor. It is one of those moments when sound diminishes, and the rest of the world fades into the background. The grandmotherly woman runs out from behind the counter. I watch her pick up the boxes and begin restacking them. I bend down to help. She doesn't look at me, obviously annoyed.

Outside, I stand under the awning. The overcast November sky has descended, ashen and full of lingering gloom. Raindrops fall thick and heavy. Shadows dance between the buildings. Again, I feel as though someone is watching me, a sensation that is becoming all too familiar. My heart rate spikes. I look left and right. A bulky man wearing a camouflage jacket and a wool cap pulled low passes by me, his broad back curved against the rain. I watch him until he turns the corner, leaving a strong scent of marijuana behind him.

The uneasiness I've felt since I got to this town persists. Since Todd's disappearance, I imagine people following me, think people are looking at me oddly. Everyone is suspect.

Is my paranoia caused by Officer Gordon and Damon and my sister and even my aunt questioning my sanity? Am I making up stuff? Or is there really something sinister happening?

I dash across the street, slide into the rental car, start the engine, then sit there transfixed, trying to decide what to do next. My head pounds with doubts about the wisdom of this whole damn trip.

But then I get an idea. I flick on the wipers and head back down the road toward the motel.

CHAPTER 24

Back at the motel, I boot up my computer, key in my location, and study a topographical map of the area. Despite, or maybe because of, the uneasiness I've experienced here, as much as I can be certain of anything, I know it's right for me to stay in this town and continue probing.

Once I get the feel of the area I want to cover, I grab a bunch of the sketches I had copied at Staples and set out for a neighborhood close to town. I park and get out of the car, shivering against the chilly air that hangs heavy with moisture. It has rained so much the last couple of days I begin to think the weather is a commentary on my life.

Glancing around, I see typical, turn-of-the-century, two-story houses accented by faded shutters and crooked porches. Blowing into my cupped hands, I squint toward the first house on the block. It is set back from the road, and its paint is peeling. Weeds choke the yard. A rope swing hangs lonely from the branch of an ancient oak, twisting in the wind.

Every nerve ending tingles. Again, I feel somebody's eyes piercing my back. I turn quickly, but the street is empty.

At the front door, I ring the doorbell, step back, and wait. Nothing happens. I ring the bell again. Finally, I hear click-clacking against wood, and the door opens.

A stout, round-faced woman, with a knitted cap pulled low on her forehead and a sallow complexion greets me. Her eyes are bloodshot, small red veins line her pug-nose. "Yes?"

"Hi," I say, flashing a bright smile.

She frowns. "Who're you?"

Rather than answering directly, I hold up the sketches. "I hope you can help. My baby disappeared along with my husband and his sister. Could you please look at these drawings and tell me if you've ever seen them?"

She ignores my outstretched hand. "Don't know anything 'bout that."

"Please, just look at the sketches."

"Why don't you call the police?" She begins to close the door.

"I did," I say quickly. "They don't believe me. Please? Just a minute of your time."

Maybe something in my voice makes her reconsider. "Fine." Her mouth sets itself in a firm line as she scrutinizes the sketches. "And what makes you think they'll be in this area?"

"I have my reasons. Have you seen them?"

She looks past me, eyes flicking back and forth. And before I know what's happening, she slams the door in my face. From the other side of the door come the sounds of a chain being pulled across and a double bolt snapping into place.

For the next few hours, I trudge from door to door, showing the sketches to people who look at me with equal suspicion as the one before and who are, at best, unfriendly. Evidently, shoving pictures in people's faces makes me look like a deranged woman.

Having reached a dead end in this neighborhood, I begin to think that maybe this approach is a waste of time. Back in town, I find a library off the main stretch and create a flyer. The headline reads, *Have You Seen These People?* Positioned above are Todd and Connie's photos and, at the bottom of the page, my phone number.

Armed with dozens of flyers, I head to another neighborhood, walking every street, taping the flyers to lampposts, shoving them into mailboxes. Then I drive back to the downtown area. There, I trudge from store to store, introducing myself and showing my flyer. At first, the shop owners are friendly, but they refuse to let me post the flyer after I show it to them, and they turn mum when I ask if they've ever seen Todd or Connie. I wonder if they're just not interested in getting involved. Or perhaps there is a more disturbing reason.

I get the opposite reaction at a women's boutique. The young manager hesitates when she hears my request, but she must feel sorry for me. She tells me she's new in town and takes great care taping the flyer to the window beside the faded poster of a smiling, pregnant woman, wearing a royal blue dress. The caption says, *Pregnant Women Can Look Nice, Too.*

I thank the young woman and return to the street, where, by now, I sense everyone watching me. A few pedestrians stop to ask what I am doing, then scowl and walk on when I tell them.

Undeterred I continue on my way. Either Todd or Connie or both of them were here. The café receipt proves that. So, someone must have seen them. Now, all I need is that person to have the courage to talk to me.

It's after six o'clock. Orange and gold bands crack the edge of the sky, lighting the top of stores and trees. One by one, shops start to close, metal grates being pulled down, padlocked. I enter the children's clothing store. A middle-aged man emerges from the back, sporting brown corduroys and a brown turtleneck. A weedy patch of brown hair sprouts off his balding head.

"We're closed." He eyes the papers clasped in my hand. "Come back tomorrow."

"I just need a minute of your time."

"Sorry, the wife is waiting with dinner, and I'm late as is."

I shove the sketches in his face. "A quick look. Please."

His eyes flutter. "What's this?"

"Have you by any chance seen these people?"

He scrutinizes the papers. Once. Twice. "Yes. No. Maybe," he says, in a rush of words, clasping his hands together.

"When exactly did you say they came in?"

"I never said such a thing." A sheen covers his pink head. He takes out a handkerchief and mops his forehead. "Now, leave."

He ushers me to the door and shuts it behind me, but not before he says, "If you come back here again, I'll call the police."

I wonder on what charges.

All this running around with nothing to show for it is beginning to drag me down. I stop at Sylvie's Diner to grab a quick bite, regroup, and recover from all the dead ends. It's after the dinnertime rush, so I almost have the place to myself, which is fine with me.

Viola approaches my table to take my order. She comes back a few minutes later and places my hamburger and mashed potatoes in front of me. "So, you're the talk of town," she says with a closed-mouth smile. "Curious, though, isn't it?"

"What is?"

"Barely here a day, and already you've created more excitement than most people around here get in a year."

I glance around the diner. No one is paying attention to me. Or they're pretending not to, at least. "People are talking? Tell me about it."

"The flyers, the door knocking, the questions."

"Really," I say, meeting her bloodshot, glazed eyes.

She shrugs. "It's just that we don't talk to people like you."

"People like me?"

"Yes. An outsider, asking questions—it rubs people the wrong way. Folks in this town are hypersensitive about their private lives. I'm sure you got the message."

I pour ketchup on my hamburger and wonder what folks in this town have to hide.

"Viola!" A voice booms from behind the counter.

"Be right there, Tommy."

"I gotta go," Viola says to me. "And please don't come in here flashing those sketches again. Tommy won't allow it."

Ten minutes later, Viola comes back with my check, which she places on the table, along with another scrap of paper. "Sorry about being abrupt," she whispers. "My phone number. Call if you need anything."

CHAPTER 25

Since it's useless trying to get any sleep, I turn on my laptop and go online, my mind abuzz with questions. The disturbing images on the flash drive continue to occupy my thoughts. Not much is revealed in the pictures. But one thing is for sure, children and young adults were marching and carrying guns. I've watched enough news specials to know that young children are too often used by adults with twisted minds to carry out their horrifying plots.

It's terrible, but it does give me a place to start to look. I begin by narrowing down my search to *children + indoctrination*. A huge amount of information comes up—but mostly what I take away is little I understand about this subject.

I continue rummaging through articles about child soldiers, until I find one that makes my heart palpitate. An image accompanying an article released by the Christian Exploit Network shows a tall woman in combat fatigues. The way she stands, leaning to the left as if weighted by something heavy makes me think of Connie. Could it be? There's nothing that identifies the woman. But she's positioned in front of about twenty camouflage-clad, pint-sized children, and the article states that thousands of children are serving as soldiers in armed conflicts around the world, a few as young as eight years old. They fight on front lines, participate in suicide missions, and act as spies, messengers, or lookouts.

As I continue scanning articles, I become increasingly alarmed by the ferocity of the hatred such groups espouse. One video features their procedures for training children of both sexes and of all ages in guerilla tactics. The narrator also explains that the children are brainwashed into believing those associated with their movement are superior to everyone else.

After a couple of hours of researching these child soldiers, I look up to see that it's past midnight. I'm still too restless to sleep, but I don't know what to do next. I rub my eyes and shiver. The cold is penetrating. As I slip on a sweater, one Todd told me he liked on me, an idea hits me: I found Todd through Dating.com. Maybe he's on there now, looking for someone new.

While the site comes up, I think about how to create a profile that would be the right kind of bait. I start by scanning profiles of women in my same age category. Desperation rolls off the screen, and there's an annoying sameness to all the profiles. All the women enjoy dining out, exotic travel, and long walks on the beach. And they're all either athletic, slender, or curvy — or all three.

Getting very little help from my "sisters" on the site, I decide to write a profile that mirrors what Todd had written previously. Mainly, I say my fictional self is *Family-oriented. Marriage-minded. Wants children.* My profile picture is of a model who does *Good Housekeeping*-type print ads. Very wholesome.

Having paid for a month's subscription to Dating.com, I turn to Craigslist, where my personal ad states I'm looking for a man, who may be from upstate New York, and include Todd's image. I post this ad in a few cities each on Craigslist Massachusetts, Canada, and New York, using the company's anonymous email address. I also upload Todd's and Connie's sketches to my long-dormant Twitter and Facebook accounts, asking if anyone knows these people.

Surely, someone has to have seen Todd. Surely.

•   •   •

I finally fall asleep just after 1:00 a.m. But I'm awakened twenty minutes later — although I'm not sure by what. I strain for a clue, some noise. But every sound seems exaggerated in the dark: the water dripping in the bathtub, an animal howling in the distance, a dog barking nearby.

I get out of bed to use the bathroom, flicking on the bedside light as I shuffle on my slippers. As I turn, I notice it something on the floor by the door glaring at me. A piece of paper.

I hesitate for a second, then grab it. With cold fingers, I unfold the sheet. Inside, someone has typed my name in red ink and these words: *Stop looking for trouble.*

Stop looking for trouble?

Razor-edged terror torpedoes through me. Who would slip this paper under my door? Is there a threat implied in that demand? For a second, I think I should call the police, but I doubt they will take me seriously.

It's so late. I hesitate to call Damon—especially as he's never replied to my email with the video I found on the flash drive. But I'm frightened and desperate. I leave a message telling him it's important for me to talk to him. Of course, given how we left things when he dropped me off at the hospital, I may never hear from him again.

Of course, I could call Luanne. But she's hours farther away than Damon—and also not a private detective. She won't really be able to help, as much as she might want to. I also consider calling Viola but drop the thought immediately. There's something about her I don't trust.

Instead, I distract myself by mapping out the neighborhoods I'll cover next, all the while, keeping an eye on the clock, anxiously hoping Damon will call back. Next, I visit Dating.com, only to find lewd responses such as, *Wow u r just gorgeous. I'd like climb on you,* and *hi gorgeous – how do you like sexy texting?* but none that will bring me closer to Todd.

As I shut down my laptops, I hear footsteps echoing outside my door. I tiptoe to the window and part the shades slightly. At first glance, I don't see anything. Then I notice him. A man is standing outside and staring at my window.

I throw open the door and rush out, but the man has disappeared. For a moment, I thought it was George. But why would it have been? George doesn't know where I am. And Noah's loss has nothing to do with him.

I stand in the parking lot, looking around for any clue of the person I saw. Suddenly, I realize how vulnerable I am out here, and hurry back to my room. Whether the man out there was George or not, someone was staring at my window. And someone slipped a note under my door.

To make myself feel less alone, I turn on the television to a local news site, where a male newscaster is speaking from behind a gleaming desk. But what catches my eye is the banner streaming at the bottom of the screen which states, *Baby drowned in bathtub*. My pulse throbs in my ears. *Could it be Noah?*

I force my mind into the closest resemblance of calm. Todd wouldn't hurt our baby. Not after going through so much deception to create him. I cling to this hope. But it's been fourteen days, and it's becoming increasingly hard to stop my imagination from getting the best of me.

CHAPTER 26

Wandering through the small-town streets, knocking on the doors of houses in desperate need of repair, I get no more response than I did yesterday. But today, I also drive along the back roads, searching for the gate and barbed-wire fence I saw on the flash-drive video. The woman's grainy image keeps poking at me. I'm convinced she looks familiar.

Towards the end of the day, my fear of driving is re-ignited when I find myself on a dark country road far from the Lakeview Motel.

I glance at my dashboard clock—it's ten past six. The road has become slick with misting rain, and the sky is darkening rapidly. Fir trees tower on both sides of the road, creating a dark tunnel. I shiver. Except for the occasional glimmers of lights bleeding out from distant farmhouses, the darkness is thickening.

When my GPS shows I'm close to the main road that leads directly to the motel, I relax a bit, yawning and twisting my head to remove the kinks in my neck. Then, clenching the steering wheel, I lean forward to see through the mist. So rapt is my attention that, at first, I don't notice the headlights winking in my side view mirror. But when I do, I realize they are closing in quickly.

With increasing apprehension, I glance at the rearview mirror. The speed with which the car is approaching makes my stomach clench. Because of the limited visibility, I'm driving below the speed limit, but the driver could easily pass me. Instead, he shadows my rear bumper, his headlights snapping between bright and normal.

I press on the gas, hoping to put a comfortable distance between myself and the other car, and look for a place to exit. When I see my chance, I veer onto a secluded road, and the vehicle behind me rushes past.

Relieved, I press on the brakes, but the pedal feels soft. I pump it and try again. This time it feels fine. Perhaps the level of brake fluid is low. I make a mental note to stop at a service station and have it checked and pull back out onto the highway.

Then, with a leap, the car accelerates on its own. I hit the brakes, but the pedal goes all the way to the floor without any resistance. Panicked, I grip the steering wheel and turn onto the grassy shoulder, hoping to slow the car down enough so I can jump to safety. But the grass does nothing to reduce the acceleration. I pump the brakes again, but there's no response. If anything, the car seems to be picking up speed.

My hands are clammy, my scalp damp. Seconds churn past—time warps, stretching like elastic. I realize I'm going to die.

But I can't die now, not now when I haven't yet found Noah. I brake repeatedly, but it's no use.

Then, in an instant, it comes to me: Hearing my father's voice in my head, I reach for the gearshift, shift into low, and pull the emergency brake, pulling it with all my strength. Metal shrieks in an ear-splitting wail as the transmission grinds down, and in the yellow glow of the headlights, black smoke boils up from my tires, filling the car with the stench of burning rubber.

I'm lucky the road is clear of traffic, as I send the car into a spinning slide across it. A field stretches out on the other side, and I plunge across the shoulder, still skidding sideways, and crash into the fence, wood splintering. The car sideswipes a thick-barked oak tree, and clods of dirt fly in all directions as the car shudders to a stop, throwing me forward, and triggering the airbag, which explodes into my face and chest, slamming me back into my seat. A rush of pain crushes my belly. It takes my breath away, and a cloud of powder releases into the car. My throat closes, my eyes burn, and I begin to cough.

I black out for a minute, maybe longer. When I open my eyes, for a few frightening moments I have no memory of what happened. I'm still trapped behind the steering wheel. I check my arms and legs to see if I can move them and search my face for blood. Unbelievably, I'm all right. But I'm a prisoner in the car. Within minutes I am trembling from the cold—and from the fear of being alone in the middle of nowhere.

As I sit here, weak and dazed, the swipe-swipe of the windshield wiper grating on my nerves, the reality hits me—someone has tampered with my brakes.

Just then, there's a knock on the window. I jerk in my seat, lift my head, and stare into the creased face of a man who looks to be in his late sixties. He gestures for me to roll down my window.

When I do, he leans forward, peering at me intently. "Are you all right?"

"I think so," I manage.

"How 'bout getting out of the car. Can you do that? The talc or cornstarch the airbag released is dangerous to breathe for too long."

I slip out from under the seat belt, ease open the door and step tentatively onto the muddy ground, forcing my knees to stop from shaking.

The man springs forward, slides an arm around me. "You're hurt?"

I shake my head, and take a few deep, steadying breaths. "I'm okay, now."

"I saw you run off the road. Are you sure you're all right? You hit that tree mighty hard."

"My brakes failed."

His eyes widen. "I have a cell phone in the car," he says. "I'll call my brother-in-law. He has a tow truck. Where you headed?"

"The Lakeside Motel."

He shakes his head. "Oh, yeah. Billie Bickerman's place. Sore on the eyes, but he keeps it clean enough to feel comfortable."

"Could I bother you to give me a ride?"

He flashes a smile, exuding natural warmth. "I was going to offer."

He heads back to his truck.

While I wait for him to make the call, I limp around the rental car: two flat tires, a dented front, and the passenger door is pretty much crushed. I pivot slowly, continuing to take inventory of the car, red flags waving wildly in my head: No, this was definitely no accident.

CHAPTER 27

The next morning, after long contemplation about whether to get the local police involved, I call Hertz and arrange for them to drop off another car, thankful I'm fully insured. This time I request an all-wheel drive. After last night's episode, I want a vehicle that provides good grip and control under all road conditions. At nine o'clock, the black Dodge Journey is waiting for me in the motel parking lot. Just when I'm about to head out of the room, my phone rings.

Damon. Finally.

There's so much to tell him, to ask him. But I start with the most important thing. "Did you see the video?"

He snorts. "Getting right to the point, aren't you?"

"Well, I'd better, because you seem to be short on time, since it's almost impossible to reach you."

"Where did you get the flash drive?"

"I found it on the floor of my Mustang a couple of weeks ago, stuck it in my coat pocket, and forgot about it until today."

"And what do you think it proves?"

"I don't know. But Connie did use my car one day. Maybe the drive is hers."

"Still doesn't prove anything."

"I know," I say, frustration creeps into my voice. "More questions than answers. But there has to be a connection between Todd and what's on the tape."

"What I see is a bunch of kids playing soldiers."

"This video wasn't supposed to be for general consumption," I say, trying not to sound defensive. Now that Damon's called me back, I want as much of his help as I can get from him — and getting irritated won't help. "The images are pretty damning."

I also tell him about my research on child abduction and indoctrination. Damon doesn't answer right away. I imagine him narrowing his eyes in concentration.

"Okay," he says. "How's all this connected to you and your baby?"

"I don't know. But could you just humor me." I try my best to sound reasonable. "Let's assume Todd's involved in a sketchy business and that the video does have something to do with him and Noah. Because right now, this is what I've got.

"Do you still doubt me? Is that why it took so long for you to get back to me?"

"Bree …" he hesitates.

"What is it?"

"I know how to find people online," Damon says. "Your husband doesn't exist. He doesn't show up anywhere. No networking sites. No PayPal account. He's not on any mailing lists. He doesn't show up on the people-finding sites. I even checked alumni lists."

"We've already gone over this."

"And there's something else I have to tell you." He hesitates. "I took the liberty to run fingerprints the other day."

"What? You went into the house without my permission?"

"I had to find out."

"What did you find?" I'm angry at the violation of my privacy, but I need to know.

"Just yours, Bree. No one else's. Doesn't look good for you. Most of the surfaces are perfect for prints. Great if anyone has left a trace behind. There are no traces, except for yours. Means that no one else lived there, except for you. Bree, I'm sorry. These are the facts."

How is it possible?

But it is possible. I remember reading about how some criminals alter their fingerprints either through skin grafted from their feet or by having layers of skin removed from their fingertips.

My throat constricts as a cold dread grips me. Another nail hammered into the coffin of my reliability. There's nothing I can do to change his mind. Not that I care to do that anymore.

I click off.

I've suspected he didn't believe me all along. Now, I am more than sure. I try not to hate him for it. He has simply pulled the gauze off my eyes, I tell myself.

Now I see: If neither the police, nor Damon, nor my best friend, nor my family believe me, I'm left to rely on myself. There's a small measure of relief in that. Somehow, this understanding is making me stronger and filling me with resolve.

• • •

The phone rings at three in the morning. The cell phone displays "Private."

"Hello?"

Silence.

"Hello?"

Nothing but breathing.

Then the line goes dead. I glance at the caller ID. It's blocked.

CHAPTER 28

I take a final look at my baby and press a gentle kiss to his warm forehead, in awe of his innocent beauty. Reluctantly, I leave his room. I want to take him into my bed with me so nobody can get near him.

A door slams. My head shoots off the pillow, and I stare around me, momentarily forgetting where I am. After several deep breaths, my eyes adjust to the shadow-filled motel room.

From the thin slits between the curtains, the yellow light of the parking lot lamps creates an abstract pattern on the room walls. I glance at the clock. 6:30 a.m. My dream has brought me full circle, wide-awake in a dingy motel room in the too-early morning.

I slide out of bed and peek out of the window at a view of a nothing-gray Tuesday morning. The rest of the world is tucked safe under the covers, next to the ones they love, while I'm busy thinking about how to find the man who stole my baby. I pull a sweatshirt over my tights and head toward the kitchenette area to fix myself a much-needed cup of coffee.

Returning to bed with the coffee and my laptop, I pull up Dating.com, again. Heart racing with anticipation, I skim through the responses and click through the profiles, eliminating men with a first glance at their profile pictures. None of them even remotely resembles Todd.

My Facebook post generated more responses than I'd expected, but they all seem to be a waste of time — people writing to say they'd seen a baby resembling the description I gave, none of them saw a birthmark, and the sightings are from all over the states.

Where does this leave me? Stumbling around the internet with no answer in sight.

Unlike Damon, I'm not skilled at finding a missing person. And I don't even know what I would do if I found Todd.

Deep inside me, a burning hatred has rooted — and with every day that passes, I am nurturing that anger with thoughts of sweet revenge. In my imagination, I picture myself as a cartoon avenger, capable of flying through the air and shooting daggers down at Todd.

I jump as the ringtone makes my phone skitter across the small table. I grab it, thinking it might be Damon — calling for what reason? To apologize? To say that he's found evidence to corroborates my story?

But it's not. It's Margaret.

"How're you?" she asks.

And without stopping to think, I tell her. "I'm angry, furious, Margaret. I want justice, Jungle justice. I want to torment that man for what he's done to me. And I want my baby …"

"Bree." My sister interrupts me, stretching out my name.

"Don't 'Bree' me!" I shout. "You have no idea what I'm going through." My eyes zero in on the sketch of Todd lying on the bed next to me. If I tried, I could burn him with my stare.

"Right. So, in your mind, how far are you willing to take your crazy thoughts?"

"Crazy? I'm not crazy. If you were a mother, how far would *you* go to find your children? To make the person who took them feel just one tenth of the pain you'd feel? Huh? How far, Margaret?"

"I wish you'd snap back to reality. Where even are you?"

"You still don't believe me, do you?"

"To be honest? No. You're obviously not thinking rationally. And not for the first time."

I make no move to stuff the silence with words.

"Sorry, I didn't mean to hurt you." Her apology sounds reluctant.

"I'm tired. I have to go now."

"Bree?"

"What?"

"I hope you know what you're doing."

•   •   •

As dawn brightens the sky, my new rental lurches along, splashing through puddles from last night's rain. They delivered the car with only a half tank of gas, so I pull into a gas station to fill up, then go inside for a cup of coffee and a muffin. Upon seeing me enter, the man behind the counter picks up the phone and whispers into it. He's done with the phone call by the time I step up to the register to pay for my muffin and coffee. He throws the change on the counter without making eye contact.

As I head for my car, a shadow peels away from the far wall of the building, and a man staggers towards me. Wisps of greasy hair, of a color that remind me of motor oil, sprout out from around his baseball cap. He is thin and wiry, with stooped shoulders. He has one finger coiled inside the loop of his jeans, and his jacket hangs loosely on a frame.

I step back. "Can I help you?"

He smiles, a calculating gleam in his flat eyes, then moves to stand between me and the driver's side door. The scent of liquor rushes at me. His eyes narrow, touching each of my features. I feel dirty.

"I don't have any spare change. Please get out of my way."

He reaches under his cap and scratches his head. "You looking for someone, right?"

"If I were, it wouldn't be you." I try to dodge around him, but he manages to keep blocking my way.

"Get out of my way or I'll scream," I tell him, ready to let all my frustration out by making a huge, public scene.

He raises his hands. "Yo. Yo. Take it easy. Your posters are all over town. I might be able to help."

The man is an alcoholic. His breath reeks and he can hardly stand on his own two feet. "I doubt it."

"You'd be surprised. Name is Folston." He extends a bony right hand.

I ignore the gesture.

He chuckles. "Too uppity to touch the likes of me, eh? Ask anybody where to find me when you ready to talk." He finally moves so I can get in my car. But he hasn't finished. "And what I have to say will cost you. But it's worth it."

CHAPTER 29

Light winks through the window blinds, as I pull into the lot of the Lakeview Motel, after spending the entire day posting flyers and asking questions. I grab my things, open the driver's side door, and get out of the car.

"Bree."

The familiar voice is as sharp to my ear as a paper-cut. Dry mouthed, I look to the Jeep Grand Cherokee parked in front of my motel room. Leaning there, an ink splotch against the Jeep's gleaming paintwork, is the last man I ever want to see again: George, clad all in black.

Pushing off the Jeep and glancing around the parking lot, he says, "What a dump. Couldn't you have found a better place?"

My heart pounds, but I try not to show fear. "How did you find me?" I ask, although it's a stupid question. The guy is a stalker.

He steps forward, intercepting me before I can make my move for the hotel room.

"Don't even think about it," he warns. "We need to talk."

"I'm done with you," I say and push at him, but he grabs my arm and starts twisting. When I scream, his hands shoot up and close around my throat. Fighting for breath, I claw at his wrists.

"Shut up. Damn you. I didn't come here to hurt you. You and I both know you don't want this sort of attention. I'll let you go if you promise not to scream."

I stop trying to twist away and nod.

"That's better." He releases his grip on my throat. Then he stares at me and raises his eyebrows. "You look like shit."

I massage my neck. "What're you doing here, George?"

"I miss you." He's so close I can see the broken blood vessels in his eyes. "Believe it or not, I worry about you." As if to corroborate this, he pastes an anxious veneer on his face, then reaches out to me.

I snatch my hand back, repelled. Whatever attracted me to this man? If I ever believed I could read people, George put the lie to the notion. He is a master manipulator. Just like Todd.

After all the pain George has put me through, I'm not about to buy this routine. I glare and say, "You don't have to worry about me."

"Oh, yeah?" He kicks a pebble toward me. "Well, look at where you are, at the dump you're staying at."

"I have a restraining order against you. I can have you arrested."

"But you won't. You don't want the police in your business right now, do you?"

"What do you mean?"

"You know what I mean," he says, stroking his chin.

I clench my jaw. Sweat gathers under my arms. I eye the door to my room.

He gazes at my motel room and pushes out a heavy sigh. "Can we talk inside?"

"Maybe another time," I answer, slipping my hand in my pocket and squeezing the car key in my fist.

"We were good together." He lets his eyes droop. I know the look all too well, the look that gives the impression I should feel sorry for him.

"We were not good together."

His nostrils flare at that, and I make a move toward the door, but he grabs my wrist again and drags me toward him. This time, I stamp on his foot, hard.

He lets out a yelp. "Why are you treating me like this?" His whiny voice crawls like a spider. "I don't know how you could have forgotten."

"There's nothing to remember."

"Look, I don't want to talk out here." His eyes flick my motel room, again.

Oh. It must have been George, after all. "Why did you do that?"

"Do what?"

"Why did you slip that note under my hotel room door?"

He attempts a puzzled look. "What note?"

"The one that says, *Stop looking for trouble*. You expect me to believe that wasn't you?"

He chuckles as if making a joke. "Yeah, yeah, of course it was me. It's always me, right, Bree? Believe it or not, all I'm doing is trying to protect you."

Suddenly, I'm uncertain. Was it really him? Or is he just messing with my mind? Maybe he does know something. "What do you think you have to protect me from?"

"Do I need to answer that?" His thick fingers tap the hood of my car. The bastard is taunting me. "Let me protect you. Take care of you."

I've had it with George's games. I side-step him, but he counters that and plants himself even closer to me than before.

"Bree, Bree," he clicks his tongue and shakes his head. "How quickly you forget all we've had together."

"We had nothing," I spit, wanting to take a baseball bat to his head. "You're delusional. Now, tell me what you want."

"I wanted to see you."

"You saw me. Now get out of my way."

He stands straighter and puffs out his chest. "Now, now, you know I can't do that. You and I are meant to be together."

I swallow a hard lump. There it is, his obsession, which led to his relentless stalking. Until I met Todd. Then George disappeared — and Luanne reported he'd been found beaten. Since then, though, nothing. Except for the sensation I've had of being followed. And now, this.

"Don't you get it? I'm not interested in you."

When his eyes bulge in what appears to be disbelief, I find myself heating up. "Here's the thing, George." Spittle sails out of my mouth. "I never ever want to see you again. Ever."

At this, his face breaks into a predatory smirk that reminds me of a hyena I once saw in a zoo. "Sweetheart, I'm trying to help you. Just listen to me for a moment."

A quiver rips up my spine. My earlier fear has transformed into a ball of rage. I point my finger at his face. "Get out of my way, George."

I enunciate every syllable through gritted teeth and try again to skirt around him.

This time, he slams me back into the hood of my car. Bellowing, I launch myself at him, ramming my knee into his groin. When he sinks into a half crouch, gasping, I follow through with a kick at his face, which misses, as he sways aside just before my foot connects.

Fighting the urge to kick him again, I spin around and sprint toward my room. My hands shake as I fumble with my key. I hazard a look back. George is still clutching his groin.

"Bree," he yells between huffs and puffs. "I have something to tell you."

I yank the door open and bang it behind me, double locking it and checking to make sure the windows are secure.

CHAPTER 30

For a few moments, I stand motionless by the door, listening. I hear a car pull away with a screech, but I can't shake the feeling that George is out there somewhere, watching me. I peer out through the crack in the shade to be sure. In the silent parking lot, there are only a few cars. George's Jeep is nowhere to be seen.

I sink to the floor. My anxiety makes the wretched motel room seem more wretched — as do my memories of George and his reaction to our breakup: the relentless ringing of the phone, the damage to my aunt's garden, and, worst of all, the loss of my job when Gene said he was sorry, but he felt continuing to have me working at the garage put his business in jeopardy.

I grab my cell phone, but realize I have no one to talk to. I'm still holding the phone, when it rings. I don't recognize the number. Could it be someone responding to one of my flyers?

"Bree. Right?"

"Who is this?"

Silence.

I tighten my hold on the phone.

"Are you going to tell me who you are?"

"It's Folston."

A sudden memory of alcohol-drenched breath invades my brain. "What do you want?"

"Wrong question. You should ask, 'What do I know?' Like I said at the gas station, I have information for you."

"What information?"

"Has to be in person."

The guy is a drunk. Why should I trust what he has to say? I also recall there's money involved. He's got to be desperate. Still, he's first — the only — person to come forward in response to my inquiries.

"I'm listening," I finally say.

"In person, right? Meet me in the parking lot behind the Black Horse, a bar just outside town. Twenty minutes to get there, tops."

Thankfully, I've passed the bar on my travels. I don't know whether it's a wise move, but what do I have to lose? I suck in my breath. "Okay."

As I'm getting ready to hang up, he says, "And like I said, it'll cost you."

"Cost me?"

"Five hundred dollars."

I stare at the phone, considering.

"Hello?"

"I don't carry that amount of cash on me. If I like what you have to say, I'll give you one hundred."

"Two hundred."

"One hundred. Not a penny more."

"One and a quarter."

It's a small price to pay if it leads me to Noah. I agree. After I hang up, I grab my gun and dash out to my rental car, placing the gun carefully in the glove compartment. Just in case.

My foot is heavy on the accelerator as I speed toward my rendezvous with Folston. As I switch lanes to pass a slow-moving pickup, I realize something has changed: Gone is my phobia of driving. Gone is the feeling of being a victim. Each have been replaced with anger that drives me to lengths I never thought I could go. For one, meeting a strange man in a bar parking lot, in a town whose citizens exhibit not only suspicion towards me but hostility, too.

I acknowledge to my new, brave self that it is possible Folston's information will end up being no information at all, that the man is simply scamming me. Still, I understand that I have no choice but to follow up. At worst, it will cost me a bit of cash and an hour of my life. At best?

Lost in thought, I don't notice the large car behind me, its beams bearing down on me, until it's right on my bumper.

"What the hell?" *Not again.*

It's a late-model SUV. I hadn't given it a second thought when I saw it as I exited the motel parking lot. But now, the way the vehicle is following makes me break out in sweat. I zip into the McDonald's parking lot and am relieved to see the SUV hasn't followed.

I glance in the rearview mirror, again. It seems that looking over my shoulder has become a way of life.

Eventually, I crank the car around and head toward the Black Horse. Despite my misgivings, anticipation rolls through me at the notion that I might soon be talking to someone who can help me get closer to Todd, to Connie, to my darling baby, Noah. But, as I turn off the main road and into the dimly lit parking lot, my mood darkens to match my surroundings.

It darkens even more when a slow drive around the lot, peering between the motorcycles and large pickups that fill the small lot, reveals no sign of Folston. Minutes slip away, and I begin to doubt my own good sense. Why did I agree to meet a drunk in a bar parking lot at night?

There is a flurry of activity by the back door of the bar. A bunch of people wearing black leather jackets alternate between drawing deeply from their cigarettes and slugging from bottles. Two bikers leave the group. They hop on their motorcycles, throttle their engines, and burn rubber as they turn onto the street.

Feeling the vulnerability of my situation—a lone woman in the parking lot of a biker bar—I remove the gun from the glove compartment, tuck it in my jacket pocket, and wait. After a few more minutes, somewhere behind me a car door squeaks, then slams shut. Seconds later, a tap on my hood announces Folston, who is holding a beer. I roll down the window.

He nods at me, and I climb out of the car, my jacket held tight to my body, the bulk of my gun a comfort. Out in the open, the smell of fertilizer and exhaust fumes mixed with cigarette smoke makes my stomach turn.

"I don't have much time. What do you have for me?" I ask.

He takes off his baseball cap. The single streetlamp reveals wispy tufts combed over a bald spot. He is a gray man with a slight build, stooping shoulders, and a soft voice. A ghost of a man. I tower over him. He holds out his hand.

"What?"

"The money."

"Not until I'm satisfied with the information you claim you have."

"Gee, you're a mighty tough lady. But at least …" He raises his beer, licks his lips, and turns to stare at the bar.

I dig into my jeans pocket and pull out a twenty, which I hand over, sending Folston dashing toward the bar. He nearly collides with a huge, leather-jacketed man, who looks to be wound tight as a guitar string.

"Watch where you goin' you drunkard bustard." The man pushes Folston who stumbles, but regains his footing, and slips into the bar.

Minutes later, Folston returns with a beer can and a bottle of whisky. His breath comes hard, sounding like a whistle, and the streetlamp casts a funereal light on his face.

"Okay," I say. "You've got your drink. Now, I'm all ears."

"It's my sister, Della." He takes a gulp from the bottle, then chases it with the beer. "She knows something." His glance flicks around the parking lot.

"And?"

He coughs and clears his throat. "Her and Johnny can tell you more than me, and I can take you to them, is all I can do."

"I thought you were the one with the information." Is he stringing me along for the booze?

His bloodshot eyes search my face. "I do. I swear I do. Everybody in town knows who you're looking for. Trust me, no one will talk to you."

He guzzles the whiskey like he is chugging water. I fight to hide my cringe.

Then, as if emboldened by the liquor, he says, "The guy on your flyer? He looks like a guy who came to Johnny's garage. Only he had a mustache and a beard."

He takes another gulp from his bottle, wipes his lips with the back of his hand. "There's no explaining that shit away, know what I mean?"

"No, I don't." I wait for him to explain.

"The point is, we both have an interest." He winks.

Focusing on his jittery eyes, I lean toward him. "I know *my* interest. What is *yours*?"

"You've got money. I got my sister and her husband. They know things."

"What do they know, Folston?"

"Plenty. They live not too far from the compound."

Compound? Images from the video on the flash drive spring into my mind. I shiver involuntarily.

"Funny stuff's going on in this town. Everybody knows it. Everybody's in on it."

"In on what?"

He slurps down the last of his beer and hurls the can toward the dumpster, where the colliding clatter of metal echoes. Immediately, a motorcycle rolls out from where it had been hidden beside the dumpster and rumbles to a stop beside us. A large, bearded man with a black bandana wrapped around his skull leaps off the bike and stands, big hands clenched, chain hanging from the loop of his low-riding jeans jingling.

"Hey, moron, I look like a garbage can to you?" He snarls at Folston.

He looks familiar. Those bottomless black eyes. It's Wayne, the man I bumped into at the Lakeview Motel and the diner.

Folston steps back and blinks up at the biker. His lips move like a fish in a pond.

"Answer me, boy. Do I look like a garbage can?"

I feel panic welling up. I don't have much confidence Folston will be able to talk his way out of this. He seems to have shrunk to half his size and is swaying on unstable legs.

Folston raises his hands. "Hey, man, sorry. I don't wanna fight."

"You don't wanna? Too bad." Wayne lands a punch that sends Folston stumbling back into the fender of a pickup, where he issues a grunt and slides to the ground.

Next, Wayne turns his attention to me. He assesses me from head to toe, as if examining a side of beef hanging in a butcher's window. "Hello, little lady. I might forgive what that asshole did to my bike if you give me a little of your sweetness."

I scrutinize his apparently unscathed bike, wondering where the said damage might be.

He cocks his head to one side and squints. His eyes are like a pair of glass marbles. "Wait a minute. I know you. You the bitch asking too many questions."

I back toward my car, but Wayne only moves closer toward me. This is the second time in one night I've been forced against my car, I think—and this feels a lot more dangerous, suddenly, than whatever game George was playing.

"The most beautiful blue eyes I've ever seen," Wayne growls out.

We're about the same height, and his hot breath—foul with cigarettes and alcohol—crowds me. I take a breath and let it out slowly.

His eyes zero in on my chest. "Not much in the boobs department, but that's okay. How 'bout we play some music together?"

I step back, but he grabs my hand and pulls me towards him with such force my breath escapes me in a rush. Thinking fast, I say, "Okay, big boy. Sure, I'd love to have sex with you. It's been a long time."

He bangs the hood of my car with his fist, producing a metal clang. "Hot dog! I like 'em feisty. I knew you wanted it."

I scout the parking lot to assess my situation. Besides Folston, apparently unconscious on the ground, there's only one other person in the lot, a drunk who is urinating up against the wall. Not my idea of a savior.

"Just let me know what you like, big boy," I tell Wayne, fluttering my eyelashes.

"So, you ain't uptight, little lady. A quick fix is what I need." He winks twice.

I want to bash my fist in his face and see if he keeps on winking. A salty smell of sweat lingers in the air, the scent of my fear that's quickly replaced by anger. Feeling the weight of the gun, my hand moves to my pocket and jerks it out before my brain catches up.

Wayne gazes at the gun in disbelief. "Really, now? What you wanting to do with that, little lady? Do you even know how to use that thing?"

"I don't want to hurt you," I say through gritted teeth. "Just let me get in my car and go."

He laughs. "And what are you going to do if I don't? Shoot me?"

In the split second that I waver, he charges, head-butting me. As I stumble backward, the gun clatters to the ground, and Wayne dives for it, kicking me when I try to beat him to it.

Roaring, I spring to my feet and, like a tsunami, I storm him.

Then, there's a lightning flash — and the sound of my skull cracking on the ground.

CHAPTER 31

I awake on a narrow cot at the police station. The cell reeks of unwashed clothes and sadness. As for me, my head feels like it was used as a soccer ball. I sit up, stretching with care, and test my range of motion, only to find I can hardly lift my left arm. Twenty minutes later, a young officer leads me to the bathroom, standing guard outside. I peer into the cracked mirror and take a deep breath. My nose is swollen and, sure enough, dark bruises have formed under my eyes. I wash my face with care, rinse my mouth, and gulp water from the faucet.

Once I emerge, the officer ushers me to a small room at the end of the hallway. There, a man seated behind a cluttered metal desk greets me with a dour "good morning" and, without introducing himself, motions me into the chair opposite his.

Immediately, I go on the offensive. "Where's my gun? And why am I here?"

The springs of his chair squeak as he leans back. "Bree Michelson, right?"

I nod.

"I'll be the one to ask questions. Why do you carry a gun?"

"My ex-boyfriend stalks me. My life is in danger."

"Nothing wrong with carrying a registered gun, but your actions last night were reckless."

"I was accosted by Wayne. He was going to rape me."

He leans forward to reach for a pad of paper. "That's not what I heard."

"From whom?"

"Witnesses."

"No one was in the parking lot, except for Folston, and a guy urinating on the wall. And Folston was unconscious. Wayne knocked him out."

He glances at his notes. "You originally from Albany?"

"Why am I at the police station? Who brought me here?"

"We got a phone call about a deranged woman with a gun."

"As I said, my life was in danger."

"Can you tell me why you think that?"

My mind races. Maybe I should tell him what I've gone through. Seek his help. But that hasn't worked to my advantage, so far—so I just shake my head.

He licks his thumb and forefinger and flips through his dog-eared notebook. "I see here you're looking for a person named Todd Armstrong and a woman named Connie Bridgestone. You also claim they abducted your infant son."

When I don't answer, the man I assume to be a detective looks at his pen as though he finds it intriguing. He's no more than forty, all shoulders, no neck.

He sighs and says, "I'm going to hold on to your gun until you leave town."

"But I need it for protection," I protest. "Somebody tampered with the brakes of my car. And to make things worse, a threatening note was shoved under the door of my motel room."

"Is that so?" He closes his note book with an air of finality. "You want my advice? Stop stalking people in this town."

"I'm not stalking."

"What would you call showing up at people's doors asking about two individuals who don't exist?"

"I have sketches to show that they do exist."

He leans forward and clasps his hands together on top of the notebook. "First of all, Ms. Michelson, sketches are not proof of anything. Second, you need to look at this from our perspective. Two days ago, you had an automobile accident. Since then, you've had an altercation in front of your motel room and been involved in an incident involving a gun, in the parking lot behind a bar."

How does he know about the fight with George?

"Luckily for you, Mr. Grogenus decided not to press charges."

"Mr. Grogenus? Charges?"

"Yes, Mr. Wayne Grogenus. And those charges would be for harassment. Maybe you should think about moving on. We don't need the likes of you disturbing our peace."

He pauses, as if waiting to be sure I understand what he's just said.

"I was the one accosted. I wasn't looking for trouble," I stammer.

"We're done here, ma'am." He rises and motions for me to follow him. I try to keep up as he hurries down a short hallway, whose walls are covered with announcements for upcoming civic events and photographs of police officers. The woman at the front desk is pencil thin, with pinched lips and glazed eyes. She scowls when she sees me.

Just as I reach the door, she hisses, "The faster you leave town, the better for all of us."

I trip over the doorsill on my way out.

CHAPTER 32

"Bree?"

I look up to see Viola standing over me with a menu in hand. Her glassy gaze lingers on my face. I've covered my bruises with foundation, but not enough to hide them entirely. "You look terrible. But from what I heard, you put up a good fight last night."

I raise my hand to my face, remembering the moment of impact with that brute. Then I make a mental note to wear thicker concealer. "How do you know?"

"You kidding? News travels fast in this small town. And about the car accident, too."

I shrug. "That wasn't an accident. Someone tampered with my brakes."

She gives me an odd look. "Really? Why would someone do that?"

I shrug. "I think I might be close to getting answers."

She looks around quickly, then slips into the seat across from me. "You better be careful. You might not make it out so well, next time."

"Why is that?"

"I don't know … Listen, it's horrible to lose a child." She reaches out and gently rests her hand on my arm. "When your baby is taken, you'll do anything to get it back. Believe me, I know."

Is she talking about herself? I'm not sure how to ask. Then something else occurs to me. "Viola, I've seen almost no children around here. Why is that?"

She drops her sympathetic hand from my arm. "I don't know what you're talking about."

I decide to let it go. Instead, I say, "I can't get over the people in this town. They all act so suspicious."

Her response surprises me. "Look around you. What do you see? Boarded up storefronts, people out of jobs, hanging on by a shoestring."

When I nod, urging her to continue, she leans in and lowers her voice. "There's a lot going on around here. All kinds of crap being sold to help numb people, help them forget how miserable they are. This town is poisoned."

I frowned. "How do you mean—poisoned?"

"You know, lots of colorful pills, easy to come by. Lots of white stuff, if you know what I mean."

It takes me a minute to absorb the implication. Who supplies these people with drugs? And if they barely have enough money to survive, how are they able to afford drugs?

"This is a rustbelt community, stuck in recession for decades," Viola continues. "The area was a major steel producer. Now, the steel mills are just rusted monuments to better days." She stares off into the distance. Then, as if remembering where she is, she turns her frozen gaze back to me. "So, what's your next move?"

My intuition tells me not to divulge too much, so I just shrug. "I'm not sure yet."

"I see," she says, nodding slowly, watching me a little more cautiously, now. "Well, like I said, if I were you, I'd be careful."

When I direct my gaze at her questioningly, hoping she'll disclose specific source of danger, she just shakes her head.

"Forget it, I shouldn't have said anything. I hope you find what you're looking for."

She stands up and pulls out her order pad. "So, what's it going to be?"

I tell her I'd like a hamburger and a cup of coffee. Before she turns to take my order to the kitchen, I ask one last question. "Do you know a guy named Folston?"

She gives me a sharp look. "Folston? Why?"

"He says he has information for me."

"I don't think you want answers from the town derelict," she says, and starts to walk away.

I reach out and grab her hand. "Viola, I can't ignore anyone who might be able to help me. Before that brute biker beat me up, Folston was telling me about a compound. You know anything about that?"

"Compound? I don't know about any such thing." She looks at me with what seems compassion, but all that she offers is a warning. "Do yourself a favor, stay away from him." She tugs her hand free and turns toward the kitchen—but just then, she jolts to attention.

It seems she's spotted something out on the street, something I'm not able to see. She tenses, and her forehead furrows. Before I can ask what it is, she hurries toward the kitchen's swinging doors and disappears behind them.

CHAPTER 33

Waiting for Viola to return with my meal, I peer out onto the street, trying to see what might have frightened her. The view through the window is bare and gray. Cold needles of rain blow sideways, the awning of an antique store flaps in a sudden gust, as a woman holding her purse over her head scurries into the shop.

Nothing unusual. Not at first.

Then I spot a tall, angular woman, standing on the sidewalk next to an old black Cherokee, outfitted with oversize tires. The woman's cargo pants are tucked into work boots and are topped by her white sweater and black down vest. Despite the overcast day, she wears large sunglasses, and her knitted hat is pulled down to her eyebrows, under which, straight, black hair snakes to her chest.

She glances around quickly, then leans toward the passenger window of the Cherokee and says something to the driver.

My heart pounds and every nerve ending tingles. It takes a moment for my brain to catch up with my instinct. She reminds me of Connie. But it can't be her. Not only does this woman have long, straight hair, rather than the mass of short, curly hair that made Connie look like an aging Annie Hall, she seems younger, perhaps in her mid-thirties? And Connie was definitely in her sixties.

At least, that's the impression I was under.

But what did I really learn about her during the few months she was in our house? Preoccupied with the worry of a possible miscarriage, I paid little attention to her. She seemed to blend with the furniture. When she came to the bedroom with a meal on a tray, her eyes, behind large, tinted glasses that practically covered her face, were kept averted. She never stayed in my room longer than she had to, and she hardly spoke to me.

As I'm reviewing what little I knew of Connie, a truck pulls up behind the Cherokee and parks under an oak whose roots have lifted the narrow sidewalk. The black-haired woman, glances at the driver of the truck. When he hops out. She waves at him, and he waves back, before heading down the street.

Then the woman checks her watch, bids the man behind the Cherokee's steering wheel goodbye, and, as he pulls away from the curb, starts to walk past the antique store. That's when I notice her slight limp. Todd told me once that Connie had been injured in a car accident that left one of her legs shorter than the other.

I never bothered to ask how he knew this. That was the old me. Dependent and gullible. Not any more.

At that moment, as if she can feel my gaze, the black-haired woman looks across to the diner. My heart rate kicks up as her eyes lock on mine. It happens fast, a flash of recognition, before she continues on her way.

Is it Connie? Could it be? I fight the urge to confront her.

The woman pulls out her phone and appears to dial a number as she hurries down the street, stopping at the bank, where she disappears behind the tinted glass doors.

Just then, Viola places my burger in front of me. Her look tells me she saw me staring out the window, but neither of us mention it. Instead, I thank her, and, hungrier than I realized, devour my burger — keeping my eye on the bank at all times. After a few bites, I see the black-haired woman rush back out, holding her phone to her ear.

Not wanting to make eye contact a second time, I slump down in my seat. When I cautiously raise my head, I see her hop into the driver's side of a black Range Rover parked in front of the bank and speed away.

Spurred by a sudden, inexplicable instinct, I throw a few bills on the table, dash out of the diner, and hustle to my car. Although my hands are shaking, I'm able to fit the key in the ignition, and I rev the engine and pull out onto the street.

My hands clutch the steering wheel tightly, as I follow the woman's taillights, mimicking every turn. My eyes are glued to her bumper, when the traffic light ahead turns red, but I hit the gas and power through the intersection. As she speeds out of town, I manage to stay a dozen car lengths behind her, but traffic is light out here, making it tricky. I need to hide behind other cars to mask my presence, while at the same time not falling so far behind that I might risk losing her on these twisting, narrow roads.

She's pulled ahead a bit, now, and the Rover disappears briefly around a bend, before I get her in my sights again.

After about thirty minutes, she turns left onto a dirt path. Rather than follow too closely, I swerve to the shoulder and wait before making the same turn.

When I finally do, I find nothing: The Range Rover is nowhere in sight. There are no houses back here. There is nothing but silence — and the rustling of leaves.

CHAPTER 34

I pull back out onto the road, reluctantly. The same instinct that brought me to this place, tailing a woman who might or might not be Connie Bridgestone—or whatever my midwife's real name is—also tells me that not only is Noah alive, but that he is not far from here.

Remembering the images on the flash drive of the fence and gate, I drive up and down nearly deserted country roads trying to find a spot that matches the description in my mind. The terrain is typical of what I've seen so far, hilly, with fields stretching to tree-lined horizons. Properties with barns and tractors and the occasional wooden farm building are surrounded by fencing to keep livestock from roaming.

But I'm looking for another type of fence: heavy with barbed wire, meant to keep people out, not to keep animals in.

After driving around for several hours, fueled by now-waning hope, I notice something familiar. Pulling to the side of the road, I see, behind a recently repaired wooden fence, a mature oak that displays a bad gash in its bark.

This is it. This is where I plunged off the road after my brakes failed. A foot to the left, and this is the tree under which I might have died. My skin prickles.

Having exhausted myself enough for one day, I pull back onto the road and drive back the way I came.

CHAPTER 35

I'm sitting in my car in a lot next to an abandoned building. Folston called last night, and we agreed to meet here. Now, I wonder for the hundredth time whether I should trust the man. Then I remind myself that I can't afford to ignore any information that comes my way.

He said he'd be here at three. It's almost four, and the sun has weakened, letting shadows take over. I decide to give him another ten minutes. I take a sip from my Styrofoam cup and grimace when the cold, bitter coffee slides down my throat.

Then, Folston's image materializes in my rearview mirror. When he gets to the driver's window, I see he is sporting an inflamed jaw and dark sunglasses.

"Where's your car?"

"No gas. I hitched." His slurred words transmit what he had for lunch. He points at my face. "I see the motorcycle dude did a job on you, too."

I ignore his comment. "Before I let you in the car," I say, "I need to know what makes you think your sister has information for me."

"It's not just my sister. It's Johnny, her husband, too. They say they hear gunshots coming from the compound."

"And?"

Then he confirms what I've noticed on my own. "You seen any children runnin' around in this town?"

Exactly what I asked Viola about. If children are disappearing in this town, where are they going? And how is my son involved? As if the question flipped a switch in my brain, I recall the internet articles I read about snatched babies and images from the flash drive start playing in my head. Is it conceivable that in a few years Noah could be marching with a machine gun slung over his delicate shoulders?

My fear for my baby morphs into terror, and I begin to hyperventilate. Then, the sound of a bang against the window returns me to the here and now.

Folston.

After several failed attempts, he opens the passenger's door and crawls into the car, bringing the stench of alcohol and body odor with him. I do my best to breathe through my mouth.

"What's wrong with you?" he asks. "Why you cryin'?"

I ignore this and answer his question with one of my own. "Are you going to stay awake long enough to tell me how to get to your sister's house?"

He nods, then points. I pull out of the parking lot in the direction he's indicated. The drive takes me past a vacant shopping center, small country homes with abandoned work sheds, which give way to horse farms and pastures. The two-lane road twists like a fishing line, unreeling through the forested mountains in sharp curves. Occasional farmhouses rise from the earth like dislocated caskets. We see few cars traveling in either direction.

Folston slumps in the seat next to me, barely awake. I poke him several times to get directions.

After we've been driving for forty-five minutes, I ask, "How much longer?"

"'Bout fifteen minutes."

When sharp doubts poke my belly, I focus on the hope that at the end of this journey I will have answers that will bring me closer to my son.

The overcast sky lets loose, and rain rattles on the car roof like pebbles. I turn on the radio. The weather lady says a storm is moving in from the west, leaving in its wake uprooted trees and damaged roofs. I shiver and grip the steering wheel tighter, concentrating on navigating the now-slippery road.

Seeing an upcoming driveway, I poke Folston. He jerks up, spittle running down his chin, and points at a metal mailbox ahead, with no number or name. I swing into a sharp turn and fishtail up a narrow, mud-crusted drive.

Dangling branches whack the windshield. After several breath-holding moments, the house comes into view.

"Needs a lot of work," Folston murmurs.

He isn't wrong. As we pull up beside the scruffy lawn, I can see that the house's gray paint is cracked and flaking so badly it reminds me of a reptilian's crusty skin. On top of that, several missing shingles expose black holes. Parked beside the house is an old, rusted, green Pathfinder. The detached garage is open to reveal a classic truck with its hood open.

I cut the engine. "Are you coming?"

He shakes his head. "You go on," he says and, turning away from me, seems to fall into a deep and immediate sleep.

I sigh and grab my jacket as I get out, leaving his flaccid form embedded in his seat.

A blast of wind sends a cluster of dead leaves across the lawn. I wrap my arms around myself. I'm following the tip of an alcoholic, the town derelict, according to Viola. This is all wrong, I think, and have an urge to turn around and flee this sad-looking house.

Instead, I straighten my shoulders, step around a fallen tree-trunk, march up the porch stairs, open the screen, and knock on the door.

A lock turns, a chain slides, and the front door opens, revealing a woman, who, despite the cold, is wearing pajama bottoms and a short-sleeved white t-shirt. Her dark hair hangs loose, and she's clutching a baby to her chest.

My breath catches as my eyes sweep over the infant. The child's black, silky hair is the same color as Noah's. I stand rooted to the spot.

Is this Noah?

The air comes out of my lungs in a whoosh. This baby looks bigger than Noah, and he, doesn't have my son's wonderful, rounded forehead. But only sixteen days ago, I held my baby, just as this woman is holding hers.

The woman stares at me over her baby's head. "Yes? Can I help you?"

As if on cue, the infant begins to cry.

That's when a terrible realization pummels me. My breasts, which had once leaked whenever I heard a baby cry, are dry.

"Shhhh," the woman cooes at the baby. "Hush little one."

I take a deep breath. Over the baby's fussing, I ask, "Are you Della?"

"Who's asking?" Her gaze is glued to the welts on my face.

"My name is Bree." I tear my eyes away from the baby. "Your brother is in my car."

She steps to the side and peers at my car. "I don't see my brother."

"He's sleeping."

With her free hand, she pushes me aside and steps out to get a closer look, then steps back into the house. "I suppose he's drunk again," she says.

"Had a hard time keeping him awake long enough to get us here."

She shifts the baby and raises her eyebrows at me. "What's that good for nothing up to now?"

"Please. May I come in? There's something I want to talk to you about."

She frowns. "It's almost dinner time, and Johnny will be home soon."

"I'll only take a few minutes, I swear."

"What's my brother doing in your car?"

"Please, may I come in?"

"Fine." She turns and walks inside, leaving me to follow. The small house is warm and thick with the smell of cabbage and onions.

"Excuse the mess," she says over her shoulder, nodding at the scattered mounds of laundry clothes. She settles into a rocking chair and motions me toward a worn, green velvet sofa, before putting a pacifier between the baby's sucking lips.

I ease myself down, avoiding the sagging middle, and look around me.

"We're going to fix it up," Della says, noticing my stare. "What with Johnny working such long hours, there isn't time for him to do anything around here."

"It's beautiful," I say. "And peaceful. What's your baby's name?"

Della smiles. "Jake. Named after Johnny's grandfather, may he rest in peace."

I smile, my lips feel strained. "He's cute. How old is he?"

"Four months."

"Still keeping you up nights?"

"Yes." She sighs. "And there are the never-ending diapers and changing and feeding."

"I have a little boy, too. He's only twenty-three days old."

The baby's pacifier hits the floor, and a wail issues from his lips. Della quickly picks up, the pacifier, wipes it with a corner of her t-shirt, and sticks it back in the baby's mouth. His eyelids drift shut over flushed cheeks.

"You didn't come here to talk about the baby." An open bag of potato chips sits on the table next to Della. She digs into it and pops one in her mouth.

I take a second to compose myself, then say the words I've heard myself repeat over and over for the past two weeks: "I need your help."

She raises her eyebrows. "I'm not sure I can possibly be of any help. I don't even know who you are."

I rummage in my purse and produce the sketches. "Have you by any chance seen these people?"

Della averts her eyes from the drawings, hand them back to me. "I know why you're here. Everybody in town knows about you."

I place my hands on my knee to stop my foot from jittering. "Have you seen them?"

She hesitates, then shakes her head. "No. Sorry I can't help you."

"You see this man?" I tap my finger on top of Todd's face. "He kidnapped my baby. Your brother said you might know something."

She frowned. "He did? Know what? How would he know what I know?"

"He didn't give details. He only said that you hear things."

"I hear nothing. Don't know what he's talking about. You should leave now."

"You have a beautiful, healthy boy. You're a mother. How would you feel if someone took Jake away from you? Surely, you understand why I'm here."

She shrugged. "Maybe. But I don't know how I can help you." Her chair creaks in protest as she begins to rock nervously. "I need to protect my family. I don't want any trouble at my door."

She knows something. It's written in her stiff posture.

"How much did my brother tell you?"

"He told me about a compound you live close to." I dig my fingers into the fabric of the sofa. "Please. Tell me what you know."

A pocket of silence grows between us. She picks at a small scab on the back of her hand.

"I feel bad for you," she finally says. "God knows how I would live if someone took my Jake, but there are certain things best not to talk about."

She digs into the bag of chips, again. Several seconds of crunching fill the silence in the room. Then she licks her fingers one by one.

I wait.

Finally, she croaks out, "You get your answers and leave. I get to stay in town and deal with these people."

Jake stirs in her arms. She kisses him on the cheek, smooths his cottony hair, and places him in the bassinet. His feet paddle the air in a dance to silent music. A picture of Noah's little fists waving as soon as I approached his crib flashes in front of me. Just as quickly, I push this image out of my head.

In the kitchen, the oven timer beeps. "I need to check on the roast."

"Do you mind if I wait for Johnny to come home?"

She presses her lips. "He can't help you."

"I'm a desperate mother, Della. I know you understand."

She starts to leave the room. But she stops in her tracks, turns, and snatches the bassinette with Jake in it.

I don't blame her.

"May I please have a glass of water?" I call after her.

Her flip-flops slap the floor as she marches away. The sound of lids clattering on saucepans rings out from the kitchen. Several minutes later, she emerges with a glass of water. "Here," she says, and clanks the glass onto the table.

I gulp the water and force my gaze away from little Jake, who is again in Della's arms. Though I try to keep my mind as blank as I possibly can, I see Noah's face in Jake's features.

Please, please, please don't let me forget what you look like — my little angel.

The short silence is interrupted by the crunch of tires and the clattering of an engine wheezing up the drive. Della stares at me for a long moment. Long enough for Johnny, who is visible through the front window, to leap out of the pickup, walk over to my car, and shake his head when he sees Folston slumbering in the passenger's seat.

Long enough for Della's husband to clomp up the steps and enter his warm house, where his wife and son are waiting for him.

The man's face lights up as soon as he sees them, and a stab of loneliness shoots through me. I miss my son with an ache, like a rock, the longing seats in my throat.

"Johnny," Della says, flatly, "this is Bree. She has a few questions for us. But I told her we don't know anything."

He nods at me, studies my bruised face, then says, "I see."

Della's sigh pierces my ears. She settles in the rocker, scowling, arms holding Jake tight. "She's looking for her baby," she tells him. "But I told her we don't know anything. Right, honey?"

"Folston said you might have information," I say.

"How do you know him?" Johnny asks.

"I don't. He called me after I posted sketches all over town."

He runs his hands across the stubble of his face and settles in a chair across from me. "Okay, I get it," he says. "I don't know what he told you, though, and I don't know how I can help. What exactly did he tell you?"

"Something about a compound."

Johnny shakes his head and looks away.

"I'm looking for two people who took my baby. Noah was six days old when they stole him from me. I need your help."

Della holds up her hand. "I told you already we got no information for you."

Johnny glances at her. "That's a shame. I'm sorry to hear it. But Della is right."

"Folston says you own the only garage in Handrock."

He nods.

"So, you see a lot of people who need their cars fixed." I wave the sketches in the air. "Maybe you've seen the people I'm looking for in your shop."

He studies me for a brief second. "Sorry," he says. It sounds like he means it.

I place the sketches back on the table. The tension in the room feels oppressive, the silence only broken by Della's squeaking rocker. Can she imagine the crippling grief of a mother whose child has been torn from her arms? How can she? No mother should experience not knowing if her baby is alive, or might be dead.

Then Johnny sighs. "What happened exactly?"

I'm so grateful he's willing to listen, I almost cry. But I don't. With Della glaring at me over Jake's sleeping form, I tell them everything, starting with the morning Noah disappeared.

When I finish, I meet his eyes, hoping to find sympathy there.

Before Johnny can respond, Della lifts herself out of the rocker, tucks Jake in his bassinet, and says, "Johnny, can I talk to you in the kitchen for a moment?"

I know that if Della talks to Johnny alone, that will be the end of any chance of my getting whatever information they're keeping hidden.

In a gambit to keep Johnny here, to get him on my side, I say a bit wildly, "Johnny, when you pulled in, I noticed your exhaust rattling."

Caught off guard, he blinks at me.

Having gotten his attention, I push my advantage. "From the sputtering I heard, my guess is there's a hole in the system, somewhere."

He looks startled. "How would you know that?"

I shrug. "Years of helping my father fix cars. And I was a mechanic."

He expels a long breath and turns to look out at his truck. "You're right. It could be I need an exhaust component replacement."

"Simple. Reattaching a loose pipe—"

"Or replacing a corroded pipe section or attaching a new muffler." He grins, then scratches his head.

Della, on the other hand, is not grinning. She wants me out of here. Now. My presence is a threat. Just my being here puts her family in jeopardy.

Thinking fast, I say something I'm pretty sure will buy me a few minutes and a bit more of Johnny's good will. "By the way," I say, trying to sound off hand, "that's a 1979 Chevy 350 pickup sitting in your garage, isn't it?"

The man's eyes widen. "Yes! But … not all mechanics are familiar with the classics."

"I used to work in an auto restoration shop in Albany."

He snaps his fingers. "Wait a minute. You didn't by any chance work for Gene at Classic Auto, did you?"

"I did," I say. But I don't elaborate. I don't tell this man, who is warming to me, that I lost that job because of George.

"Damn. My cousin's blue 1967 Chevy Nova was restored there. Did you work on it?"

I nod. That Nova was the last car I worked on before they fired me.

"Great job. She looks like new. Not a problem with her since he got it back."

"Thanks," I say.

Della, lips drawn into a thin line, turns around and stomps toward the kitchen.

"Well, you didn't come here to talk about cars. But I don't know how I can help," Johnny says, after Della's out of earshot.

"I'm not sure," I respond. "But I'm at my wits end. And, like I said, Folston told me you and Della have information that can help me find my baby."

He shakes his head. But there's something in his face that tells me he does know something. He opens his mouth to speak … but before he can get a word out, Della interrupts.

"Johnny, dinner's ready."

He turns toward Della, who stands at the kitchen door.

Feeling opportunity slipping through my fingers, I plead my case one more time. "Della, Please. You love your baby more than anything in the world, don't you?"

Della shrugs. "Yes. What's the point?" she snaps. "My baby is the one I'm trying to protect."

"Protect from what, exactly?"

"Sorry. I have nothing to tell you. We have nothing to tell you."

At this, I see Johnny shake his head. "Wait here," he says to me softly, and crosses to Della, takes her hand, and leads her back to the kitchen.

Nervously, I pick a romance novel from the chipped wooden coffee table — and see the headline of the newspaper underneath it: *OPIOID EPIDEMIC TAKING OUT TOWNSPEOPLE.*

Viola told me about the drugs. And Folston talked about a compound. He might be an alcoholic, but he seemed clear about that one fact. I think about the guarded, hostile people I've encountered in Handrock, about the restaurant check that brought me here. About the missing children. About the disturbing images on the flash drive. And now, Della, who is obviously hiding something.

Do Todd and Connie fit into all of this, somehow? Are Noah and I connected to it at all? A thousand scenarios whirl in my head, and none of them are good. I'm about to pick the paper and read the article, when Johnny appears from the kitchen, resting against the doorframe.

Arms folded, he says, "This is hard for me. I want to help you, but …"

When he doesn't finish, I say, "I'm sorry if I've caused you and Della trouble."

He turns and looks out the window. I watch his jaw tighten. A vein bulges at his temple. The rain, which has started again, beats on the roof.

"I have to protect my family," he finally says.

"All I'm asking is if you've seen these people." I pluck the sketches from the table and wave them at him. "Just tell me if you know who they are."

"I've seen the pictures already."

Of course, he has.

He wipes his hands down the front of his jeans, as if his palms are sweating. "You need to know what we're dealing with here," he says firmly. "This town is struggling to survive. What's left are empty storefronts and corner bars and a lot of desperate people."

Dread crawls along my spine. What is it he's not telling me? From the kitchen, a glass shatters and utensils clatter to the floor.

Johnny jumps. "Sorry, but you have to leave now."

I know I won't learn anything more tonight. As I walk out the door on heavy legs, I hear Johnny following behind me. I look back, and he smiles.

"Have to get the bum out of your car."

We hurry through the rain, and I hop into the driver's seat, while Johnny goes around, tugs open the passenger's door, and shakes Folston, who moans in his sleep. Johnny glances at the house. "I didn't want to talk in front of Della," he says, quietly. "But I want to help. I understand what you're going through."

He slips me a piece of paper. "My cell number. Call me tomorrow, and we'll set a time and place to meet."

With that, he hauls his brother-in-law out of the car, slings him over his shoulder, and heads back to the house, where Della, who has appeared in the doorway, awaits him.

CHAPTER 36

As I pull out of Della and Johnny's treacherous driveway and onto the road, my phone rings. It's Margaret, with bad news.

"Auntie is in the ER. She's had another attack."

"How serious is it?" Slowing, I pull over to the shoulder, where I sit, heart pounding. Along with the chill of concern, the primary emotion I experience is guilt. I haven't been thinking much about my aunt lately.

"She's asking for you. Hang on a second." I hear muffled voices, then Aunt Rachelle, saying, "Honey, is that you?" in a faltering voice. In the background, the faint beeps of a heart rate monitor punctuate my fear.

"Yes, Auntie, it's me. I'm so sorry …" I imagine my aunt lying beneath the unforgiving glare of fluorescent lights, and blink away tears.

More muffled voices, and my aunt says, "Honey, talk to your sister. The nurse is here."

"Wait," my sister says as soon as she gets on the line.

I hold my breath, as the sound of her heels click like daggers. Then she clears her throat. "Um, we need to talk. Where are you?"

"I'm not home."

"Is it a secret? Are you okay?"

Weariness settles over me. "I'm fine. And I'm close to finding answers."

In my mind's eye, my sister raises an eyebrow at me. "Answers to what?"

"Why ask, when it's obvious you don't believe me." If my tone is sharp, I feel she deserves it.

"You're just like Dad."

"What does that even mean?"

"Oh, never mind. Look, I've been hard on you, and I do believe you now."

"Why the change of heart?"

She answers with silence.

"Margaret?"

"Okay, I hate to admit it. It makes sense. Why would you go through all this trouble if you didn't actually have a baby?"

Although this about face is completely out of character, I want to believe her. So far, all I've gotten are questions and mistrust everywhere I turn. It feels nice that someone is finally starting to believe me. I cast my doubts aside, tell myself that everyone is redeemable.

"Listen, Auntie isn't doing well." Margaret's words tumble out in a rush. "You need to get here right away."

"I'll be there as soon as I can." I rub my gloved hands together and glance at the clock. It's almost six. "By nine-thirty."

I have mixed feelings. I'm finally getting somewhere. My sixth sense tells me my meeting with Della and Johnny has brought me a giant step closer to finding my son. But my aunt's perilous condition takes precedence. At least for tonight. If Aunt Rachelle is stable tomorrow, though, I'll call Johnny and pick up where I left off.

Comforting myself with that compromise, I swing my car out onto the main road and head toward Albany.

• • •

Only a few cars are parked in the visitors' lot, when I arrive, and I find a spot close to the ER. I crash through the swinging doors of the emergency room, to find the lobby eerily empty and dimly lit by a fuzzy-reception TV tuned to FOX News. A quick glance shows a series of rooms around the periphery.

My sister comes running out of one of the rooms.

"Here you are," she calls out. She is dressed in an elegant silk suit — not suitable for today's weather — stockings, and high heels. Her makeup, as always, is perfect. Hours of sitting in a hard plastic chair in a hospital waiting room have done nothing to mar her fastidiousness.

"Can I see Auntie?" I ask.

"In a few minutes. The nurse is with her. But let's talk."

When she produces a tissue from her purse and blows her nose, I imagine horrifying complications in Auntie's condition. Then I notice the bags under Margaret's eyes and the wrinkles bracketing them. Briefly, I wonder if she's settled things with her husband. Her foundation conceals whatever, if anything, is left of her bruises.

Shoving her tissue back in her purse, she grabs my arm. "Come on," she says, and leads me back into the room she came from. There are several chairs, a table, and two vending machines.

"Do you want coffee?" she asks.

When I shake my head, she sits on one of the dull, gray plastic chairs. I remain standing, waiting for her to say her piece.

My sister's cheeks redden. She shifts in her chair. Finally, she clears her throat.

"I have to be honest with you. Auntie is going to be all right. You're the one we're concerned about."

"What? Why didn't you just say so on the phone? Why drag me all the way to Albany?"

"Sorry, I …"

I shove my fisted hands in my jacket pockets. My mind is spinning a litany of curses to direct at my sister.

"It's not that I don't believe you. It's just that . . ."

"That's exactly what it is. Neither of you believe me."

"Look, we … we just think you need help."

I feel the color drain from my face. "And this is what you want to talk to me about? I drive three hours to hear another accusation, another commentary on how my loss is invalid?"

"You need to stop chasing something that doesn't exist," she says softly.

I begin to shake but I bite back the anger boiling inside of me. "My baby exists."

The look Margaret gives me is sly. I recognize it from when we were growing up, and she was trying to get me to participate in one of her schemes. That look should have prepared me for what she says next. But it didn't.

"This is an excellent opportunity to check yourself in voluntarily."

I can't believe this. Who does she think she is? I pace from one end of the room to the other, blood boiling, as I try to decide what to do.

"Sit down," Margaret says. "You're making me nervous."

I spin to face her. "Go to hell. You make it sound like I'm out of my mind."

For the first time, she makes direct eye contact. "I never said that."

"You said plenty." I head toward the door. I've decided. I'm going to head back to Handrock, tonight, and I'll call Auntie in the morning.

"Don't walk away from me." Margaret steps to the door beside me. Her voice softens. Out at the nurses' station a few nurses mill around sipping cups of coffee. Quietly, my sister says, "Maybe you've been damaged by our parents' death, but believe me, you're letting that damage go too far."

Against my will, my mind flickers back. After the accident, I tried clinging to my sister, but she hadn't been able to carry that burden. Now, all these years later, she acts as if she cares? I don't think so. Besides, the situation with Noah and Todd has nothing to do with our parents' deaths, and I tell Margaret so.

"Oh, no? But that's what made you try to commit suicide." The fluorescent light casts a pallid light on her face, making her look more tired than I've seen her before. For whatever reason, I feel sorry for her. But I'm too angry to acknowledge it.

"That was an accident."

She raises an eyebrow. "Unlikely. Swallowing a bunch of pills is a willful act."

"I was too young to realize how lethal they were. I just wanted the pain to go away."

"And what about the false pregnancy?"

"That's finished. I got help. You can't hold it over my head for the rest of my life."

"And what about our phone conversation the other day? You said you're looking for revenge and willing to kill Todd if you find him. And you own a gun."

"My God! That was only my frustration talking. You don't have to take every word I say literally."

"Okay," she says, holding her hands up. "Come back, sit down." I waver, but her gentle touch on my arm convinces me.

"Fine." I go and sit beside her.

She leans back in her chair, arms folded. "I'm only looking out for you. If you admit yourself, you can get the help you obviously need."

I try to see it her way. But I can't. I grit my teeth and cast my gaze around the room, letting her comment dangle between us.

"You're looking out for me," I finally say. "That's nice of you. But what I need is not a stay in the hospital. What I need is to find my baby. And all you've done is impede that process. We're done here." I can feel my temper flaring again.

I stand, but she stops me. "It would be a mistake for you to leave now. I've petitioned the court to have you forcibly admitted if you won't do so voluntarily."

"You did what?" Spittle flies out of my mouth. I yank at the chair I'd been sitting on and smash it to the floor.

Margaret leaps from her own chair with a yelp. "Calm down, Bree. You're scaring me."

"You should be scared! Who in the hell gave you that right?"

She twirls the gold chain around her neck. "Be reasonable. It's for your own good. I've arranged a bed for you and spoken to the head of the psychiatric unit."

"Fuck you, Margaret." Adrenaline pulsing through my veins, I kick the toppled chair out of my way and dash to the door, but my sister is right behind me and grabs onto my jacket.

I jerk out of her grip, then, without thinking, and with five inches on her, I push my sister away, hard. She teeters on her high heels and, tripping over the upturned chair, crashes to the floor and bangs her head.

I'm not sure if she's conscious or not. But when I bend over to check, her arms snakes out, and she grabs my ankle.

"Margaret, let go," I shout, and pull my foot away.

Her grip loosens, and I rush again toward the door. Behind me, my sister is screaming like an ambulance siren. "Stop! Stop! Stop! Stop!"

Just as I dash across the threshold, a strong hand blocks my way. I swing forward and slam my fist into a white-lab-coated chest, and the man—a nurse? an orderly?—sinks to his knees. I've got to get the hell out of here. The icy claws of adrenaline rush through my veins, and cold sweat tickles my forehead as I dash toward the exit, shouts and pounding footsteps following me.

"Bree Michelson?" An overweight male nurse leaps in front of me, blocking my way.

I bolt in the other direction and elbow my way past a flock of medical residents making evening rounds. I hear footsteps thudding behind me, gaining, on me. I throw a glance over my shoulder and catch sight of a tall police officer giving chase.

I'm halfway down the hall when another officer leaps out from nowhere and grabs me. "Stop right there," he orders.

The overweight nurse materializes in front of me, huffing and puffing. "She's being committed," he tells the officer. And to me, he says, "You need to come with me."

"No, I don't."

"Bree," I hear Margaret call from down the hall. "Please cooperate."

"Bree," says the overweight nurse. He smiles, then hitches his scrubs before extending his hand. His grip is firm and warm. "I'm Leon, and I'm a mental health nurse. Your sister and aunt asked us to talk to you because they're concerned about your mood."

"My mood? I'm in a great mood. My *mood* doesn't warrant a stay on a psych ward."

Margaret hobbles to Leon, and the two of them exchange a knowing glance. The second police officer edges closer.

"That's okay," Leon tells him. "I can handle it from here."

"Margaret?" My voice comes out in a shout. "Tell them to leave me alone."

"It's for your own good," she says.

"Please calm down." Leon's voice is soft and soothing. "We just need to talk to you. Everything will be fine."

I turn away from Leon. He steps into my path.

"You think you can stop me from leaving?" I demand.

"It will be all right," Margaret says, soothingly.

Leon, echoing her tone, says, "I think you and I should go talk about this."

A nurse appears at my other side. "Let's go," she says. "It'll be easier for you if you comply."

This can't be happening. Just when you think you've hit rock bottom, you realize you're standing on a landmine. My cheeks sting from the tears I didn't realize were dripping down my face. There has to be a way to get out of this. I'm a drowning woman on a mission. I have to get out of here. I have to go find Noah.

When the police officer steps in front of me with hands on his holster, I charge forward and drive my fist into his stomach. Then I continue pummeling him, until a pair of strong hands restrain me. The next thing I know, I'm cuffed and shoved forward.

With a nurse on each arm and one pushing my back, I can't help but move forward. "Where are we going?" I cry.

Leon's hand tightens around my arm, which isn't necessary because I'm cuffed. "You need to calm down," he says, voice sterner. "You've just assaulted a police officer. We're going to take you for an initial physical. After that to an interview room."

The crisis triage unit is located beside the emergency room. A phone on the wall outside the locked door connects us with the nursing station inside the unit. The electronic lock clicks, and Leon pulls the heavy door open.

When we reach the nurse's unit, Leon removes my handcuffs, and I slide into the chair. The other two nurses take their leave, and a new nurse, middle-aged, with a smile that engages her whole face says, "Hi, I'm Tanisha. You're in good hands. We promise we aren't here to hurt you."

If that's supposed to be reassuring, I'm not reassured.

Her large hands move deftly as she loops the blood pressure cuff around my arm. As it tightens, I feel my pressure rise. She sticks a thermometer in my mouth and talks as if to divert me from what she's doing.

"You have an appointment with the doctor tomorrow for a full physical." She wipes beads of perspiration from her upper lip with the back of her hand.

"I shouldn't be here," I manage to say around the thermometer.

She removes the thermometer and hands me a sheaf of papers. A quick glance shows them to be questionnaires and tests.

"We need for you to answer all of these, okay? Can I have a contract with you that you won't hurt yourself with the pencil?"

"I'm not crazy."

She's slowly shaking her head. "No, you're not crazy. I can see that. But do yourself a favor and agree with everything they say. It'll be easier this way."

Half an hour later, Leon pops his head in. "Finished?"

When I nod, he escorts me into the hall. My legs feel heavy. Anger and confusion simmer in my head. I feel alone and vulnerable. We pass several windowed rooms, each with a table and two chairs. Finally, he ushers me into a room. Paint, porcelain, laminate, and linoleum all in shades of gray. Then the smell of body odor that's fused into the gray walls hits me.

A man behind a desk smiles and points to one of the chairs facing him. He looks as tired as the décor. "You can sit there," he says.

I sit, and Leon leaves the room, closing the door quietly behind him.

The man behind the desk smiles again. "I'm Dr. Ladlow. And I want to welcome you to Soundview Hospital Psychiatric Unit." He speaks slowly, enunciating each word carefully, and I wonder if he thinks I'm hard of hearing. His narrow face is surrounded by a bush of curly, mud-colored hair. He's a man who wouldn't elicit a second glance. But it's his intense, emerald eyes that draw attention to him.

He takes the sheaf of papers from me, then glances at a file spread open in front of him and clears his throat. "Bree Michaelson, right?"

I nod and pin my elbows against my sides to keep myself from unraveling. My notion of who I am and how I ought to conduct myself is eroding, and my anger, which flows close to the surface in an ongoing stream, threatens to bubble up and explode.

"How are you feeling?"

"Confused."

"Do you know why you're here?"

"Not a clue."

The doctor picks up his pen and scribbles something in his notepad. "Your sister and your aunt think you need help," he tells me.

"I don't need help. I'm perfectly fine."

He stops writing, sits back in his chair. It squeaks. "They must have a reason."

"I want my lawyer."

"You haven't been examined yet. It's not necessary. And this facility is not a prison."

"In that case, can I leave?"

"Not yet. You're categorized as a 'temporary admit,' which means your stay here is at least seventy-two hours."

I know what it's like. At the end of a seventy-two-hour hold, a patient gets a hearing, complete with attorneys on both sides, witnesses, and expert testimony. Too many days lost. Johnny is expecting me to call tomorrow. He has information. And I have to find Noah. I'm running out of time.

I want to scream in frustration. But I know what I have to do instead. Stay calm enough to convince Dr. Ladlow that I don't belong here.

As if noticing my displeasure, Dr. Ladlow explains, "We have a court order obtained by your family. You'll be with us until Monday morning. During your stay, we'll evaluate your mental state."

"I haven't done anything that endangers others or myself."

He shuffles a few papers in my files. "You have a history of trying to commit suicide, and —"

"Excuse me? That was a long time ago."

"And," he says, emerald eyes glued to the file, "your attack on your sister and a police officer complicates things. We have no choice but to admit and evaluate you."

My silence chokes the room. I don't trust myself to talk.

"You have rights, you know."

"Except the right to walk out of here." I clench my jaw. No one believes that Todd stole my baby. No one believes that there is a Todd or a baby. And this is what happens. I find myself in a loony bin.

"I understand," he says. "People get angry about involuntary commitment, even when it's in their best interest. No one likes to give up control." Dr. Ladlow's index finger taps the file. "Bree, I understand you own a gun."

"I do. And it's registered."

"Do you often find yourself angry?"

"Wouldn't you, if your child was abducted?"

"To what extent are you willing to act on that anger?"

"Not enough to kill somebody. But I would certainly use my gun for protection."

"Why do you feel you need protection?"

I clamp my lips together, not wanting to sound defensive.

"Bree?"

"An ex-boyfriend turned stalker. That's why."

"How old are you, Bree?"

"Thirty-one."

"Have you been crying a lot lately?"

"No."

"Do you have any problems sleeping or eating?"

"I'm good, thank you, but I appreciate your concern."

"Do you sometimes think that life is not worth living?"

"I love life."

"Do you hear voices telling you to hurt yourself or others?"

These questions he's asking comprise the standard depression inventory, suicide assessment, and mental status exam. "Heck no."

He glances at the file, again, and shifts in his seat. "I see this situation isn't new to you."

My blood chills as the reality sinks in. I'm in their system. Again. I clench my hands on the tabletop, knuckles white with tension. What is my aunt's role in all of this? I love Aunt Rachelle, but I'm devastated that she doesn't believe me. Truth is, given my past, I don't blame her. But that doesn't make me feel any better.

I push out of the chair and start pacing, feeling my inadequacy, the depth of my helplessness. I come to stand before the barred window. An ambulance pulls under the portico with a squeal of brakes. EMTs leap out and run to the back of the vehicle. The doors fly open, and a gurney is wheeled out.

"Bree."

The doctor's voice pulls me back, but I'm not ready to turn around yet. My hands are fisted. My anger is deep. Margaret. I'm sure she orchestrated the whole scheme. But then I remember. Only a week ago, during my visit, my aunt urged me to seek mental health. She threatened if I didn't, she would have me committed. And she has. Both of them have.

"Bree, can you hear me? You're experiencing anger right now."

Damn right. How can I put out the red-hot fire I've got burning in my heart?

I turn slowly. He narrows his intense eyes at me. "Please sit down," he says. When I do, he adds, "I've made you angry. Do you get angry often?"

I swipe my hair from my forehead and remind myself I'm being evaluated. If anyone can have me released, it would be this twig of a man with the penetrating eyes.

"I'm sorry," I say, injecting remorse into my voice. "I don't usually get angry. But I'm having a difficult time. I have actually had a baby, although I understand that my previous, um, situation makes that questionable. And my baby has been abducted. The fact that no one will believe me, never mind help me, is making me angry."

I've expressed this as sanely and as calmly as possible.

Before responding, he jots something in his notepad and places his pen deliberately on the table. "The report from your previous stay mentions that you've experienced pseudocyesis in the past.

Examination at that time showed symptoms, everything from an elevated presence of pregnancy hormones to enlarged breasts."

Yes, I know. What's missing from this scenario is a heartbeat, an actual picture of the baby, and delivery.

"This phenomenon," he continues, voice lifeless as he recites the facts, "is symptomatic of low self-esteem and tends to occur in women who, additionally, misinterpret reality and have a strong desire to have a baby." He pauses, then asks, "Can you tell me everything about yourself since the last time you were here?"

I silently catalog those unhappy years and debate how to make myself sound rational. I opt for an abbreviated version, telling him just briefly about my work at Gene's auto shop, about George, about moving to Becket, and about Todd. And Noah.

"And where do you think Noah is now?"

The last thing I want is to lose my composure. I must be careful. "With Todd."

His pen scratches at the paper. "And where do you think Todd is now?"

A loud scream comes from somewhere down the hall. The doctor taps his pen on the notepad. "Do you have any idea where Todd is now?" he repeats.

"No. I don't." My mind spins. It has been, what, just over two weeks? But it seems like a lifetime. I have no idea what to do next. Maybe I should call Damon. "Can I make a phone call?"

"Not now, but you will have reasonable access to the unit's pay phones to make and receive calls between eight-thirty a.m. and ten p.m. daily, with a few exceptions."

"What about visitors?" Again, Damon is who comes to mind.

"You have the right to have visitors at all reasonable times and to have privacy when they visit. You also have the right to refuse visitors."

Good. Maybe Damon will be able to help me out of this mess.

"I've got a bed for you. Consider the next three days a rest. To regroup yourself." Dr. Ladlow sounds conciliatory.

"I'd like to leave now."

"Not possible." He pushes himself to his feet. He has no more questions.

As if there's been a signal that I missed, Tanisha enters, gives me a gentle smile, and removes the shoe laces from my boots, my necklace, and my watch.

"I'll show you to your room," she says. I have a strong sense of déjà vu, of the last time I was committed. It's a disagreeable familiarity. Nothing has changed. The same mustard yellow walls, the same worn linoleum.

Only I've changed. Or have I?

I'm being held here without my permission. I've been stripped of my privacy and dignity. I'm even beginning to question my own sanity. Could Margaret and Aunt Rachelle be right? Am I experiencing another mental break from reality? Did I really have a baby? The memories seem so real. But ... maybe ...?"

The room Tanisha leads me to is painted white. Its twin-size metal bed is bolted to the floor. "I'll get you a nightgown," she tells me. Then, "Do you think you'd like something to help you sleep?"

"No," I say. "Thank you."

"You'll find most of what you need in the bathroom." Tanisha gestures to the bathroom door. She smiles, again. Her dark skin has a blue hue to it. I think I see sympathy in her eyes. "One more thing. If you need anything in the night, there's always staff available to talk."

When the door closes behind her, I realize the extent of my solitude. I sit on the edge of the bed, my shaking hands held loosely in my lap. How am I here right now?

All it took was one hour, and I'm officially a mental patient. Again.

CHAPTER 37

When I hear Noah's gurgles, a rush of tenderness catches in my throat. Although he's stopped coughing and doesn't sound as congested as he did, I still want to have him checked by the pediatrician. I reach down into his crib to lift him, but only come up with air. His gurgles turn to wails.

I scream. And scream. And scream.

When I open my eyes, two nurses breeze in. One is holding a hyperemic needle. It doesn't take long before I start feeling drowsy.

I wake in a panic. Darkness has given way to dawn. It's the beginning of another day, but the last vestiges of that dream, already fragmenting, send new waves of heartache through me.

It takes all of my willpower to climb out of bed, to push into the bathroom, to shower, to stare at my face in the stainless-steel mirror. Not so good, I decide, studying the dark circles that hang heavy under my eyes. I look like someone who is disintegrating.

My encounter with Dr. Ladlow has left me exhausted and confused, but my mental gears are churning out things I can say in my second evaluation. Knowing how the game is played, I rehearse lines that will impress them with how sane I am. And I must avoid taking any more medication — that shot in the night was enough of a reminder of how the meds take away any semblance of control.

The problem is, none of my rehearsed lines sound good.

As much as I want to crawl back into sound sleep and enjoy the bliss of avoiding the misery my life has become, I pull on my jeans, slide into my sweater, shove my feet into my now-laceless boots, and soon find myself following a group of drugged patients to the cafeteria. The heaviness in my heart slows my steps so that I shuffle as if I'm one of them.

The most important person in my life has been snatched away from me. All I had was six days with him, to cuddle and feed and love him as only a mother can. Or did I? Doubts plague me, again. Did I really deliver a baby? There must be a good reason why I ended locked up in a psychiatric ward. I must be losing my mind.

I shake my head and fill my plate with rubbery looking eggs, then grab an empty seat.

"You can have anything you want—as much as you want. You have to eat," says the curly-haired woman sitting across from me. A network of fine white scars run along her inner forearms. She's a cutter. Perhaps she scratches at her surface to find what lies beneath.

I pick the plastic fork and let it drop again.

"It isn't good to not eat," she says. "If you don't eat, if you don't look happy all the time, they force you to take medication. Believe me, you don't want that."

But the thought of my second evaluation roils in my stomach.

"Really," the woman insists. "If you don't eat at least eighty percent of what's on your plate, they put 'food refusal' in your chart. You don't want that."

She's right. I know this from my previous admissions. So, I swallow the overcooked eggs and charred toast—but the ache in my heart remains.

At nine o'clock, a tension headache and the fading edge of my dream follow me into a room at the far end of the corridor. This psychiatrist is a bulky man with hair the color of dirty WD40. He's wearing a blue-checked shirt and a green vest, a combination that suggests he's color blind. A pair of glasses hanging from a chain rest on his overstretched middle.

I read the name tag clipped just above his vest pocket—Dr. R. Pinsky.

"Good morning. I'm Dr. …"

"Pinsky?"

He smiles quickly and motions me to an armless wooden chair across from his desk. "Please, sit."

I take a deep breath, bracing myself for what's to come.

"I don't belong here," I say as soon as I sit down.

"What I find interesting," he says, "is that everyone who has walked through that door has said exactly the same thing."

His voice has a nasal quality that has already gotten on my nerves. He lifts his bifocals, sets them on the tip of his nose, and glances at my file. "Well, let's talk about it."

Yes. Let's talk about it.

"How are we feeling today?" His demeanor is relaxed, but his eyes are alert.

"I have the *feeling* my sister has convinced you that I'm delusional."

"People can only be admitted to hospital against their wishes in the interest of their own safety or that of others."

"I'm not a dangerous person."

"I understand you had an episode last night."

I roll my eyes. "Not an episode. I had a bad dream."

"I also understand there was an incident in the ER, when your sister tried to reason with you. And with a police officer."

"I have no idea what Margaret's motive is, but I assure you I'm sane." As the words come out of my mouth, I realize I am trying to convince myself as much as I am him.

His gold cufflinks snatch the light as he scribbles in his notebook, then, "Tell me about your dream."

A drop of moisture crawls from my armpit down my side. My gut tells me not to talk about Noah. What if I was wrong about having a baby? "Um, I don't remember. I just know the dream was disturbing."

"Why do you think your family is concerned about your mental state?"

"They should mind their own business," I tell him.

His arms rest on the desk, fingers interlaced. "Do you have an idea what worries them?" He directs an expectant gaze at me. Something about this expression annoys me. In my opinion, anyone who decides to become a psychiatrist needs a psychiatrist themself.

But I've got to play the game. I sigh. "Okay. Let me come clean. I do realize I need help. Sometimes I let my anger run my life."

He steeples his fingers. "Some people hide truths about themselves from themselves — as a coping mechanism."

I resent his textbook evaluation. How can I possibly tell him I'm in mourning and about the conflicted feelings that go along with that — the cherishing and the remembering and the sorrow, which has turned to anger? And the guilt that I've let my infant be taken away from me.

Or did I?

"What do you expect to gain by holding on to your anger?"

I clutch the sides of the chair. What do I have to gain? *Lots. Revenge. I want to find Todd and kill him.*

When I don't answer, Dr. Pinsky brushes an invisible piece of lint from his jacket and continues. "Let's talk about your parents."

"Why?" An image of my parents trapped in the fiery car flashes through my head.

"Your sister told me about the accident ..."

"My sister, the busybody."

"That's a lot to cope with," he says. "Especially for a child." Several tense moments pass. "Let's talk about that." He clears his throat, sits back in his chair, blinking his pale lashes at me.

I have spent seventeen years arranging and rearranging a variety of facts and words and memories until it has all become nebulous. According to Dr. Palmer — the psychiatrist who treated me after the accident — the trauma caused me to experience "dissociative amnesia," or "recall gaps" regarding the incident. Yet, I can still see the flames shooting up from the car and spreading in the autumn wind.

I clench my jaw. No good can come from excavating the past. "Let's not," I reply firmly.

He doesn't seem to hear me. "When the parent-child connection ends violently, there's discontinuity. A survivor of such a soul-shattering experience could confuse fiction with fact."

I wrap my arms around myself. "Noah is not a fictional character."

"Oh, that," he says, raising his eyebrows. "Your sister told us about that."

My chest tightens. *That?* Did he just refer to my son as "that"?

"Emotional shock is a proven cause of a jumbling of reality." I watch him stroke the side of his nose. "Because we tend to block memories of trauma. Does that make sense?"

I count to ten to keep from saying something I'll regret.

"You were just fourteen. It must have been terrible to lose your parents when you were so young."

I raised my brow at him. "What do *you* think?"

"Indeed. Indeed."

"I want to know the status of my impending evaluation."

"Too early to tell," he says.

"I don't want psych meds. They gave me something last night. I don't want any more."

"Fine. If you don't need them, we're not going to give them to you."

Dr. Pinsky glances at his notes, yet again. "I understand your mother was five months pregnant at the time of the accident."

His words skyrocket me back to the past. At twenty-three, I entered a three-month in-patient program for women who have experienced false pregnancy. I was obsessed with giving new life and had convinced myself—and my body—I was pregnant. To salvage the third life lost in the accident? Maybe. To undo what happened to my parents? Probably.

So, the real question is this: Am I crazy, now? Are my sister and aunt right? *Is* Noah just a figment of my imagination—a "fiction" as Dr. Pinsky suggested? I'm teetering on the edge. Am I delusional? I've had one false pregnancy. Why not a second?

The room is swirling. I tuck my head between my knees to ward off nausea.

Dr. Pinsky walks to the door of his cramped office. Cheap Venetian blinds clatter as the door swings behind him. He returns with a plastic cup of water.

I take a long gulp. "Thank you."

He squeezes back into the creaky chair behind his desk. "You want to talk about it?"

I don't. I don't even want to think about it. I don't want to remember how my parents celebrated the new life growing in my mother's belly. About the brother or sister I never got the chance to meet.

"During your stay," Dr. Pinsky says, gently, "we can help you face the memories."

Heat burns my cheeks. Obviously, he's going to keep talking until I get on board. Fine, I think, and give him a nod.

As unpleasant as this all is—and as worried as I am that I may have imagined Noah's very existence—I suddenly remember that I have something perhaps even more terrifying to worry about. If the doctors here come to the decision that I'm not crazy, and that I did deliver a live child, then their next logical step will be to wonder if I killed him. Like Officer Gordon does. And if so, what would stop them from charging me for it? Could they have even spoken to Officer Gordon? Aunt Rachelle did.

My panic rises rapidly, but I take a few deeps breaths to calm myself. No matter what, crazy or sane, I have to figure out a way to get the hell out of here. Unfortunately, they took my purse and the keys to the car in it.

I turn my attention back to Dr. Pinsky, who is still drawling on. "Daily group therapy will help a great deal. I strongly suggest you participate. It shows a willingness to get well."

I nod and smile, giving it all I have.

"May I make a phone call?" I ask before walking out of his small office.

"Indeed."

I call Damon and tell his voice mail that I'm in the Soundview Hospital Psychiatric Unit, and that I need to talk to him as soon as possible.

CHAPTER 38

"Group starts in twenty-five minutes," Tanisha says, as soon as I walk out of Dr. Pinsky's office. "But you have a visitor."

My heart leaps. How is it possible he made it here so quickly? "Is it Damon Morgan?"

"No. It's George Ragner. Do you want to see him?"

At the mention of George's name, chill bumps pimple my arms. He's the last man I ever want to see, but I'm alone right now and hopeless.

"If you have to think about it that long, I suppose that's answer enough," Tanisha says, with a caring look on her face.

"No, no. I'm all right."

She cocks her head. "You sure?"

I nod.

"Okay, then."

With Nurse Tanisha escorting me, I roll my shoulders, push open the glass door, and step into the visitors' area.

The room contains brown sectional couches and chairs, a faux leather ottoman, several tables, and the lingering smell of perfume. As if on cue, a baby starts crying. I fight the urge to turn and run back to my room. Instead, I scan the room and see a couple sitting quietly at one of the tables. The woman holds the crying infant on her lap, but she's staring into space. There's sadness spelled in the hunch of her skinny shoulders and the droop of her mouth.

Behind the couple, a tall man paces the floor, mumbling to himself. He circles the room once, picking things up and putting them down.

Throwing glances at the door, he alights briefly on a chair, then jumps up and resumes pacing.

I spot George on the sectional, holding carnations that look a bit wilted. He's wearing pressed jeans, a Red Sox baseball cap pulled low, and a Red Sox jacket over a crisp white shirt. Looking at his chiseled chin and high cheek bones, I can't help but notice how handsome he is.

I inhale deeply, forcing a veneer of calm.

When I stand in front of him, he gives me a once over. I must look dreadful. My hair feels like straw, and my clothes need a wash.

"What's with the baseball cap?" I ask, knowing how proud he is of his thick head of hair.

"I'll tell you later." He points at my face. "Your chin. You have a piece of food stuck there."

I force a big smile and wipe my chin with the back of my hand. "How did you know I was here?"

"Need you ask?" He taps the couch. "Sit."

I take a seat next to him.

He shoves the flowers toward me. "I worry about you, you know."

"Very thoughtful of you," I scoot a little closer. The warmth of his thigh gives me a tiny bit of comfort. The devil you know is better than the devil you don't. "So, how are you?"

"Much better than you. You got yourself into a mess. How did you manage that?" He raises his hand to shush me. "I know. I know. You don't have to tell me."

"Dumb, huh?"

His eyes pin me. "It is."

"But I was angry at my sister."

"I'd say that's an understatement." He frowns and crosses one long leg over the other, revealing spit-shined, brown calfskin shoes. "I haven't always approved of your choices. Still, I don't blame you. I understand she tricked you to get you here."

"She did."

"You're a mess." He looks around quickly, then whispers, "What were you thinking, roaming around at night? That was dumb. At night at a biker's hangout?"

"You were there? In the parking lot? Why didn't you help me?"

"I got there too late. I was just about to help when the police showed up."

Across the room, the baby issues another cry. I turn and see the child squirming in the woman's arms. The husband strokes his mustache as if considering what to do next. I ache for the distressed baby, and my arms tingle with anticipation.

"A mess," George repeats, shaking his head. "For your sake, I hope you've learned your lesson."

"Me, too." I give what I hope is an encouraging smile.

A thought creeps into my mind. But I need to step carefully.

"That's why I'm so happy to see you," I say, sweetly, smile frozen on my face. "You've always protected me."

"Damn right, I have. But you? You never appreciated me."

An elderly woman seated at a table next to us is folding and refolding her napkin. The young woman across from her places a hand on her arm, as if to calm her. But the older woman jerks away with a scowl.

"I really am glad to see you, you know," I say, bending over so I can gaze up at him, wide-eyed and guileless.

"Oh, yeah? Why is that?" His eyes soften.

"I've had time to think since the last time I saw you. I'm sorry about that, about what happened between us."

A shadow crosses his face, and I understand he wants a different answer.

I think fast.

"And I've missed you a whole lot," I add. "You're right. I didn't appreciate you."

"Well, that's not what you said the other night at your motel."

"I know. It's just that you caught me off-guard. And I was, um, having my period. You know how that affects me." I blush and glance down at my lap.

When I look up, George is frowning.

"How much?" he asks.

"How much, what?"

"How much did you miss me?"

I can't believe it. He's hooked. "A lot more than words can express," I say meaningfully.

"Is that so?" He fixes me with a steady gaze.

I fight the impulse to squirm.

"Yeah, right." He folds his arms, shakes his head.

Maybe he's not as easy as I thought. But he's my only hope at the moment.

"I don't like how you treated me and the way you left."

"I'm sorry," I say, with the most contrite tone I can muster. "I'm serious. We should've stayed together. It was such a mistake to leave you."

His face begins to soften.

I wait. The other night, in front of my motel room, he said he had something to tell me. I wonder if he was telling the truth. On the other hand, he could have been lying, baiting me. Either way, now is not the time to ask. If I do, he might get suspicious.

He laces his fingers behind his head. "Yeah. You wouldn't have been in this muddle if you'd stayed with me."

Now's my moment. I scan the room. "Then let's get away from here. The fact that you're here when everyone else has forsaken me shows how much you care. I promise not to let you down again. I owe you a lot, and the last thing I want is to hurt you again."

He considers me a moment. I hold my breath.

"We'll be good together; you'll see," I say.

He leans over and whispers, "As a matter of fact, I do have a plan to get you out of here."

"You do?"

"Of course." His eyes sparkle. "You see? I'm nice to you. You'll be nice to me. Right?"

I nod, not trusting myself to speak, in case I break the spell.

His eyes flick to the deserted nurses' desk. Then he points at a shopping bag on the floor, and scoots closer, wrapping his arms around me. I lean into him, and he whispers his plan into my ear. Then he shoves something into my hand, which I tuck surreptitiously into my bra.

When he releases his embrace, I shape a shaky smile.

"Oh, and one more thing. Look for the same car you saw the other night."

"What happened to your Corvette?"

"Yeah, well ... Can't talk about it right now." He checks his watch. "I have to go." He glances at the nurses' desk again.

"Okay." He pushes out a breath and squeezes my hand. "You did well to trust me to get you out of here."

I nod. I smile. My heart is beating faster than it ever has.

He rises, letting his gaze skim over me one last time, as though trying to make certain I'm being truthful with him.

My most dazzling smile sends him out the door.

Once he's out of sight, I exhale deeply. The irony hasn't escaped me: the only person who will rescue me from this black bottom is my stalker.

CHAPTER 39

After changing into the clothes George brought me, I stand in the bathroom, holding my breath. By now George should have left the hospital. I'm ready to make my move. Will his plan work? I know him to be—for better or worse—clever and resourceful, so chances are good that it will. However, in my desperation to escape, I'm afraid I'm falling into another trap: George's. But what if I am? There is freedom in surrender. He will keep me safe. This I know to be true. I also know there will be consequences. I am living proof of this fact.

I let out my breath and step out of the bathroom and into the hall, wearing a baseball cap pulled low on my forehead and a Red Sox jacket zipped to the top, and creep down the beige linoleum toward the visitors' area. Before me, two elderly women are also making their way to the locked door that leads off the ward.

Boldly, I stride up beside them.

The women glance at me briefly.

I smile and say, "How are you today?"

"Doing well, thanks," one of the women says, her tentative smile deepening the hollows around eyes.

"This is a beautiful facility, isn't it?" I comment.

She cranes her head up to gaze at me. "Indeed, it is."

She's carrying a large, paper grocery bag. "I brought my son food from home, but I have to take the empty containers back with me," she explains when she sees me eyeing the bag.

The closer we get to the door, the more I want to turn around and wrap myself in the safety of the psych ward. It would be so easy. I could stay here for years, eating bland food and being guided through my days. But I gather my courage and continue alongside the women, shaking slightly as we approach the door.

"Are you okay?" asks the woman carrying the bag. She fixes her eyes on me. Even though they are kind and soft, like melted chocolate, her look makes me wonder if she can see right through me.

In that split second, when it seems my freedom hangs in the balance, the woman, tips the scales. "Who are you visiting?" she asks.

Sighing inwardly, I say, "My husband. "He's lucky to be here. He's making significant progress. Here, let me carry that bag for you. It looks cumbersome."

She hands me the bag. "Thank you, dear."

I stay close to the small group as the nurse buzzes us off the ward. And no one singles me out for attention. George was right.

At the next corridor, I hand the bag back to the woman and bid her a pleasant day. Then, I continue toward the exit with a casual stride, as if I have no cares in the world—although I am simultaneously mentally exhausted and cranked up on adrenaline. If I'm caught before I get out of the hospital, I'll be hauled back and medicated and my stay will be extended.

"Hey," I hear someone call, as I approach the exit. I glance back. A few hundred feet behind me, a nurse is making her way rapidly towards me.

I hasten my pace.

"Hey," she calls again. "Come back. Come back, now."

I ignore her and begin to sprint, heart pumping hard, until I push through the main doors, and scan the curved drive for George. But he's not there, and the nurse is on my tail. I take a chance, turning to the right, running as fast as I ever have, grateful for the length of stride my long legs give me, my footsteps a metronome for my panting.

Then, from the street that parallels the wood beside the hospital, George's car squeals into view.

"Stop!"

Turning to see two male nurses flying towards me, I swerve off the main path toward a half-empty parking lot and glance over my shoulder again. They are gaining fast.

I redouble my efforts, but without their laces, my boots are clumsy. With a leap, one of the nurses grasps the back of my jacket. I jerk loose, turn and slide my foot behind his leg, punch him in the chest, and send him sprawling.

Before I know it, the second nurse has me pinned to the ground. I flail under him, but he's much stronger than I am. Suddenly, his eyes open wide, as if in disbelief, then he cries out and falls away from me. I look up to see George standing over the second nurse and holding his hand and wincing from the blow he's given my assailant.

"Hurry," George says, grabbing my arm and pulling me to his car. He shoves me into the passenger's seat, then takes off with another squeal and the smell of burnt rubber. I brace my hand on the door as he swerves out onto the main road.

"You owe me big time." George says. "I stuck my neck out for you."

I don't reply right away. The ramifications of what I've gotten myself into are beginning to sink in.

"Aren't you going to say, thank you?"

"Thank you," I say. But my voice sounds more like the sad girl who saw her parents trapped in a burning car than it does my new, competent voice. Perhaps that resolute, courageous Bree is gone, too.

"That's more like it."

"Where are we going?"

"To my motel room."

The wipers slap against the windshield. I keep glancing at the side view mirror, and George glances in the rearview. "If we get stopped, follow my lead," he says.

"Whatever you say." My initial panic has subsided, but a feeling of disorientation remains bright and red-hot in my head.

George drives several more miles before speaking again. "You can't trust anyone else. I won't let them catch you. You'll only be safe if you realize you have to depend entirely on me to keep you that way."

The disorientation is being replaced by numbness, as I realize that I may have chosen this, but I'm not safe. Maybe I never will be.

Then George ruptures the tiny hope I didn't even realize I was holding onto.

"Even Damon can't help you."

I bow my head. There's no need to ask how he knows about Damon. He's a stalker. My stalker. He's been following me all along.

Suddenly, a new thought occurs to me. If George knows about Damon, he knows about everything else. He even knows about Todd ... if there is a Todd.

"What else do you know about me?"

He raises his eyebrows. "What makes you think I know anything else?"

We drive another few miles in silence. Then I get an idea. "Let's stop at a liquor store," I say. "We need to celebrate."

He narrows his eyes at me.

"After what we just went through," I say in a soft voice, "we need to relax and have fun. Don't you think?"

He reaches over, takes a fistful of my hair and yanks it lightly. "That's my girl."

•   •   •

Half an hour later we approach the motel, liquor in hand. My body tightens with the irrefutable knowledge that I am going to have to do the last thing I would ever want to.

"Come." A command.

When I hesitate, George grabs my elbow and steers me toward his motel room, shoving me inside. As soon as the door closes behind us, he reaches for me.

I smile and dodge his advance. "Give me a minute," I say.

His face shifts, his features, tightening into something threatening. His voice, low and seemingly polite, sends chills down my spine. "What's wrong?"

"I'd like nothing more than to make love to you." I smile again. I seem to be doing that a lot lately. "Let's have a few drinks, first."

A playful smirk replaces the threatening expression. "Be right back," he says. "Going to brush my teeth."

As soon as he disappears into the bathroom, I'm tempted to escape. But I have nothing to get me to where I need to go. I left my gun in my rental, which is now parked in front of the ER. And they took my purse, which I'll have to figure how to get back.

I do a quick scan of the room for anything that would help me get out of here. His small duffel is on the bed. I risk a quick peek, but see only clothing. When I hear the toilet flush, I step away from the bag.

Just in time.

George emerges, smiling. He holds two plastic cups in his hands. "I'm really hot for you," he growls.

I plop to the edge of the bed and remind myself to breathe.

When he pours the vodka into the two cups and hands me mine, I smile broadly, and give him a wink. "Cheers," I say, and take a sip.

He down his drink in one gulp. While he pours himself another, I dump the rest of mine on the carpet behind the bed and hold out my cup again. He grins and fills it.

We repeat this routine four times, and each time I take a sip and pour out the rest.

By now, George is definitely feeling the effects of the alcohol. His gaze slides over my body, and, pulling off his clothing, he comes for me, swaying for a moment before pushing me down across the bed — a horrible reminder of our time together. Then his hands are kneading my breasts, making me clench with discomfort. I stiffen instinctively, but he continues, pressing his mouth into my neck, his hands reaching from my breasts to my behind.

I grit my teeth to keep myself from pulling away, hoping I calculated correctly. And it seems that I did, because, eventually, the persistent, fervent movement of his fingers and body against me slows, and then stops, and George lies next to me, snoring softly.

I spend several moments staring at the ceiling and wondering how long I should wait. When his steady breathing suggests he's in a deep, alcohol-induced slumber, I ease out of the bed, gather my clothes, and tiptoe into the dark bathroom to get dressed.

A disturbing weight sits on my shoulders. By escaping, I have broken the law, and the police will have been alerted. But I'll worry about that later. Now, I move softly around the room, in search of

George's wallet and car keys. I go through his pockets and softly open the drawers in the bureau and night stands. Nothing. Where could they be?

George rolls over and mumbles. I freeze. Then his renewed snores tell me the alcohol hasn't worn off yet.

I think for a moment. George went right away to the bathroom. Why? To brush his teeth? That's unlike George. I tiptoe back to the bathroom, where eerie light from a full moon glows through a crack in the window shade. I check the medicine cabinet and the bathtub. Nothing.

One room and a bathroom. Where could the wallet and keys be?

I creep back to the bed and, hoping George is as deeply asleep as he appears to be, slide my hand under the pillow. Nothing.

Silently, I run my hand under the edge of the mattress, trying not to cause any shift in the bed that would awaken George. Then I get down on my hands and knees and look under the bed.

George shivers and flings out an arm, but his snores recommence. *Take a deep breath, Bree, and think.* I've checked everywhere. But his keys and wallet have to be here.

Then I realize there is one more place to look.

I tiptoe back to the bathroom and, slowly, so as not to let the porcelain clank, I lift the lid from the back of the toilet. There they are: his cell phone, wallet, and keys, all ensconced inside a plastic baggie.

Back in the bedroom, I see George hasn't budged. Noticing his duffel on the second bed, I gather all his clothes and stuff them into the bag. Lifting that quietly, I tiptoe to the door, turn the deadbolt and the doorknob and pull the door toward me a fraction of an inch at a time.

Holding my breath, I step through the door and pull it closed as quietly as I opened it. A quick look at my watch tells me first light is in two hours. Since I left my laptop in my motel room back in Handrock, that will be my next stop.

CHAPTER 40

Back at the Lakeview Motel, I park out of sight of the lobby but in view of my room and scan the area before slipping inside. I grab my laptop and other belongings and hurry back out, my breath escaping in frozen puffs in the unforgiving November air. I toss my things in the back seat of George's car, jump in, crank the engine, then lurch out of the parking lot and head north.

I find myself checking my rearview mirror every few seconds. Stabbing at the radio buttons, I try to find something to calm me, but, finding only static, talk-radio callers arguing politics, or the bullying sound of a thumping bass, I turn the stereo off, leaving nothing but the hum of the road to soothe me.

Twenty miles out, I spot an abandoned gas station, and pull in, parking amid the weeds and discarded fast food bags. I take inventory of George's wallet, counting seven, crisp, one-hundred-dollar bills, in addition to a few twenties and several smaller bills. I heave a sigh of relief. It's enough to last me a few days—no need to leave an electronic trail with my credit card. I stash the wallet in my knapsack, shove the large bills into a separate compartment, and place the rest of the money in my jeans pocket.

Then I eye George's iPhone.

After I broke it off with him, he made it clear he would never let me go. He choked my voice mail with messages about the life we could share together; his gifts littered my mailbox. He showed up at Gene's shop, at my favorite coffee shop, and at my aunt's house. I was thankful that his constant harassment hadn't escalated to more dangerous behavior. But it hadn't stopped me from worrying that it might happen.

I researched measures to protect myself. One of the things I learned is that stalkers are above average in intelligence. They're capable of hacking into computers, tapping telephone lines, and will even travel thousands of miles to find their victims.

And they take photos.

Luckily, George's phone is unlocked. I click on his photo album and start scrolling.

My breath catches when I see the pages and pages of photographs of me. Looking through them is like watching the last couple of years of my life played out in reverse.

There are photos of me knocking on Agnes's door, at Damon's door, going for a run, outside the police station. But the most importantly, he has photos of Todd: at our house, at the supermarket, with a woman who resembles me, but isn't.

And one of me, pregnant, standing on the front porch, my arms encircling my huge belly.

So, I'm not crazy. The thought sends a huge wave of relief through my body. There is a Todd. I had a baby. Here is the proof, right in my hands — courtesy of George, my stalker.

Dropping my gaze to the phone again, I think back. His harassment stopped when he was beaten and ended in the hospital, shortly after I got pregnant. After that, I thought he was out of my life for good. I was wrong. He continued to watch my every move and photograph it. As much as I am shaken by the intrusion, I also feel a rush of giddy excitement at what the fruit of that intrusion has borne.

I continue to shuffle through the photos. I see myself at the garage, bent over the engine of a classic Ford street car. And there are Todd and Connie, standing next to her Jeep, Connie's arms tightly crossed at her chest, while she scowls at Todd. I see myself exiting the house, in mid-scream, looking for Todd and Noah. There are Luanne and me, at the Manhattan coffee shop. And more. Much more.

What grabs my attention is a black Suburban parked alongside a barbed-wire fence, like the one I saw on the flash drive. And in another picture, a black Range Rover — is it the same one the black-haired woman was driving the day I followed her out into the country? — is pulling through a gate in that same fence.

So, George has been following me this whole, horrifying time. Conceivably, he tracked me down in Handrock to tell me something about Todd. But I doubt it. I'm certain his plan was to manipulate my misery in the hope I'd return to him. And he came close to succeeding. But I managed to turn the tables on him. I've used his game to help me, instead of allowing him to perpetuate the victim status I've held onto for far too long.

Chilled, I start the car and crank up the heat, then continue scanning the pictures. There must be thousands of them. I come to a group of photos of houses and what seem like army barracks. Behind the barracks, there are a few larger buildings, airplane hangars, by the looks of them, where men with machine guns draped around their shoulders stand beside a pile of crates.

I look up from the phone and start adding all these images together. Quickly, my logical brain gives me the only answer that makes sense: This is the compound Folston was talking about. Not only that, but there is a reason George took these pictures. This place has something to do with me.

My emotional heart makes the leap: Todd is there. Noah is there. My chest tightens, as I imagine my son crying out for me.

After viewing all these pictures, I cast aside any lingering doubts and allow the escalating urgency I feel to propel me forward.

I flash on George for a moment. Somehow, he can always find me. But, I reassure myself that, right now, he'll try to keep as low a profile as possible. After all, he's complicit in my escape from the hospital, and he beat up a male nurse, who, I'm sure, would be happy to testify against him. Plus, he's got his hands full for the moment trying to figure out how to buy clothes without money, not to mention what to do about getting another car.

Yup. George's current problems will buy me time.

Squeezing the steering wheel, I stare through the windshield into the stormy early morning. A slash of lightning sears the sky.

No time to waste.

Continuing north, away from Handrock, I find a Walmart and buy a pay-as-you-go phone. Then, I pull up Google Maps on George's phone. Deciding on my destination, I start the ignition and nose the car toward the town of Summit.

Forty-five minutes later, Summit announces itself with an old, clapboard sign. The main drag through town boasts a single stop light, halting traffic at the intersection of the narrow state road that bisects the town.

I pull off at a motel that advertises "Clean Rooms," and pay cash to a sleepy young girl whose body is decorated with tattoos. Does she know that particles from the ink end in the lymph nodes, or that tattoos can cause infections fifteen years later? I don't get the chance to tell her, because she's busy on her cell phone during our entire transaction. Evidently, she's breaking up with her boyfriend and getting another tattoo to celebrate her newfound freedom. All for the best. I wouldn't want her to remember me, if she's ever asked.

The two-story motel forms a horseshoe built around a swimming pool. I follow the covered stairs up to my room, lock the door behind me, and plop on one of the full-size beds. Immediately, I transfer all the pictures from George's phone to my laptop. Next, I remove the battery and SIM card from George's phone, flush them down the toilet, and toss the shell in the trash.

Then, I email Damon the file I've created for the photos to prove I did have a baby, and that Todd and Connie *were* in my life. Next, I call Damon on my pay-as-you-go phone and leave him a message, alerting him to the email with the photos and asking him to call me.

With all that in place, I pull the slip of paper Johnny gave me with his cell number on it and dial it. When he doesn't answer, I leave a message, for him, too.

Since, Damon doesn't have a great track record of answering my calls, and I just have to wait for Johnny to get back to me, I move on to the next item on my list: I need to stash George's car out of sight and get myself another vehicle, just in case the police have been alerted by the two nurses who pursued me — oh my God, was it just yesterday? — and who could have memorized his license plate number.

CHAPTER 41

Johnny's auto body shop is on a narrow side street in a rundown building. Thinking I can kill two birds with one stone — in this case, talk with Johnny and get a lead on a replacement for George's car — I park off to the side, where a young man in cowboy boots leans against the wall, smoking a cigarette. He nods at me as I pass. Inside the garage, one of Johnny's crew is changing a flat on a minivan, while another is bent over the engine of a black Mustang. I get closer and see the mechanic is holding the transmission in place with one hand and bolting it in with the other. Standing here — surrounded by cars on lifts and the scent of axle grease and burnt oil — makes me nostalgic.

One of the mechanics throws me a questioning look. I smile and step through into the small office. A wiry man sits behind a desk strewn with papers, which he's busily shuffling. According to the name embroidered on his blue coveralls, he's Otto.

"Hi." I say.

Leaning back in his swivel chair, Otto appraises me, eyes stopping at my breasts. His smile widens, but his eyes remain on my chest. "What can I do for you, honey?"

I suppress the urge to walk over and kick him in the groin. "Is the owner here?"

"You're looking at him."

"But isn't this Johnny's garage?"

His interest turns guarded. "So what?"

"Where is he?" I demand.

"Ain't here." He shrugs and straightens his chair and begins shoving the papers purposefully.

"Can you tell me where I can find him?"

He lifts both hands, palms up. "How should I know? What do I look like, his mother?"

"Your attitude," I say, as my rising blood pressure pushes the remark up and out, "needs adjustment."

Otto considers me for a moment, smirking. "Hot tempered. That's a turn-on." His tone makes me squirm slightly inside. "Now, leave before I call the police."

There's a metal trash can in front of Otto's desk. I kick it with everything I've got. The metallic clamor it makes as it crashes into the wall is pleasing to my ears.

I turn on my heels and leave, a plan already forming in my mind.

CHAPTER 42

Della opens the door, clutching her sleeping baby. Anxiety covers her pale face, and the buttons on her green sweater are unevenly fastened. She stands squarely in the doorway, as if to bar my entrance, and challenges me with a stare from her red, swollen eyes.

"I know why you're here."

"I need your help."

Her eyes flash anger. "No, you don't."

"Please, just hear me out."

"I thought I saw the last of you."

The statement is harsh, but I don't react. She's clearly upset about something—something other than my appearance on her front stoop.

"May I come in?"

"It's all your fault," she says, eyes brimming with tears.

I frown. "Della, what's wrong?"

She continues to cry quietly, and little Jake stirs in her arms.

"Tell me what's going on. I was just at Johnny's garage," I say, and tell her about my interaction with Otto.

At that, Della lets her tears fall and hugs her baby tighter. When I wrap an arm around her shoulders and gently guide her into the house, she doesn't resist.

The living room is a mess. Clothes, dirty and clean, are draped over furniture, and a plate containing a half-eaten apple and an untouched sandwich sits on top of the crowded coffee table.

"My Johnny disappeared. I'm afraid he's dead." Two great tears slide down her sunken cheeks to bear witness to her distress.

I open my mouth, but the words stick in my throat. I feel sick and faint. "Here," I say. "Let me put Jake down." She allows me. I tuck a pacifier in his mouth and set him in the bassinette.

Della collapses on the couch, shoulders hunched, sobbing.

I cross to her and put my arm around her. "I'm so, so sorry. How long has he been gone?"

"Two days." Her chin starts to quiver, and fresh tears slide down her face.

When she catches her breath, I ask, "What do the police say?"

She sniffles, and wipes her eyes. "I can't even file a missing person's report for 72 hours, Bree. He's an adult."

"I'm so, so sorry," I repeat.

The pressure in the room weighs me down, and I begin to pace. Outside, a bird flits past the window, and its tweeting dies away.

Della twists her wedding ring. I sit down next to her and take her hand in mine. She wipes her eyes with her sleeve. "He left for work, as usual, at six, yesterday," she tells me. "Said he'd call later in the day to check up on me. He always does that, my Johnny. He worries about me and Jake." She turns a soft gaze toward her baby.

I wonder if there's a particular reason for him to worry about Della and the baby, but I keep the question to myself.

"But when I didn't hear from him during the day, I knew something was wrong. I called the shop. No one answered. I called his cell. No answer. And he didn't come home last night."

She straightens up and pulls her hand away. "I have no idea how you're involved. I don't know if Johnny's disappearance has anything to do with you, but the timing tells me it is."

I think she's right. "All I can tell you is that I'm a pawn in a heartless game I don't understand. I have information, but it's partly a hunch. I don't know if Johnny's disappearance has anything to do with me, either, but it may have. If it does, I'll find out where he is — and I won't quit until I do. That's a promise."

She's biting her lower lip. Her gaze shifts to Jake, who's fast asleep in the bassinet.

"I need to ask you a favor," I say, quietly. "The car I'm driving isn't mine. Long story. You don't want to know. But I have to hide it, for now. Last time I was here, I noticed an old Chevy pickup in the garage."

"My Johnny is always tinkering with that truck. It's his pride and joy."

"Does it run?"

"Not right now. He pulled it apart again."

"Let me put it back together. I just need it for a few days. I'll take good care of it."

She looks skeptical.

"Look," I say, before she can tell me no. "I'm on the trail of something. But I need a vehicle no one can trace to me. If you let me ..."

Della interrupts. "I don't want to get involved with you. You're toxic."

"If Johnny has gotten caught up in the mess I'm in, I'll find him. I promise."

She stands and walks over to the bassinette, then she lifts Jake gently, kisses his forehead, and hugs him to her chest. She turns. "All right," she says, slowly.

"Thank you," I say.

In the garage, I find a rebuilt fuel pump, which I install first. Next, I put in the new fan belts Johnny has sitting on a shelf. As I clean the spark plugs, my mind begins to tumble through all the parts of this puzzle I've gotten myself involved in: my son's disappearance; Todd's; now, Johnny's, too. The images on the flash drive; the lack of fingerprints in the house I occupied with two other people. The hostility of the people of Handrock. I know Todd figures into all of this, somehow. If only I could figure out exactly how.

"Sure, looks like you know your stuff."

I jump involuntarily.

Della steps in front of the open hood, where she can see me.

I straighten up, stretching my lower back.

"Luckily Johnny did most of the hard work." I grab a shop rag and begin to wipe at my hands. "This is a great truck. The Chevy 350 engine is one of the century's best."

Della watches me as I try to get the grease off. "Johnny used barrier cream to keep his hands clean," she says. Then, "I don't know why I'm thinking about that, now. I'm so worried." Her eyes well up. She lowers herself onto a stool as if her legs can't hold the weight of her sadness. She wipes her eyes on her sleeve.

"I understand there are a lot of drugs in town."

"I have no dealings with those people."

"What people?"

"The druggies."

"Does Johnny have any dealings with them?"

She chooses her words carefully. "My husband does business with all kinds of people. They drop off cars and pick them up. Maybe a few of them are shady. Maybe he knew … knows something. But he never told me anything about it."

I'm listening with my gut as much as my ears. Her words are weighted with unspoken meaning. What is she not saying?

She sighs. "As much as I blame you for Johnny's disappearance, I can't hate you. You're looking for your baby. God knows, if Jake was taken from me, I would climb the highest mountain, claw at the earth until my fingers bled to bring him back home."

She pauses for a moment, then says, "And now Johnny … We even started talking about adding another little person to our family." She buries her face in her hands. Her shoulders rise and fall.

I stand quietly, giving her time to grieve, although neither of us know if she's grieving for a dead man or one who is missing and will be found.

When she looks up, I say, "I want to ask you about something."

She looks wary.

"I notice that there are no children in town. Only infants." The images of children marching and chanting come back to me. Are all of Handrock's children in the compound George captured on his phone?

Della holds my gaze and nods. "It's true," she starts, but just then, her cell phone rings. She pulls it out of her back pocket and glances at it. Her face goes pale. Then the phone stops ringing.

"Finish what you started to say," I press.

"About what?"

"You were going to tell me about the children, why there are no children in Handrock."

Her eyes slide away.

"Please, Della."

She hesitates, then, "I'm risking my life here. If they ever find out I told you anything, they'd kill Johnny for sure—if they haven't already."

I hold my tongue, not wanting to spook her more than she is already.

"Rumor is that the babies and youngest children get moved around pretty often."

I start to ask another question, but when I open my mouth, she shakes her head. "I'm sorry, Bree. I have to check on Jake." She rises. "A word of caution, though: Don't trust anyone in town, no matter how friendly they act."

Halfway to the house, she turns. "And watch for that glove compartment. It pops open every so often."

I scrub up at the garage sink, getting as much of the grease out from under my nails as possible, and think about what Della said. If she's right about babies being shifted around, what are my chances of getting to Noah before he's been moved on? If what she's heard is fact, I am now in a race against time.

Quickly, I drive George's car around back behind the garage, where it's not in plain sight. Then I hop into the pickup, intending to go back to where I spotted the barbed-wire fence.

Before I turn the key in the ignition though, I reach over to check the glove compartment. I touch the knob, it falls open. When I scoot over to close it properly, what I see inside stops me cold: a .38 revolver. I pull the gun out gingerly and open the chamber.

It's fully loaded.

CHAPTER 43

Ninety minutes later, I pull off the road, then turn Johnny's truck around and reverse into a hidden spot under a group of trees, just on the edge of the woods. Across the highway, wooden signs are posted along the now-familiar barbed-wire fence: *NO TRESPASSING. VIOLATORS WILL BE SHOT*. Extreme language for such a bucolic site.

Should I take the gun? No. I'm just going on a reconnaissance mission. No need for firearms. A blast of frigid wind slaps me when I climb out of the Chevy. I hoist my backpack over my shoulder and start across the field.

Something is different. Something has shifted. The air carries a scent I almost recognize—but I can't quite put my finger on what it reminds me of. I turn around, sprint back to the Chevy, and retrieve the gun.

I make it across the road and, turning onto the trail, I trudge along in muddy tire tracks that stretch back as far as I can see. A quick burst of gunshot echoes, and I halt, holding my breath. It comes again. And again.

Of course, it could be hunters. But after seeing George's pictures of the compound, I think it's unlikely. Besides, Folston mentioned that Della and Johnny often hear gunshots not too far from their home, even out of hunting season. I wish I could tell which direction the shots are coming from, but soundwaves ripple out in all directions, and the discharge of a firearm travels for miles.

The shots seem to have ceased, so I keep going, keeping close to the edge of the trail, ready to slip into the woods if I hear a vehicle coming. A few minutes later, I come to a wide steel gate, secured with a heavy chain and oversized padlock. Below my feet, a heavy steel grate serves as a bridge over the irrigation ditch that runs alongside the dirt road. To my right, there's a driveway—overgrown with weeds—that I can see leads to a weathered farmhouse, with gaping holes for windows.

I run my fingers through my shaggy hair. My uneasiness increases as I watch the harsh winds whip the trees into submission.

In my pocket, my cell phone vibrates silently. It's Damon.

"Where are you?"

"Near Handrock," I say, in a whisper. "Did you get the pictures?"

"I did. And you were right. About everything."

"What does that mean exactly?"

"I've learned some disturbing information. I'm in a case involving child trafficking, and—"

"Wait. Are you saying Noah is …"? I can't finish my thought.

"No. that's not what I meant. I came across something different. It involves Connie."

My stomach tenses at the sound of her name.

"I spoke with a buddy of mine at Abduction Response Deployment, which is a branch of the FBI. Apparently, your Connie has been on their radar for years—involved in child abduction. She's quite the slippery chameleon."

"Do you know where she is?"

"No, I don't. She's elusive. From the sketch you gave me, we constructed her bone structure and built the rest of her face from there. But she's a master at changing her looks. I know you said you thought she was in her sixties, but she can appear older or younger—she even disguises herself as a man."

I'm stunned. No wonder I couldn't get a bead on who she was. "So, where do we go from here?

"Tell me your location. I'm coming."

"I found the gate shown in the flash drive."

"Are you sure you're in the right place?"

"Looks identical." A flicker of movement catches my eye. I scan the pine-covered terrain. Nothing. I tell myself to relax.

"You shouldn't be up there alone. You're dealing with people who have a lot to lose, and that makes them dangerous."

"I'm just going to scout the area."

I hear him sigh in frustration. "That's insane. You're talking about going into a fortress that's guarded by heavily armed men. Bree, you've got to listen to me. Leave the area immediately and wait for me in a safe location. I'll be there in a couple of hours."

"I'll be careful, but I'm not going to quit until I get answers. I'm close to my son. I can feel it. And there's something else: In all my driving in different neighborhoods, I've hardly seen any children. Someone told me today that the children are shuffled to different locations. I don't know why or how. But if Noah is here, I have to move fast before he's taken someplace else."

"Don't you understand? There are armed guards standing outside the inner gate. On the inside, they do actual military training exercises."

That would explain the gunshots.

"But I'm standing outside the gate now, and I don't see any guards."

"Then you must be in the wrong place. Bree, give me your exact location."

I describe where I am, and we agree to keep our cell phones handy. He'll be here as fast as he can, he says — and hangs up.

Directing my attention back to the gate, I pull an industrial strength bolt cutter out of my knapsack. I picked it up at a hardware store, on my way. It takes effort but I eventually manage to cut through. On the other side of the gate, I plod on, my head bowed into the steady drizzle. Shadows hover over me like vultures. I hear a low rumble. Thunder? No. It's a diesel engine behind me, bucking its way over the rain-soaked ruts.

I run directly into the woods, hiding in the foliage just before the truck rounds the bend that kept me from the driver's view. I decide not to follow the track any more. Instead, I push through the trees. The air smells of decaying leaves and wet earth. Chill has penetrated my boots, and my back is soaking wet.

Suddenly, I have the distinct sensation I'm being watched. Every cell in my body freezes. A loud crack sounds somewhere to my right, but I don't see anything. Eventually, I start to move again—only to reach the edge of the woods, where I find what must be a sixteen-foot high barbed-wire fence.

Somewhere there's a loud thud, a car door slamming closed. I crawl a few yards on my belly and settle myself against the cold, hard dirt. Through the denuded trees, I make out several buildings with corrugated-metal doors.

Then I see what appears to be a guard shack. And the guards, six of them, sweeping through the complex and around its perimeter—alert, and armed.

I press even closer to the ground. There! Footsteps, slow and steady, coming closer. Slowly, I raise my head. Three guards, two men and a woman, all with automatic rifles, laugh softly as they joke and share a quick smoke.

One of the guards turns as if sensing my gaze. He can't see me—I'm well hidden, but still, I hold my breath. Then I hear more voices, and two men hurry by with flashlights. Their voices are low, and they're talking fast.

It was one thing to watch scenes like this on a video from the safety of my motel room. But up close … I'm beginning to realize that Damon was right. I should never have come alone.

CHAPTER 44

I whirl around, but not fast enough. Something slams into my skull, and pain explodes in my head. I shoot to my feet. In an instant, I realize my assailant is Wayne, the biker who attacked me at the Black Horse bar. He is holding the revolver that fell out of my hand.

Then, from behind me, I hear another man say, "Well, well, lookie here." I know who he is by the smell of his chaw: Billie, from the Lakeview Motel. "Another gun? What does a pretty little lady like you need a gun for?"

Two to one. I'm outnumbered. What are my chances? I remember my aunt once saying I'm stronger than I think. Maybe I am. Maybe not. But I am burning with fury. That makes my heart pump harder, my adrenaline shoots higher.

"No!" I scream at the top of my lungs. "Stay away."

My shriek seems to throw them off balance. I start to back up, but my right foot finds empty space, and I fall. Before I can comprehend the impossibility of this, Wayne seizes my arm and yanks me toward him, then grabs me by the neck.

He chuckles, his breath foul on my face. "Sticking your mug in places you don't belong, again? What do you expect, little lady?"

He turns to the other man. "Hey, Billie. Think we should have some fun with her before taking her in?"

"Nah," Billie says. "Keep it in your pants. She's off limits. You know that moron."

Strong arms grab me, a large hand covers my mouth.

There's a sting. Then, nothing.

CHAPTER 45

My senses return in small increments. My tongue is dry and thick. Pain sears through my limbs. Before I can pry open my eyelids, I hear distant voices echoing. The sound of a truck backfiring causes me to jolt, and that's when I realize my hands are tied.

Damn! I lost another gun.

What's happening to me? My head is spinning. I focus on taking several deep breaths. Eventually, the shock fades, and I regain focus.

I'm in a small, concrete room, harshly lit by a single, bare bulb dangling from the ceiling. On the wall across from me hangs a flag emblazoned with a Celtic cross. It looks disturbingly familiar, but I can't remember where I've seen it. Weak sunlight penetrates the small, high window. There's a mattress on the floor beside me and the chair I'm sitting on. Then I realize someone else is in the room. The aroma reminiscent of smoky pine and rain-soaked earth can belong to one person.

"I'd stay still if I were you. Unless you want your wrists to bleed."

I aim my blurry vision toward the familiar voice. Leaning against the wall, one leg propped on a second chair, is Todd.

"Good morning."

I can't believe my eyes. Despite my desperate hopes of finding Todd here, I am speechless—but my body buzzes with loathing for this man. He drags his chair over and sits right in front of me, assessing me. I try to imagine what he sees: my mud-caked clothes, filthy hair, the bruises on my face.

Todd looks different. His longish, gray-streaked blond hair is now a side-swept undercut. But his large golden eyes are unmistakable, as is the straight ridge of his nose. There's a toughness about him I haven't seen before. His shoulders seem fuller and wider, and his skin is leathery and darker than I remember — as if he'd been spending his time outdoors. He looks intimidating, yet the desire to claw at him sends burning impulses along my nerves.

As if he can guess my thoughts, he laughs. "You want to kill me, don't you?"

"I'd like to tear out your guts," I spit.

He just shakes his head and looks amused.

"What day is it?" I ask.

"Sunday morning."

That means I've spent the night in this chair. "What did you inject me with?"

His shoulders lift in a shrug. "Nothing strong. Just enough to get you here in the most expedient way."

He leans forward and roughly lifts my chin with his forefinger. "I told the fools not to tie you tightly," he says, in a tone of faux concern. He releases my bounds, and I topple off the metal chair. He waits for me to get up, then hands me a bottle of water. "Here, drink."

"Where is my son?"

He gives me a long look, then sits back and interlaces his fingers behind his head.

Somewhere a door slams. Shakily, I take a few sips from the bottle. Some of the water spills on my chin and crawls down my chest.

"Are you okay?" he asks, not bothering to hide his smirk.

A hammer would be nice, I think. Something to bash his teeth in with, now that my hands are free. "I haven't been okay since the day you took my son."

"Our son."

"Where is Noah?" I ask again. It's just the first of many questions: the why, the how. Most importantly, the why.

His golden hair catches the light when he shakes his head. "Patience."

I leap from my chair in a fury and pound on his chest. "How could you?"

"Sit," he says, and shoves me back down.

"You … you, selfish shit." My voice trembles with rage.

His eyes go hard. "Foul mouth. Refrain from using that language around me." He pushes the beads ahead, one at a time, with rhythmic clicks. The air between us burns with our mutual hostility. A moment passes.

I clear my throat. "I have to use the toilet."

He hesitates. "Okay, stand up."

He shoves me toward the door, which opens into a narrow, low-ceilinged corridor. He pushes me to the left and points to a door.

"There's no lock," he says. "You have three minutes."

Once inside, my eyes sweep the closet-sized room, which contains only a toilet and a sink—no window. My chances of breaking out of this place are zero. Resigning myself to whatever is going to happen next, I flush the toilet, wash my hands, and open the door to find Todd standing guard. But before I close the door behind me, I glance back into the bathroom at the odd-looking flag with the Celtic cross hanging on the wall. Where have I seen a flag like that?

Once we're back in my cell, he motions me to sit again.

"Todd, how could you do it?"

"My son is where he belongs, now."

"I want to see Noah." My scream is a scorching flame that has been burning for days. "I'm his mother. Damn you! I have a say. Why did you do it?"

"It doesn't matter why. What is important is that he's home."

"This is absurd." I smack the side of my chair, hard.

A muscle near his eye twitches. "Calm down, or else."

My stomach tightens. "Or else, what?"

He doesn't reply.

"I don't expect you to understand," he finally says. "But I hope that in time you will."

"Try me." My foot taps the floor, a nervous impulse that started nineteen days ago, when I awoke to my new reality.

"I wish things could have been different," Todd says.

I catch a faint trace of emotion. Regret? Nostalgia? No. I'm projecting my own emotions onto Todd. But I'm not projecting his decisiveness. He's making it clear that he doesn't intend to let me have Noah. I'm slammed hard by the understanding.

"Our son's name means 'hope,'" I say. "Hope for a better future, for a stable home, for a safe environment. But you know that already. How do you figure that by doing what you did he'll be better off? And without a loving mother. I am prepared to do everything in my power to get him back."

"Erroneous thinking," Todd says, rubbing a hand over his chin again — it's his own nervous habit, I think. "You have no proof we were ever a couple. I am a figment of your imagination. There are no records of my existence in any government file or system."

The mind-lulling tapping of my boot bridges a long silence, during which all the signs from the past year come rushing in on me — from the wig, to Todd's persuasive arguments that I should detach myself from everyone I ever knew, to Damon's revelation that there were no fingerprints in the house other than mine.

I stare at Todd's fingers.

He follows my gaze and turns over his palm. As if reading my mind, he says, "we wiped every surface in the house with bleach."

"So, you erased all traces of yourself and Connie and Noah. You sure did a good job of that." I take a deep breath and exhale slowly. "You undermined my credibility. But, you see, I do have proof that we were together and that I gave birth to our son."

Color leaches from his face. His voice — seemingly quiet and pleasant — sends chills down my spine and raises the hairs on the back of my neck. "What proof?"

"Are you going to tell me where my son is?"

He shoots from his seat. He towers over me, looking as if he is about to explode. "You're lying. What proof?"

I have seen him angry, been the target of the menace in his eyes. But by then I was a few months into my pregnancy and wanted to believe it was my imagination. Another failure of mine. Now, despite the rage in his eyes, I don't flinch. Still, I do consider my situation. Maybe telling him I have evidence of his existence wasn't smart. I backpedal. "Maybe I have proof. Maybe I don't. But I don't know your real name? Who are you?"

He sits again, then scoots his chair towards me until our knees touch. I meet his challenging gaze with my own.

"You think I'm a monster," he says. "You think I have no soul."

I exhale a long-held breath. The guy is unstable. How is it that I lived with him for nearly a year and didn't realize that? I have to ask him, though: "Was that always the plan? To get me pregnant, then steal the child?"

"And you fell for it hard," he says, with a wide smirk that lights up his face.

"Why me?"

"Our son has strong genes. Don't you see? Like his mother, our son is going to be brilliant and tall. Like me, he will have a warrior's heart and strength." He ticks off his motives on his fingers.

Confused, I interrupt him. "But I'm not brilliant. Not by any stretch of the imagination."

"I beg to differ. Before meeting you for the first time, I took the liberty of finding out about your family. Your parents were extraordinary people. Physicists. Professors. Geniuses."

Todd is right. My parents were eminent physicists, involved in the discovery of string theory — a branch of mathematics that attempts to link quantum mechanics to Einstein's theory of relativity.

"But," he says, "your father quit his job at fifty. Do you know why?"

My father was disillusioned with academic research. He felt it slowed scientific development. But that isn't something I want to discuss with this lunatic, who has reduced Noah to some sort of a genetic experiment. I also won't discuss the fact that my father had a breakdown and was hospitalized for several months. I'm surprised Todd didn't discover that on his own. I wonder if he would have included me in his little plan if he had.

"Discussing my genetic background makes motherhood sound so clinical." From my pocket, I pull out the little sock, which I've carried with me for every one of the last nineteen days. I wave it in Todd's face. "You see this? We're not talking about a lab experiment here. Noah is our flesh and blood."

He resumes speaking—continuing his train of thought.

"In addition to your high IQ, which I was looking for in a woman who would carry my seed, you were an easy target. No real friends, except for Luanne. Other than your aunt, no family close to you. Your only your sister lives in California."

Evidently, though, while I may not have had many friends or much family, I had had another stalker. How lucky for me. Two stalkers. At the same time.

"How long have you been following me?" I demand.

He looks thoughtful. "Lots of research went into this project. I shadowed you long enough to know everything about you."

"So, that's what Noah is to you? A project?" If there wasn't so much at stake, I would leap on this madman and tear him apart—or die trying.

Instead, I ask another question. "What does this all have to do with our son?"

"It has everything to do with him. He has a great future ahead of him. He's destined to become an important leader for our cause. And, thanks in part to you, he has the genetic makeup to fulfill his role."

He's frightening me. "What leader? What cause?"

With chilling calm, he says, "It's a matter of perspective, Bree. We all protect our interests. We will protect our interests."

"It would help if I knew what your interests are." I feel completely baffled. I have heard this talk before and it's making me feel uncomfortable.

No matter how often I have anticipated this moment, no matter how well I thought I had prepared myself to confront Todd, right now, all my planning is lost to me. Since I was fourteen years old, I've allowed myself to be swept along by the current. As an adult, I've let the men in my life steer my fate, be it the boy I dated in college, who turned out to be verbally abusive; or George, who raged and threatened and ultimately proved to be a stalker; or Todd, who lied and hid his identity and stole my son, I've put myself at their mercy.

No longer. I am going to figure out what is going on here and reclaim my son—and my own life, too.

But not right now.

I hear the murmur of voices in the corridor, and the door opens. The moment the black-haired woman enters, her hostility, like the bone-deep cold of the wind blowing through the woods outside, chills me. It's the woman I followed to this place several days ago—but I have a moment of disorientation. Except for the black hair, this woman could be my sister. My twin. She takes three steps towards Todd, walking with a limp I immediately recognize. If I had any doubts before, I have none, now. I am looking at Connie—that limp, the body that is all angles, her height, her bone structure. All of these give her identity away, despite the way she disguised herself when she lived with us.

Arms folded, she stands beside Todd, fatigues tucked into army boots and a large hunting knife hanging from her belt. She forces out a bark-like laugh and tells me what I have just realized: "We all have a twin. And you're mine. How convenient is that?"

"Convenient for you and Todd, maybe. But a very unpleasant surprise for me. It must have pained you to put on all that makeup to make yourself look so old, Connie."

She snorts, and places a hand on Todd's shoulders, her fingers tightening in a subtle squeeze. I must admit to myself that it irks me to see this display of intimacy, but I'll be damned if I show them that.

"Not really," she says. "We had a mission. And now that it's accomplished, no need for the disguise. Oh, and Bree? My name isn't Connie." She scrutinizes me from a grave-like depth with the sort of stare that could make even the strong-hearted quake. "And exactly what do you think you're doing here?"

"What do you think? I've come to get my son."

Connie and Todd exchanged a quick glance. She gives Todd's shoulder another squeeze, less subtle this time. "You don't have a son," she tells me.

Evidently, that's all either of them have to say to me right now. Todd rises, then plants his hand on the small of Connie's back as they cross to the door. I stare at them. How could I have been so blind, so much in denial? Connie and Todd are not just comrades in an insane cause that has engulfed my son. They're lovers.

Just before she leaves the room, the black-haired woman I know only as Connie pauses, throwing me a parting look that says, "Gotcha."

CHAPTER 46

After a few minutes pass, I try the door, which, as I knew it would be, is bolted. Then I eye the little window and realize why it's set so high up. I'm in a basement, and the window is at ground level. I drag over the chair and climb up. That's when I see that the window is wire reinforced. No breaking out this way—even if I were small enough to use it as a means of escape. Looking out, I can see only a packed patch of dirt overgrown with weeds, but I am able to hear truck motors revving, idling, passing by. I also hear boots clumping back and forth. Men yell what sound like orders. There's laughter.

The clock in my head is ticking, and it's getting louder with each passing minute. Whatever my fate, it's likely to be grim. Although, for some odd reason, Todd doesn't want me tied up. Maybe he feels sorry for me. Or maybe it's something else. His mind is impenetrable to me. But he must have a reason.

I take a deep breath. Try to focus. The room smells stale and musty. There are water stains on the ceiling. There's a second door, but it has no handle, and the hole where the handle would have been is plugged with wood putty. I put my ear against the door and listen to silence.

My attention again is directed to the flag. What does it mean? Eerily, the emblem feels as if it has been part of my life. But how is that possible?

I spend the next twenty minutes pacing the room with an anger that has no other outlet and which is growing too large for the space that contains it: six steps from the mattress to the wall, six steps from the wall to the door. My body aches to hold my baby. I feel like I'm so close to him. So close. And yet, I'm locked in this room with no means of escape.

I bash my palm against the wall to release the tension building up in my chest. Finally, with a sinking heart, I lean against the door, slide to the floor, and rest my head against it. The adrenaline spike has subsided, leaving me exhausted and hopeless. I can see that the life I constructed for myself over the last year is based not just on Todd's deception, but also on my own self-serving needs. Now the choices I made are paying off with horrifying consequences.

I'm lost in a downward spiral of guilt and self-recrimination, when I think I hear something. No. Couldn't have been. I give myself a mental shake. Get a grip.

But then I hear it again. My name, in a whisper. "Bree?"

And again. Slightly louder. Then, "Bree, put your ear to the crack at the bottom of the door." It's a male voice coming from the door to nowhere.

I drop to the floor and whisper to the infinitesimal space beneath the door: "Who is that?"

"Johnny."

"Johnny?" My eyes widen in disbelief. "What are you doing here?"

"They're holding me hostage."

I flash on my promise to Della to save her husband. "How did you know it's me?"

"I saw them carry you in."

"Where are we? What's going on?"

Before he can respond, I hear a crash and the thud of flesh smacking the floor — then a door slams.

"Johnny?" I whisper. "Johnny? Are you okay?"

There is a beat of silence. Suddenly, the door to my cell is thrust open and Todd strides in, his face unreadable.

"Why are you holding Johnny prisoner?" I demand.

He towers over me, the tendons in his neck protruding like columns of anger. "Sit." He points at the chair.

He scrapes the second chair against the cement floor, dragging it so close that, when he drops into it, I feel his breath on my face. "You asked what happened. I'm here to tell you."

The air leaves the room. "Where's Noah? Is he okay?"

"Yes."

"Can I see him?"

Without warning, Todd strikes me across the face so hard I fall off the chair.

"Get up."

I rise to my knees. There's a loud ringing in my ears, as push myself up.

"Why did you hit me?" I yell.

"Shut up," he snaps, "And sit."

But I don't. I stand staring at him, and the tension sparks electricity between us.

Finally, he rises himself, and, placing a heavy hand on my shoulder, pushing me down.

"Ask anything but whether you can see my son."

As I rub my throbbing cheek, I remind myself that this man is unstable. Making an effort to keep my voice level, I say, "Okay. What happened?"

Todd closes his eyes, takes a deep breath, and begins talking.

"You see, Bree, women want to be loved and have a family. You were easy prey."

My teeth clench. "You mean this has been all premeditated? You … you … bastard!"

He raises his hand as if to strike me again. I jump up and back away, but he's fast. Before I can scream, he cups his hand over my mouth and shoves me against the wall. The impact leaves me dazed.

"I'm going to teach you that every action carries consequences," he says. "Now sit down and behave in a civil manner and ask your questions with respect. I will not tolerate this kind of behavior from any woman, especially you."

I settle back in my chair.

"You may continue asking questions. This is the only chance you'll get to do that."

"Why take the trouble to clean the house? Why not just grab the baby and leave? Why not kill me?"

He studies my face for a moment.

"Too messy."

The tension in the room presses against the walls. "Let me see if I've got it right. You wanted to have a baby with me because of my genes, knowing all the while you'd take Noah away from me. But how could you know that I would get pregnant?"

"I didn't. It was a short-term gamble."

Again, I'm reminded of how clueless I've have been. It just so happened that I got pregnant immediately. The thought leaves a bitter taste in my mouth. My need to have a baby outweighed my caution. I would have done anything to have a baby, recreate the family I lost, the baby my mother lost. Maybe I'm getting what I deserve. In the end, Todd—or whatever his name is—crept out in the middle of the night, leaving me to ache and wonder. But it's not about me, now. It's about an innocent little boy who didn't ask for this.

"Noah needs me. I'm his mother. Are you going to deny that?"

"He has a mother."

A picture pops into my brain that punches me in the gut. "Would that, by any chance, be Connie?"

"Noah is a strong child. With the proper training—which the woman you call, Connie can give him—he will grow to be a remarkable man. I will make sure of that. It's up to you whether you want to be part of his future."

This is an invitation to something I'm not ready to accept. "I don't understand."

"Life is full of trade-offs."

"What do you want me to trade?"

There's the ghost of a smirk on his lips. "Your compliance, for the chance to raise our son together. If you choose correctly, we will have power over the country. You can be a part of that."

I shake my head. "I don't want to be part of your life. Or, should I say, your 'lives.' With no records, no fingerprints, I imagine it's safe to assume that you operate under several different identities?"

A deep breath fills his chest, widening his already broad shoulders. "Yes. Connie and I have been successful at staying under the radar—we are smart, we are invisible."

He brags about his exploits, about using different disguises every time he left our house—which explains why no one in Becket recognized the sketches—but all I want to think about is Noah, about wrapping my arms around him and inhaling his baby scent. However, I force myself to listen to Todd. I do, after all, want to understand what brought me to this point.

When finishes, I shift in my chair and, staring him right in the eye, say, "You're brilliant, huh? Well, that's not how I see it. You used me to carry your baby and conspired with a fake doctor to have me bedridden, so no one would see me pregnant. You made sure to leave nothing behind but the safe—which you filled with incriminating documents." I'm shaking, now, unable to control the anger in my words. The betrayal. The knowledge that he targeted me and used me from the start. "And it didn't hurt that Connie—or whatever her name is—was mistaken for me and rented the house."

"Whatever your perception, I always execute my plans perfectly," Todd says, rubbing his hands together. "I don't exist. I was born at home by a loyalist doctor, and my birth was never registered. The same is true for my son."

I shake my head again. I'm finding it hard to digest. But I have more questions. Everything about the compound is shrouded in rumor, mystery, and fear. "What is this place? It looks like an army barracks."

"We're at the center of a flourishing organization. We strive to form social hierarchies that place whites at the top. We're shaping young minds. In turn, these children will grow up to shape the country."

He rubs his hands together as if he'd just won a lottery.

The image of the children on the flash drive, marching like soldiers under the watchful eyes of men with rifles slung over their shoulders, spins through my mind. A vision of my little boy doing the same thing causes me to shudder.

Todd's words continue to slink through the room like a foul vapor. "We must protect the existence of our people and a future for white children—don't you see that?"

Is this guy nuts? I shift in my chair, unsure of how to react. I think about the Ku Klux Klan—of robed men marching, carrying torches. But it's not like that anymore. On television recently, the white supremacists I saw marching were white, certainly. But they were, for the most part, young men dressed conservatively in polos and crisp khakis—just ordinary-looking people carrying Confederate flags, spewing their brand of hatred. Gone were the white robes. They were out in the open.

"This is pure discrimination."

"On the contrary. All we want is to keep our majority in a majority-white country, hold on to our political and economic control, and have our culture maintained. The way things have been going, our white pride was being threatened. And we can't have that. Not anymore."

I hear the roar of a truck and a honk. There are men shouting.

I bring my focus back to Todd. "But you're taking an extreme position, promoting racial violence, discrimination, and antisemitism."

I suck in short breaths to fight the pressure building in my chest. "How far are you willing to push your brand of belief? And what about the innocent children, who are physically vulnerable and easily intimidated and who don't have a say in all of this?"

He glares at me. "Enough with your simplistic thinking."

I wipe away the spray of saliva he spat with his words.

"On the contrary," he says, his voice now a demonic whisper, "these children are soldiers, and they're are treated well. Grown and fully trained, we utilize them to further our message.

"You see, what's ruining the country is multiculturalism, a massive influx of non-whites across our borders. We are in danger of extinction, given the low birth rates among whites. We need intelligent white women like you to help us propagate a pure race."

I make a horrifying parallel. Like Todd and his cronies, Hitler believed that the future of Nazi Germany was its children. His youth was indoctrinated in a depraved ideology based on physical fitness and military training, meant to create race-conscious, compliant, self-sacrificing Germans, willing to die for Führer and Fatherland.

I know I can't change Todd's mind, and what I have to say will not put a dent in his twisted thinking. But I'm so angry about the injustice being perpetrated against these vulnerable kids that I have to say something.

"What gives you the right to infect young children's minds with such twisted ideology of Nazism?"

"We all have agendas," Todd says with a shrug. "Young white men now believe that they have no future. These children will be strong enough to unite a disjointed country, and my son will be at the helm."

Again, images of white men parading with guns, chanting Nazi slogans, and carrying tiki torches flashes in my head. The room is closing in on me, and I find it hard to breathe. I eye the door.

But Todd isn't finished yet. "Besides, who are you to judge me?" He shakes his head, disapproval apparent in the set of his mouth. "I experienced firsthand what can happen to good white men when manufacturing and unions have dismantled the middle class. My parents lost their factory job and their home and ended committing suicide because of that. And you? You had a privileged life. Your father was a good man. He should have opened your eyes."

"My father? How …?"

"We are being discriminated against," he says, punching his fist in the air. "A white person who prefers European culture, who prefers to be around white people? He is called a Nazi. Where is the justice in that?"

His words twist around me to fit an argument.

The dark vision Todd is painting is interrupted, when, outside, several men start shouting. There are raised voices in the corridor, too. Todd's phone pings. He brings it to his ear and listens. His face goes red.

"Did you get him?" he asks, running his hand through his hair.

He listens for another second, his forehead creasing. "Damn it. Damn you. What are you guys doing out there, sleeping?"

He listens some more.

"Be right there," he says, and heads for the door.

"Wait!" I call after him. "I want to see Noah."

He turns and curls his lip. "Noah? No. My son's proper name is R. E. Lee. My son is destined to bring back the glory days of the Confederate Army."

Just before exiting the room, he turns to face me. "And if I were you, I'd seriously consider joining us."

With that, he steps through the door and slams it behind him, leaving me to consider what sounded very much like a threat.

Another thought is looming over me. Todd made it sound as if he knew my father.

CHAPTER 47

Todd's words play over and over in my head—until the door blows open and Connie stalks in, a black cap pulled low, a warrior in her fatigues, another woman tagging behind her. I eye the rope the second woman's holding, then glance at her face. My heart leaps.

"Viola? What are you doing here?"

The waitress gives a short laugh. "I live here. This is my home." She looks to Connie, who surveys me with an expression of unconcealed disgust.

"Tie her up," Connie orders Viola. "Then leave."

Heart banging, I swipe at the sudden cold sweat on my forehead.

"Sit down," Viola orders, eyes flicking between Connie and me. "And give me your hands."

"Viola, why are you doing this?" Though I barely know her, it feels like a betrayal.

"Shut up." Her stare is as glassy as when she's served me at the diner. Is that why she's doing this? For the fix? "I'm not here to chitchat. You were too stupid to see what was in front of you. You never suspected me. Did you? You spilled your guts everywhere you went. The whole town kept an eye on you."

"The whole town is in on it?" New pieces of the puzzle tumble into place. I'm beginning to sense the shape of an answer to the question that arose after Viola told me about the drugs flooding Handrock: How do the largely underemployed townspeople afford their habit? Are they paid by Todd?

"That's enough, Viola." Connie's voice rings out in a warning.

"Give me your hands," Viola demands.

I do the one thing I can think of that might help me free myself later. I extend my hands crossed at the wrists and rotated about forty-five degrees. Then, when I straighten my wrists, I'll be able to loosen the rope and free my hands.

"Leave us," Connie says, once Viola finishes tying the knot.

Viola turns and leaves, but not without a nervous glance back.

I turn to Connie. "What does Viola mean, the whole town kept an eye on me?"

"Most of the town's residents are united in defiance of the federal government. Simple as that."

Before I'm able to process that, Connie pushes away from the wall and steps closer to face me, so close I can smell the faint tang of perspiration rising from her. "All this time you were trying to figure out what happened to the baby, and all this time you didn't have a clue."

My throat tightens. "*My* baby. His name is Noah."

"You think?" She curls her lip. "I think you mean R. E. Lee. And, by the way, he isn't yours. You'll never get him back. You know that, right?" Her expression is hard as lava rock. I never looked into her eyes before—they were always hidden by huge glasses. But now I see there's no life in them—they are eerie, soulless orbs.

"I know no such thing," I say, bravely—as if my words can determine the future of my child's life. "He doesn't belong to you." But the bluntness of her words has shaken me, summing up fears that have festered in the recesses of my mind.

Slowly, she draws her knife from its sheath and runs a finger along the blade. "In fact," she says, "the baby does belong to me now. I'm his mother. I know how to raise him properly. I will teach him how to lead a social movement grounded in the politics of respectability and followed by the elites—and there's nothing you can do about that."

The room begins to spin. The anxiety that engulfs me is as bad as any I've ever experienced. Noah cannot grow up calling another woman "mother" and giving the Hitler salute. I close my eyes, willing the nausea to pass.

"You know what they call me?" she asks.

I open my eyes and lift my shoulders.

"The She Devil. You know why?" She doesn't wait for an answer. "Because I have an amazing influence on men. I get what I want."

She's taken another step forward and now stands over me, tapping the knife on her palm. "But you? I don't know what he ever saw in you. I don't know why he's keeping you alive. I told him to kill you, but he refuses. I'm not used to being denied. And that's something you're going to have to pay for."

Todd? Is that what this is about? I swallow the bile climbing up my throat. "I'm not in competition with you," I say. "You can have that loser all to yourself."

Like a dog poised to attack, she bares her teeth and leans in menacingly. I press myself back until the unyielding chair rungs dig into my spine. "I don't like your attitude," she growls.

"And I don't like yours," I say through clenched jaws.

I'm caught off guard when she grabs my hair and yanks my head back, holding the knife blade to my throat. The tip pierces my skin. I flinch. "You are lucky," she hisses, "that he wants to keep you alive. If you know what's good for you, you will keep yourself away from him at all costs. He belongs to me."

The blade is sharp. I hold my breath, sweat drips from my armpits, and I feel a trickle of blood tracing my throat. I brace for another jab. Instead, she removes the knife and licks at a smear of my blood with her long, pointy tongue.

Hot pain pulses from the wound. I do my best to remain motionless so as not to set the woman off again. Suddenly, I hear footsteps, heavy-set, halt at the door. Connie pulls away from me and throws a glance toward the sound. She seems to breathe a sigh of relief when the footsteps recommence, and whoever it was continued down the corridor.

Since the distraction appears to have broken her concentration, I take a chance to ask a question that's puzzled me. "Who was Dr. Bryson? Was he really a doctor?"

Her brows knit. "Dr. Bryson? Oh ..." She snaps her fingers. "Well, he is in a way. At any rate, he agreed to play a role for us. He's, let's just say, 'sympathetic' to our cause."

I remember how the man I knew as Dr. Bryson had been so tense and how disapproving the deep creases at the corners of his mouth made him look. "I tried to find him. I went to his office, but someone else is occupying it. They said they never heard of him."

"We paid them royally to use their office and to keep quiet. You have no idea what money can buy."

"You went to all that trouble just for me to have a baby?"

"Todd had a special reason to want you to bear a child for us. R. E. Lee however, is not the only child we have. In Handrock alone, many people are in financial straits but still support our cause. And they're happy to have us educate and house their children. We pay them well, supply them with drugs, and keep the town solvent."

"Then why did Todd need to have a baby with me?"

A gleam appears in the graveyard of her eyes. "You really don't know, do you? Todd forbade me from telling you. He wants to tell you himself."

"What? What does he want to tell me?" I demand.

She flips her thick black hair over her shoulder and smirks. "No point of keeping you in suspense — although your father kept you and your family in the dark. I don't know why he did that, but I think it's time you learned the truth."

"You knew my father?"

"I knew of him. He was a great man. Very charismatic."

Eyes fixed on her in anticipation, I remind myself to breathe.

"Your family's dark secret." She runs her finger along the length of the blade, then sucks the tiny bead of blood that wells up from the paper-thin slice in her skin. "Your father was a revered leader when it came to developing nationalism in the minds of young, white America. He organized events and opened several chapters, centers where young men could receive leadership training. His dream was to create a white ethno-empire stretching across North America and Europe."

My face is in flames. What is she talking about? "You're lying," I spit out. My father was a brilliant man, yes, but he used his brain to solve complex scientific problems, not to impose violent social order.

She laughs. "You should see your face. And Todd? Well ... Todd was your father's star student."

If I ever thought this woman was insane, she's just confirmed it. But before I can say what I think, the corridor erupts with the sound of pounding feet, while outside, I see legs rushing past the little window and hear people shouting.

There's a sharp rap at the door. Connie marches over and opens it just enough that I get a glimpse of a young man with a shaved head. They keep their voices low, so I can't make out what they're saying, but from their forceful tone, it's clear they're arguing.

Keeping my eye on Connie, who still has her back to me, I surreptitiously twist my wrists. As if sensing something going on behind her, the woman spins and glares at me. I freeze—and only let out my breath when she turns back to the man at the door.

Unsettled by what seems to be her sixth sense, I find I'm shaking so much I can hardly make my fingers obey, but, after several tries, my hands are free. Just in time. She shuts the door on the skinhead. Having the element of surprise on my side, I leap to my feet as she turns towards me.

Her features morph from disdain to shock to anger. We stare at each other in a silence, brewing with tension. Time slows.

Raising her knife without taking her gaze from me, she shifts, so she's favoring her shorter leg. Then she smiles, but her black eyes are hard. "You don't want to do something stupid, do you? You have no chance against this," she says, flicking the knife, so it glints.

"You think? Haven't you heard about mothers who single-handedly lift cars off their trapped children? I'm just as desperate as those mothers. I will not let you have my son."

Her nostrils flare and her upper lip curls. "You may be a desperate mother, but I'm an armed soldier."

I goad her. "I'll take my chances," I say.

Her face darkens and she lunges at me, her knife slicing the air. I grab my chair and hold it before me like a gladiator would a shield, and the blade clangs harmlessly on the edge of its metal seat.

Connie stumbles then regain her footing and charges again. I focus my anger at her like a weapon and, stepping forward, swing the chair, connecting with her knife arm, but she has a death grip on her weapon.

"Bitch." Spittle flies from her lips. She rushes me, kicking at the chair, which crashes to the ground, and thrusts the knife directly at my chest. Before it connects, I manage step to the side, grab her wrist, and sink my teeth into her arm. She yelps and the knife clatters to the floor.

Giving her no time to think, I kick the knife out of reach, and, with the bitter taste of her blood in my mouth, grab the chair and smash it against her back as she dives for her weapon. She grunts, stumbles, and, recovering, whirls to face me. Feral eyes shooting waves of malice, she strikes — her right hand connects, and my head rocks back. Sheer hatred pumps through me, as blood spills from my nose, warm and salty.

Powered by a surge of adrenaline like I've never felt before, I haul the chair into the air and crack her in the face with one of its legs. She howls, and her hand shoots to cover her eye as she backs away, banging into the wall. I advance on her and swing the chair again, connecting hard with her shoulder, toppling her to her knees.

Panting, I hold the chair high and say, "Stay still, or I'll smash your head in."

At that, Connie raises her gaze and fixes me with a furious, one-eyed glare, hand still protecting her injured eye. "Go to hell," she spits out and — like lightning — grabs for my leg and yanks with such force that I tip over, bringing the chair down with me. Scrambling desperately, I manage to get to the knife and plunge it into her shoulder. Blood blooms from the wound, and she slumps with a groan. I push myself off the ground and aim a kick at her head, then watch as her good eye rolls back, and she loses consciousness.

Wasting no time, I paw through her pockets and find a keyring with four keys. Clutching the keys, I pause. How to make my escape? Surely, if I step outside this room, I'll be nabbed — and who knows what they'll do to me, now.

I look at Connie's motionless body. She's so like me in appearance. It's as if I'm looking at myself lying there in a bloody heap.

And that's when the idea hits me.

CHAPTER 48

Poised at the door, wearing Connie's clothes, armed with Connie's knife, I stand, heart pounding, and listen to the silence in the corridor. I wonder what all the commotion was about earlier — but whatever it was, it seems to have quieted down.

Connie's crumpled on the floor, clad only in bra and panties, my clothes piled beside her. I staunched her knife wound with my t-shirt — don't want her death on my conscience — but she's definitely out cold.

Tugging her black cap low on my forehead, I ease through the door, and, choosing the right key on the first try, I lock it behind me. Turning right, I find the door to the room where Johnny's being held. Alert for anyone on the move, I try the other keys on the ring. The third one produces a click and unlocks the door.

In Johnny's cell, a heaviness lingers in the air, along with the smell of sweat and urine. The room is mostly a sealed cube — no window, like in my cell, but a similar bare, dangling bulb lights the space. And the same familiar flag with a Celtic cross hangs on one of the walls. Johnny is sprawled on a mattress, ankles bound. I drop to my knees. His face is swollen and bruised, the blood congeals at his temple.

"Johnny," I whisper. "It's me, Bree. Are you okay?"

He opens his swollen eyes slowly. He's breathing hard, and his face twists. "I've been better." His voice is hoarse and soft as if talking is an effort. He motions me with his head to come closer. "You need to get out of here."

"What happened to you? Why are they holding you here?"

"They're trying to convince me to talk the others into joining."

"Joining what?"

"Their movement. And they're holding Jake over my head. If I don't help them, they'll take our son. Della and I were planning to get away. But they got to me first."

"Why you?"

"I've got some sway in the community." He tries to sit, grimaces, and slumps back down. "They want to own the entire town, but there're still a few hold-outs. And they think I can make 'em change their minds."

I consider this for a minute. It makes sense. Johnny's a good man. That much is clear. I pull out Connie's knife and cut the plastic tie that binds his ankles. He sits up with a grunt. "Do you know where they're holding Noah?" I whisper.

He nods. "In a house. Not far from here."

It's clear he's hurting—that it even hurts to talk. But I have to know.

"Where is the house?"

Slowly, he gives me directions, then adds, "Be careful. There are guards everywhere."

You're not telling me anything I don't know, I think. But all I say is, "Can you walk?" I point at his right leg, swollen to nearly twice its size.

"It's broken. You go ahead without me. I don't want to slow you down."

"I'm not leaving you behind. I promised Della I'd bring you back to her if I possibly could."

Johnny's face brightens at the mention of Della's name. He nods. "Okay."

"Here, give me your hands." I brace myself and pull him up as gently as I can.

He lets out a grunt and wobbles, fixing his eyes on me in a mute appeal for patience.

"Now," I whisper, "let's go find my son—and get you home to yours."

CHAPTER 49

With Johnny leaning heavily on my shoulder, we limp slowly down the hallway. Our luck holds. We see no one in the corridor or down any of its branches. More importantly, no one sees us. When we reach what looks to be an exterior door, I turn one of Connie's two remaining keys in the lock. It works. Cautiously, I turn the handle and nudge the door open a crack—to find that night has fallen.

Pushing the door open another inch, I glance right, then left. Difficult to see anything other than the distant flashlight beams that slice the dark. I imagine guards patrolling in pairs, blank-faced, machine guns at the ready.

I step out ahead of Johnny, who follows closely, still leaning on me. Despite a soft rain, the odor of gas and oil drifts towards us. We haven't gone ten feet when we're startled by an engine revving. A black Humvee lurches forward, swerving to a halt in front of us. Panicked, we turn and begin to scramble back the way we came.

But then a familiar voice calls out, "Wait. It's me. Damon." The passenger door flies open. "Hurry. Get in."

I help Johnny into the back, then throw myself up front beside Damon. "Johnny knows where Noah is," I say, breathlessly.

"Yeah," Johnny says. "I know the compound backward and forward. Been coming here for years to fix their trucks."

Damon glances over his shoulder. "Where do I go?"

"Make a left and follow the dirt road," Johnny says.

I turn to Damon. "Boy, am I happy to see you. How did you find me?"

Damon snorts. "Next time you're on the run, don't show your ID when you buy a pay-as-you-go sim."

"But how did you get past the guards?"

Damon grips the steering wheel and leans forward, peering at the road. "Let's just say two unconscious guards are having a nice nap in the woods." I can hear the smile in his voice.

"Won't somebody be looking for them?"

"Yup." Damon glances at his watch. "In thirty minutes, the guards change shifts."

Suddenly, headlights wash over us. "Get down," I tell Johnny, and pull Connie's cap lower on my forehead as the vehicle rolls next to the Humvee on my side. I roll down my window and give the driver a Nazi salute, hoping this is their customary greeting. Guess so. The driver returns the chilling salute and smiles at me, before driving away, tires rumbling on the washed-out dirt road.

"I suggest you turn off the headlights," Johnny tells Damon, drawing himself back upright.

Continuing on with only a pale moon to show us the way, Damon follows Johnny's directions, until a weathered-looking farm house comes into view. It sits at the end of a long drive, but there's no car out front. And except for a faint glow from the second floor, the house is dark. Deep shadows blend into the dense wood behind the building, and the ever-present barbed wire surrounds it. I shiver. To the left, I see an old, swaybacked barn. To the right and across the dirt road are several rusted trailers.

Damon passes the farmhouse, turns down another dirt road, and a hundred yards later, comes to a stop behind the house.

"You stay in the vehicle," Damon tells us. "I'll go inside and check it out."

"No, you don't. Noah is my son. I'm going with you."

"Damon's right," Johnny whispers. "Stay here. You don't know who's in there."

I put my hand on the handle and shove the door open. "No. I'm going with him." I look back at Johnny. His head is slumped against the seat, and his eyes are closed.

"Are you okay?"

"Don't worry about me," he says without opening his eyes. "I'll be fine. Just be careful."

I slip out of the Humvee and stand beside Damon.

"Wait," he says and hands me a compact flashlight. "That thing is so high-powered the intensity of the light can blind an attacker." He runs his finger over the razor-sharp, crenelated edge that surrounds the lens. "And this can cause serious damage, too."

I shove the flashlight into my left-hand pocket.

"Let's go," Damon says. "Stay close."

As we tread quietly toward the house, all my senses laser in on the single, soft light glowing from an upstairs window. Noah is in there. But we cover just a few yards when I suddenly feel something is off. I sense movement, though I haven't heard a thing. I reach into my right pocket. The cold steel of Connie's knife strengthens my resolve.

Then, "There you go, getting into trouble, again," a voice from behind me says.

I know who it is immediately. I spin, and I draw out the knife, ready to defend myself. No one is going to get between my baby and me.

Especially not George.

The moonlight is just bright enough to reveal that the man's usually immaculate clothes are a mess—his jacket is torn, and his trousers are crusted with mud.

"Bree, careful," Damon hisses.

Too late. George grabs me and yanks me backward, and the knife drops from my hand. Damon reaches for his gun, but George has anchored me against his body, his left arm wrapped around my neck, his right hand aiming his gun at my head. George's gun has a silencer.

Instinctively, I shove my chin into the crook of his choking arm and raise my shoulders to relieve the pressure. At the same time, I try to pull his arm away from my throat. Useless. His wiry strength makes his grip impossible to break.

"Toss me your gun," George tells Damon. "And don't think I won't shoot her if you don't." His voice is a low rasp, and the alcohol on his breath almost makes me gag.

Damon hesitates. "Hey, buddy. There's no need for violence."

"I won't tell you again."

Instead, Damon launches his gun deeps into the woods with the strength of a big-league pitcher. Instantly, George swivels his gun toward Damon and pulls the trigger. The force of the impact drops Damon to his knees. Blood drips from the hand he holds over the bullet entry at his shoulder. George shoots again. This time, Damon falls flat—and stays there.

A murderous rage fills my head. Blindly, I bury my teeth into George's bared forearm. He cries out, and his grip loosens. I pull away. Then, losing my balance, I crash to the ground.

George makes for me, eyes bulging, but I grab his boot, and he falls. I manage to scramble to my feet, just as he makes it up to all fours, and I slam Connie's steel-tipped boot into his ribs. He rolls away with a moan, but then rolls back and jerks at my foot, toppling me again.

Before I can regain my equilibrium, he grabs me by the throat and squeezes, choking me. My fingers claw his face, ripping, tearing, but he presses harder. Panic sets in as I struggle for air. *I'm going to die,* I think, lungs beginning to burn. Then I remember Noah, only a stone's throw away, and a rush of adrenaline floods me, giving me the strength I need. Staring into George's crazed eyes, I hook my fingers into his eye sockets, digging in as hard as I can.

He shouts and releases his hold on my throat. I roll away, scramble to my knees, and then convulse, pain searing through my throat as I cough the air back into my lungs.

"You stupid bitch!" he yells. The smell of blood hits my nostrils, as he slams into me, hammering me face-down into the ground. My breath blows out in a whoosh. Struggling, I manage to push him off of me, leap to my feet, and kick the gun from his hand. The weapon slides into the shadows, out of sight.

But George doesn't move.

What? For a moment, I'm confused. And then I understand.

There's a knife sticking out of his back. Connie's knife. And Johnny is leaning against the Humvee, panting.

Taking a deep breath, Johnny nods at Damon, who is on the ground, unmoving. Inching closer, I kneel beside him and lay a hand on his chest, hoping against hope. Then I feel it. The motion is slight. His breathing is shallow. But he's alive.

Johnny drops to his knees beside George, yanks the knife out of his back, wipes the blood on his leg pant, and hands it to me. "You'll need this," he says. Then nods to the dark edge of the woods, which have swallowed both Damon's and George's guns. "Too bad you guys got rid of the guns. Might have come in handy, right about now."

I shrug. I have a knife and a bad-ass, super-powered flashlight. And that's going to have to do.

•   •   •

Cautiously, I slip through the back yard, passing a wooden table set on the lawn, with two wrought iron chairs flanking it. When I get to the house, I duck behind a shrub and peer out. Satisfied no one is around, I dash toward the back door, cup my hands on the window set in the door, and peer in. The room is in shadows. A large sofa faces a wall-mounted television. I try the door. Locked. Maybe the last of Connie's keys will unlock it. I search my pockets. Dammit. The keys aren't there. They must have fallen out in my struggle with George.

Nothing for it but to find another way in. As I circle the house, I see a half-open window. It's screened, and its shade is pulled all the way down—but it's just a bit too high for me to see inside. Then I remember the chairs. I turn to retrieve one from the lawn when a powerful beam of light dances across the side of the house. Seized with panic, I fall to the ground and roll behind a small bush. I press myself closer to the ground, not moving. Then I see the source of the light: two guards, not a hundred feet from where I lie. With the slightest turn of their heads, they'll see me. But their heads don't turn—and they move on.

I wonder how long I have before I'm discovered.

I mop the sweat from my forehead, exhale the breath I didn't realize I was holding, and go grab one of the chairs.

Back at the half-open window, I position the chair quietly and, with a glance around me, climb onto it, which puts me high enough that I can easily slice a large X on the screen with Connie's knife. A light push on the shade reveals a small, empty bathroom. I pull myself up and wriggle through the window. It's a tight fit, but I'm able to shimmy my way in. I twist around and lower myself quietly until I'm standing on the tile floor, tightly holding the knife.

While I wait, letting my eyes acclimate to the deeper dark of the house, I catch the scent of onions and garlic. My stomach rumbles. When was the last time I ate? Then I notice something else: the faint odor of antiseptic and baby powder in the air — and I have to shove my fist in my mouth to keep from crying out.

I force myself to relax. Finally, taking a chance that no one is on the other side of the door, I slip through into a hallway. Creeping down the corridor, I ease past a small pantry and pause near the entrance to the kitchen. Then, I move through the living room and down a short corridor that leads to the front of the house.

As if on cue, a baby's desperate cry echoes through the house. Sweat rushes from my armpits. Noah. He's upstairs. His sobs tear through my nerves like a razor. I'm so close. So close.

Using the weak moonlight that shines through the windows to guide me, I tiptoe upstairs, keeping my weight off the potentially squeaky centers of the treads. My legs tremble. My palm, wrapped around the banister for support, is damp.

At the top, I find a corridor, which is pitch dark, except for the soft light filtering from under a door at the end of the hallway. I have to pass two other rooms on my right to reach it.

Keep breathing. Keep steady, I tell myself.

The door to the first room is open. I lean forward and see a queen-sized bed, night stands, an armoire. A nightgown is neatly folded at the foot of the bed. I continue down the hall to the second room. Its door is only slightly ajar. I reach out and ease it open. The room is still and quiet. Nobody here, either.

I stare at the door at the end of the hall. The baby is whimpering now. I step forward, then halt at a creak followed by a tiny shift in the atmosphere. I stiffen, breath caught in my throat, and wait, staring into the darkness.

Then the door at the end of the hall opens and reveals a woman silhouetted against the light behind her. She's no more than a sketch in the gloom. Still, I can make out her long, unruly hair. She grips the doorknob in one hand, doorframe in the other. As my eyes adjust, I see she's wearing a robe, loosely knotted.

"Who ... Who are you?" The panic in her voice is visceral. And familiar.

"Surprise," I say. "You know who I am."

Her hand flies to her chest. "You're in deep trouble."

When the baby's whimper escalates into cries, I find myself unable to breathe, as if my ribs are in a vice. "Move away from the door, Viola." My words come out in a growl.

She shakes her head. "I can't do that."

"What's going on?" Another figure steps up behind her—another familiar voice. Looming in the half-dark, he seems larger than life, his bare chest as broad as I remember.

I draw myself to my full height, my back armor straight. "I've come to get Noah."

"What ...? How did you escape?"

"Get out of my way. I'm here for my son."

Todd whispers something to Viola. She nods. I train my eyes on her, but she hasn't budged yet. Quickly, I realize I'm not going to be able to get to either of them with the knife from where I stand—the blade is suddenly a liability. I need the long beam of the flashlight to disable them from this distance. Praying it's as blinding as Damon said, I drop the knife into one pocket and slip the flashlight out of the other.

I should be afraid. But I'm not. I'm ready.

Propping his shoulder against the doorframe, Todd tries to take control of the situation—with the same, infuriatingly calm voice that I know all too well. "Now, now, Bree. Take it easy. Don't be foolish. I have big plans for us."

There it is that offer again. But I'm not his plaything anymore. He can't twist this situation into what he wants me to think it means. I'm here for one thing and one thing only.

My fingers tighten around the flashlight. I'm calculating my chances of reaching Todd before he can regain his eyesight, once I blind him with its bright glare. The distance between us is about ten feet. Close enough.

Suddenly, Viola ducks back into the bedroom, and at the same moment, Todd rushes at me. With that, the desire for vengeance that has been a low flame inside me explodes into an inferno.

I sidestep his bulk, pull out the flashlight, and blast the blue-white light directly into his eyes. When he throws up his hands to protect them, I lunge and drive the toothed bezel into his forearms, and then into his cheek. I continue slicing the bezel into his face, his temple, his ear. As his blood gushes, I deliver a hard kick to his groin, which doubles him over with a howl, leaving the crown of his head a perfect target for the circle of steel teeth, which I smash into his skull with all the adrenaline-boosted strength I can muster.

When he falls to the floor, blood seeping from his wounds, I surge into the baby's room, where Noah is howling. But before I can register what's happening, an arm shoots out and knocks me off my feet.

Cell phone in hand, Viola is ready to dial. In one motion, I leap up and launch the flashlight at her forehead. She screams and reaches for her head, eyes bulging. A dark red stain appears between her fingers and trickles down to her pink robe. Giving her no chance to recover, I dive for the flashlight at her feet, and, lifting it, send a punch into her stomach with all my weight behind it. She collapses with a grunt, and I deliver a sharp kick to her ribs. She doesn't budge.

I dash toward the crib and scoop Noah up. Holding his soft little body, I chant, "Shhh ... my sweet darling, I'm taking you home." Slowly, his sobs stop, and our eyes lock. Is it too much to think he recognizes me?

As my heartbeat slows, I let my gaze travel over his face, relishing all the details I never allowed myself to forget: the silky, hair, his perfectly shaped head, his father's large, golden eyes. Then I peek at the heart-shaped birthmark on his thigh. Whether he recognizes me or not, this is my son.

Holding Noah tight, I step over Todd's body and make my way down to the kitchen, where I notice two small magnets on the fridge. One has an image of Jesus and the other, the words, *White Power*. I can't let my sudden rage distract me. Focusing, I kiss my son's head as

I yank drawers open. He makes little gurgling noises as if he knows he's safe in his mother's arms.

Finally, the drawer closest to the refrigerator yields what I'm looking for: a lighter.

Grabbing a pile of newspapers from the counter, I head into the living room. One-handed, I crumple the paper and tuck pieces under the curtains and the sofa. Then I flick the lighter, watch the newspaper catch, and flee with my son in my arms.

Heart pounding, I run toward the Humvee. Despite the bouncing, Noah is tranquil. Mother and son are fused with a recognition driven by instinct. Glancing over my shoulder, I see an orange glow radiating from the house. Then there's mayhem, shouting. Guards converge on the house: more shouting, and distant sirens wailing their way closer.

When I reach the vehicle, I hear Johnny shout, "Hurry! We don't have much time."

I yank the back door open, hand my son to Johnny. Next to him, Damon slumps, eyes closed. "How is he?"

"Still breathing. I made a tourniquet for his thigh and plugged the hole in his shoulder. But we've gotta hurry."

"I have to do something first." It's not easy to in the dark, but I manage to disconnect the compressor relay located near the left front lower wheel well that's attached to the chassis harness—which will prevent the airbag from going off on impact.

"Bree, get in the car. We've got to go!"

I leap into the driver's seat, pull a tight U-turn, and head back the way we came, pulling off the road twice to allow other vehicles to race toward the house, amidst the shrill wail of sirens. With Johnny shouting directions, I turn right on a road he says will take us to the front gate, then, in the rearview mirror, I see the headlights of another Humvee flying around the bend after us.

I floor it. The tires rumble over the uneven road, spraying pebbles and mud. To our right, two large hangars loom in the ghostly moonlight. I weave around a massive crane, and the stacks of shipping containers piled next to it and speed on. We pass more trailers, a barn, outbuildings, and various vehicles on cinderblocks.

Finally, our headlights illuminate the closed gate. Checking my rearview mirror, I see that somehow we've put the road between us and the other Humvee.

"How are we going to get out of here?" Johnny asks.

"No way for us to stop," I say, stating the obvious. "I'll have to barge through it."

As we approach the gate, I see three more Humvees parked next to the guard shack.

"Hold tight, and make sure you have a good grip on Noah," I cry. Then I hit the gas, and the Humvee torpedoes straight toward the gate, crashing into it, but not through it. I'm going to have to back up and go again. But as I reverse, machine gunfire erupts from our right. I glance over and see where the shots came from. Tugging the steering wheel around, I floor the gas again, this time aiming at the man shooting at us. I clip him, and he falls to the side.

I reverse again, and this time, I plow the Humvee through the gate, nearly running over another armed man, who leaps out of my way at the last minute.

"Is Noah okay?" I shout over my shoulder, as we thunder down the dirt road.

"Yes," Johnny says. "He's fine."

As we careen onto the main road, the other vehicle giving us chase, the flashing lights of six police cars squeal around the corner, blocking the other Humvee's path.

Finally. I've done it. And my son is fine.

CHAPTER 50

The door sticks, but when I put my shoulder against it and push, it gives. Cautiously, I make my way down into the dark basement, where I feel for the string on the lone light bulb that hangs from the ceiling. I tug, and the bulb's sudden glare illuminates the cement floor and walls—reminding me uncomfortably of the cell I escaped not so long ago.

But instead of the harsh shouts of nationalist soldiers, from Aunt Rachelle's kitchen above me, I hear laughter and footsteps.

This morning, I woke at dawn, the sky pink and alive with promise, the birds chirping. I decided to stay in the rambling farmhouse where Noah was born. Here, my son and I are sheltered by the woods, encircled by nature. I've redecorated the nursery, returning it to the soft blue that first welcomed my baby and stenciling clouds on the ceiling. On the wall above his crib, I wrote in a flowing black script, *Be brave, Little One. You are my sunshine.*

On the drive to Auntie's house—Damon beside me in the passenger's seat, Noah tucked into his car seat in the back, and Charlie, Noah's ever-present canine keeper, splayed across the rest of the seat—my heart is heavy. I let out a sigh. Even after all this time, I'm unable to suppress a twinge of guilt.

"You're doing it again," Damon says.

"What?"

I glance over at him. He looks handsome in his crisp white shirt.

"Feeling guilty."

I stifle a yawn. I haven't been sleeping well lately. My anxiety over losing Noah again keeps me half-awake, one ear tuned continuously to him. I try hard not to let fear and guilt get in the way of my happiness at my baby's return. But I can't forget that my carelessness caused his abduction. Although Noah is the best thing that ever happened to me, ironically, by giving birth to him, I placed him in danger.

Out of the corner of my eye, I see Damon shake his head. "Just keep telling yourself that guilt is an emotion people experience when they've caused harm. You don't meet that job description," he told me. Not for the first time.

We are lucky in so many ways. Among them is the fact that George's bullets passed through Damon's shoulder and thigh, leaving relatively little damage behind. And since his release from the hospital, Damon has stayed by my side.

During this time, he's revealed bits and pieces of his life. I asked him to explain what he did since he was no run-of-the-mill private eye. "I'm the man parents of abducted children turn to when law enforcement is unable to help," he said. Then he told me about his own son's abduction: "There were scores of tips — some from psychics, who are often called in on missing-person cases. But the tension, the waiting, the not knowing was excruciating. Finally, my marriage fell apart. Jennifer was inconsolable. And still, after all this time, I have no way of knowing if my son is still alive. So, I help other people in the same situation. It helps ease the pain."

Not an hour after Johnny, Damon, and I escaped with Noah, the FBI swooped in to the compound, making arrests and confiscating computers. When questioned, the parents who'd handed over their children to Todd and Connie's nationalistic scheme told law enforcement they were coerced into giving them up. They claimed they were duped into believing their children would have good educations and bright futures. But I know better. Most of those parents were complicit. As for the children, after thorough psychological evaluations, numerous were returned to their homes, while others were put into the system.

Once the compound was dismantled, the world learned that the white ethno-empire organization stretched across North America — with more than a hundred chapters and tens of thousands of dues-paying members, plus hundreds of thousands of supporters on social media.

"I can't believe they got away with it for so long," I told Damon.

"They've been on the FBI's radar for years," Damon said. "But as long as the situation hadn't exploded into violence, the agency decided it was best to leave it alone. Until you blew the lid wide open," he added, with what I took to be an appreciative chuckle.

The FBI interrogated me for days, seeking any clues I could offer about Todd or Connie, who'd both managed to flee. I gave them everything I could, but nothing, I'm afraid, was very useful. Knowing that Todd and Connie are still out there makes me nervous. I'm always looking over my shoulder, or checking on Noah. I'm not sure if, or when, I'll ever feel he is truly safe.

Interestingly, Officer Gordon, along with several other officers from around the region, was found to have been directly involved with higher-ups at the compound. They are now awaiting trial.

And George? Well, he's stalked me for the last time. Whatever his intentions that night in the compound woods, Johnny's stabbing proved fatal for him. I am not sorry to say I am glad—and relieved—he is dead.

Luanne has all kinds of theories about why I chose such terrible men. But I think the bottom line is this: The world is full of broken people. I used to be one of them.

•　　•　　•

With all the fallout from the events of those weeks after Noah's abduction—the longest of my life—it's taken almost two months for us to make it to Albany. And now, I stand in my aunt's basement, eyeing boxes packed with items from my childhood and young adulthood.

I make my way over to the far wall and settle myself on the floor. I start with a box I had labeled, *MOM*, before consigning it to Auntie's basement. Tugging open the folded top, I find photos of my mother with her family, college friends, her first car. There are also her favorite books and a few birthday cards, my sister, and I gave her. There's also a feathered hat that she loved. All bring back fond memories—but nothing in the box indicates she knew what I know. Did *she* also bury her head in the sand?

Shoving that box aside, I pull over another cardboard carton, this one labeled, *DAD*. I'm not one for rummaging through my past. It's been too painful. But this is necessary. I take a deep breath and open the box that contains what's left of my father's belongings.

On the top, there's a flag, emblazoned with the same type of Celtic cross I saw on the flags hanging on the walls in the compound—and which I've since learned is one of the most commonly used symbols of white supremacists. This flag graced the wall over my father's desk at his garage for years. But I never thought to ask what it meant.

When she had me at her mercy, Connie made a damning accusation against my father. But I didn't believe her. How could I? My father, in some ways, had been my best friend. Faced with the FBI's confirmation that what Connie had said was true, though, I have had to reconsider every aspect of our relationship. This is the last step in that process.

I remove the flag and find unlabeled leather journals stacked beneath it. Dread spreads through me, and I have to push back the panic that' close on its heels.

Turning the pages of one after another of the diaries, I find meticulous notes, all in my father's handwriting, documenting his leadership of the white nationalist movement that is the source of so much violence in our country and around the world. He recorded the locations of the chapters he helped open, the names of the leaders of those chapters, the names and ages of the children who were inducted into the movement under those leaders—and the youngsters' aptitudes to be exploited later.

I run my finger down the lists, looking for one particular person. There. Todd's real name: Adolph Dresden, typed next to the name I knew—Todd Armstrong.

I also see detailed plans for the violent, apocalyptic overthrow of the federal government; blueprints showing the best way to stockpile arms; and my father's detailed instructions on to prepare the next generation to wage war against the System, which he perceived as being under Jewish control.

My heart is thumping hard, and my armpits are damp. When tears gather in my eyes, I let them fall. For a few moments, I sit unmoving on the cold floor, in the silence, memories swirl.

How is it that I didn't know about his nationalistic activities? It's hardly credible, even to me, that I didn't notice something of them. If I'm honest with myself, though, I realize that young as I was, deep down inside, I did feel something was wrong. Angry-looking men often showed up at the garage, as my father and I were working on car engines. Each time they did so, my father would send me to the store to buy something. But those men never came to our house.

I sigh. Having found undeniable and personal proof of exactly what I've been hoping to deny, I now have the grim task of telling my sister and aunt the horrifying truth. Clutching two of the most damning diaries, I climb the stairs on legs that feel as heavy as lead.

CHAPTER 51

Upstairs, I find Damon watching television. Noah's napping in his car seat, thumb in his mouth, Charlie beside him. Charlie flops his tail against the floor but doesn't budge. He's on duty. I walk over and gently kiss my son's beautiful head. He stirs but stays asleep.

Damon, seeing the journals, looks at me with a question in his eyes. I nod.

He rises, lays a comforting hand on my shoulder, then squeezes me in a bear hug.

"Where is Aunt Rachelle?" I ask.

"In the yard," Damon says, pointing out the window, where I see my aunt raking leaves.

Before I join her, I tuck the journals in a drawer in the dining room sideboard. I'm not ready for anyone else to see them—although it's inevitable that I will have to share their contents, soon.

I step out into the yard. Auntie's cheeks are pink with the cold. She looks at me, fondly. "You've gained some more weight," she says. "You look good."

I smile. "So, do you." Last week Auntie's doctor gave her a clean bill of health.

"That young man of yours is a find," she says, smiling. "After all you've been through with George and Todd …"

Suddenly, unexpectedly, I start to cry.

"Oh, honey, what's wrong?"

"Nothing," I say, trying to get a hold of myself. Now is not the time to tell my aunt about my father. I have to wait for my sister to get back from the grocery store.

Aunt Rachelle pulls me toward her for a hug. We stand like that for a couple of minutes, me soaking up her warmth and the scent of fresh soil until Margaret's new car pulls up.

We help her with bags and have just turned toward the house when we hear an engine backfire. I spin around to see a very familiar 1979 Chevy pulling into the driveway.

Johnny leaps out, sporting a wide grin. Behind him, Della unlatches Jake from his car seat, and their little family joins mine. Much hugging and kissing ensue, then we head inside, where Damon is pulled into the festivities, Charlie's tail whipping a frenzy beside him.

I lift Noah from his car seat, and we all move into the kitchen. Margaret starts to put away the groceries, and Aunt Rachelle offers everyone a coffee. I push the terrible news I have to share to the back of my mind, and, instead, enjoy the company of good friends and family.

After ten minutes of catching up, Damon says, "Let me have Noah. I'll take care of him while you guys make lunch." He closes his hand around mine and squeezes. Johnny follows suit, taking Jake gently out of Della's arms.

While Johnny, Damon, and the kids are parked in the living room, my sister, my aunt, Della, and I prepare lunch. My heart overflows as we work together in harmony: Aunt Rachelle briskly chopping celery, Della bustling together the ingredients for pasta sauce, Margaret efficiently stirring onions and chopped meat in a skillet.

"Bree," Della says. "Thank you again for saving my Johnny. He told me how brave you were."

"Actually, *he* saved *my* life—not to mention Noah's life."

She laughs away from the swift shadow that I saw cross her face. "So, we are forever indebted to each other."

I go over and hug her. I think she's the one person who really can understand what I went through—because she was so close to losing both Johnny and Jake.

Margaret looks up from the skillet. "Did you hear the news?" she asks.

"What news?" I reply.

"Luanne is getting married," my sister says, brushing a strand of hair from her forehead with the back of her hand. "She called me while I was on the way home from the supermarket."

"Yes," I say. "She told me yesterday. I'm so happy for her."

I pour myself another cup of coffee and sip it at the sink, gazing out the window. The sky has a jigsaw quality as the sun fights to break through the clouds. I swallow hard, hoping to ease the vise that tightens around my heart when I think about what I have to tell my aunt and sister.

I remember what my aunt said after Noah, and I escaped: "I know the truth can hurt. But you need to know. Countless nights following the car accident, I listened to your nightmares. You lost your parents. Why? Not because you argued with them, Bree. But because your father was a drunk. That's why."

When I challenged her, asking, "If that's the case, then why didn't you tell me years ago?" she studied my face. Then she said, "I'm sorry. You adored your father, and I wasn't sure which would be harder for you—to have his memory destroyed or to allow you to feel you were at fault. I believed that eventually you would outgrow your adolescent belief that you were to blame. But you never did. So, I'm telling you now."

And, she explained, he didn't leave his job because he was impatient with the implementation of his research. No. He was fired from the university because of his alcoholism.

But what I have to tell my aunt now is a lot worse than my father being an alcoholic. And learning the truth about what kind of man her sister, my mother, was married to, that is going to be as soul-destroying as any emotional damage she worried I would have experienced had she told me about my father's drinking all those years ago.

Pulling myself back into the present, I turn to my sister. "Did you sign the lease on that place you were going to rent?" I ask.

"Yes," she says. "I signed it yesterday."

"Congratulations," my aunt and I say in unison.

Just then, Johnny calls Della's name. She smiles and slips out of the kitchen.

Margaret seems to have been waiting for a moment of privacy because she turns off the stove and gazes at me steadily. "Bree," she says, "I have to tell you this. I'm sorry. I'm sorry for misjudging you. For not believing you. For having you institutionalized." She stops for a moment, then continues. "I can't tell you how sorry I am for blaming you for so many years. Our parents' death wasn't your fault. And I think I always knew that."

My sister's apology catches me off guard. An upwelling of gratitude overcomes me.

"I accept your apology," I say. After all, my sister and I suffered the same loss. And we orbited around the same pain, never coping with the truth.

"In truth, I was jealous of you. Jealous that Dad favored you. Jealous he spent more time with you, tinkering with cars. The thing is that I wanted a family of my own, just like you did, and ended saddling myself with a controlling and abusive man."

"Are you still jealous of me?" I ask although I'm not sure I want to hear the answer.

"I don't want to be," she says, tears welling. "But there are days I can't help it. You got to spend their last day with them. I'll never have that. You know?"

For a moment, we're silent. The only noise is the chatter in the living room.

"I understand," I say. And I do.

Suddenly, my sister starts laughing, and then I start laughing, too. Our laughter seems to wash away the pain, the misunderstanding, and the years we lost of sisterly friendship.

But the anger I feel at my father rages underneath. How will I be able to put out the red-hot fire burning in my heart? It's a funny thing about memory. At fourteen, I was old enough to have seen the truth — if I had wanted to. Instead, I chose to fictionalize my father, something I've continued to do with men until all too recently.

Della rejoins us, and we finish preparing our feast. Later, after she and Johnny and Jake head back to Massachusetts, and Auntie and Margaret and I clean the kitchen, I consider how, lately, I've stopped thinking so much about how things would have been different if I'd never kept that date with Todd. If that hadn't happened, there would be no Noah. I needed to recreate the family I lost when my parents died. But Noah is not here to fulfill my needs. It's my duty to meet his. And with that understanding, I decide I need to learn to forgive myself for all the mistakes I thought I made.

Noah has given me the gift of life. And that's what I owe him, the gift of life and motherly love.

Just then, Aunt Rachelle hangs her dish towel and pulls Margaret and me into a hug. In their embrace, I make another decision: I will take the box of my father's belongings—all the notebooks—and burn them. I will carry the burden of his terrible secret myself.

Following my sister and my aunt into the living room, where Damon and Noah and Charlie wait, I glance back at the basement door, and then I flip off the kitchen light.

ACKNOWLEDGMENT

It takes dedicated and talented people to help breathe life into a novel. I am fortunate and grateful to all of those who helped me with such a challenging endeavor. The process hasn't been a solitary experience.

First, thanks to Reagan Rothe, for believing in this story. And thanks to my editor, Jamie Morris, for zeroing in on the heart of the story and trimming away the distractions.

Thanks to all my friends who offered love and encouragement.

Gratitude to my writing group, Two Bridges, who offered insightful read and support: Walter Cummins, Talia Carner, Laura B. Weiss, Joanna Laufer, Susan O'Neill, Tony Gomes, Astrid Cook, Pamela Walker, Victor Ranger-Ribeiro.

My love and appreciation to my husband, Art Drescher, who offered advice and support, and to my son, Danny, who backed me up and supported my vision.

ABOUT THE AUTHOR

Henya Drescher is often found reading a book, and that book will most likely be a psychological thriller, which she writes. Writing novels was always her wish, and now, with *Stolen Truth*, it will soon become a reality. When not absorbed in writing her fourth novel and spending too much time on the computer, Henya's passions include lifting weights, cultivating her large garden, and driving long distances. She and her husband live in New York City.

NOTE FROM THE AUTHOR

Word-of-mouth is crucial for any author to succeed. If you enjoyed *Stolen Truth*, please leave a review online — anywhere you are able. Even if it's just a sentence or two. It would make all the difference and would be very much appreciated.

Thanks!
Henya Drescher